A SURPRISE FOR CHRISTMAS

A SURPRISE
FOR CHRISTMAS

And Other Seasonal Mysteries

edited and introduced by
MARTIN EDWARDS

First published 2020 by
The British Library
96 Euston Road
London NW1 2DB

Introduction, selection and notes © 2020 Martin Edwards

Cataloguing in Publication Data
A catalogue record for this publication is available from the British Library

ISBN 978 0 7123 5337 3
eISBN 978 0 7123 6747 9

Front cover illustration shows a detail from a Dunlop Tyre advertisement in the *Illustrated
London News*, 23 December 1933 © Illustrated London News Ltd/Mary Evans

Typeset by Tetragon, London
Printed in England by CPI Group (UK) Ltd, Croydon, CRO 4YY

CONTENTS

A Surprise for Christmas is the fourth anthology of classic crime stories with a wintry theme to be published by the British Library. Christmassy mysteries have enjoyed a remarkable surge in popularity during the last few years, and this is largely due to the efforts of the British Library, which set the ball rolling back in 2013 with the publication of Mavis Doriel Hay's *The Santa Klaus Murder*.

Hay was, at the time, a highly obscure writer who had enjoyed a brief crime writing career in the 1930s, publishing three light detective novels before retiring from the fray. Her novels had been out of print for about three-quarters of a century, and at first their reappearance made only a limited impression. The original cover artwork for *The Santa Klaus Murder* had a black background and an image of Father Christmas dripping blood, but a new series style was then adopted, making effective use of vintage railway poster artwork. Whilst one should never judge a book by its cover, the commercial reality is that cover artwork does make a difference, and is important in attracting the interest of booksellers. The railway poster style offered a pleasing combination of elegance and nostalgia; sales shot up, and the reputation of the series continued to rise. A Christmas crime novel with a lovely cover picture of a train in a snowdrift, J. Jefferson Farjeon's *Mystery in White*, became a huge bestseller in the UK, and it was followed by the first Christmas-themed collection of short stories, *Silent Nights*, which also enjoyed exceptional sales.

These successes did not go unnoticed in the publishing trade, and in recent years bookshop shelves have overflowed with Christmas mysteries, their covers invariably blanketed with enough snow to

cover a multitude of criminal sins. The British Library followed up
Silent Nights with *Crimson Snow*, and then, two years ago, with *The
Christmas Card Crime*. At this point I began to wonder if there was
scope for a fourth book. The demand from readers was there—but
what about the supply? Would there be enough material of interest
and quality? Some stories that seemed to fit the bill could not, for
various reasons, be included in this book; even so, I was delighted to
find that extensive research and discussion with fellow enthusiasts
for the genre yielded rich rewards. This book is the result.

As with other anthologies in the series, my aim has been to try to
strike a balance, and to offer as much variety as possible. So there
are stories by well-known authors and others by writers whose
names have long been forgotten. There is one very long story and
several very short ones, one or two that are fairly familiar and several
that are likely to be unknown even to devotees. I've also striven to
showcase a mix of writing styles. So we have the lively, what-you-
see-is-what-you-get prose of Ernest Dudley and the elegant writing
of authors such as Cyril Hare and Carter Dickson. Novels by two
of the contributors, Carr and Anthony Gilbert, have previously
appeared in the Crime Classics series, although Gilbert's Christmas
mystery *Portrait of a Murderer* appeared under a different pen-name,
Anne Meredith.

One of the great pleasures of acting as consultant to the Crime
Classics series is the opportunity it affords for me to talk to and
correspond with fellow admirers of traditional mystery writing. In
compiling this book, as previously, I've been particularly grateful
for the advice and encouragement of Nigel Moss, Jamie Sturgeon,
and John Cooper. It's also fascinating to receive messages and emails
from readers of the series based all around the world; the series

has attracted large and loyal following, not only in Britain but also in many other countries. A good many people are collecting the whole series, and again the attractive artwork undoubtedly plays a part in their enthusiasm. But of course, the story is the most important thing, and the great achievement of the British Library Crime Classics, I think, has been to show the remarkable range and quality of traditional mysteries. Correspondents often make recommendations for titles that might merit reprinting in the series and I'm always interested to receive these suggestions.

My thanks, as usual, go to the team at the Publishing Department of the British Library who have worked tirelessly over the past few years to build the success of the series. Above all, I'm grateful to you, the readers whose enthusiasm has ensured the extraordinary resurgence of crime fiction from "the Golden Age of Murder" between the wars. Long may it continue!

MARTIN EDWARDS
www.martinedwardsbooks.com

THE BLACK BAG LEFT ON A DOORSTEP

Catharine Louisa Pirkis

Catharine Louisa Lyne was born in 1839 and married Frederick Edward Pirkis, a naval officer, in 1872. She published her first mystery novel, *Disappeared from Home*, in 1877 and regularly contributed stories to magazines. Over the next seventeen years, she produced fourteen books before deserting her literary career for activism. She and her husband were prominent campaigners for animal welfare. They supported the anti-vivisection movement and helped to found the National Canine Defence League.

"The Black Bag Left on a Doorstep", which introduced Loveday Brooke, first appeared in *Ludgate Monthly* in February 1893. Loveday's exploits were collected in *The Experiences of Loveday Brooke, Lady Detective*, published in 1894. Joseph A. Kestner discusses the book in depth in *Sherlock's Sisters* (2003) and describes Loveday as "one of the most important female detectives at the end of the nineteenth century in England". Loveday, as Kestner points out, "often goes under a different identity or in disguise. She appears as someone's niece, as an amanuensis, a nursery governess, as an interior designer…" Unlike Sherlock Holmes and some of his contemporary rivals, she did not have an equivalent to Dr. Watson to narrate her adventures. As Kestner puts it, Loveday is "completely self-defining and self-determining" and "assertive, courageous, defiant and self-reliant when confronting murder" and other crimes.

"IT'S A BIG THING," SAID LOVEDAY BROOKE, ADDRESSING Ebenezer Dyer, chief of the well-known detective agency in Lynch Court, Fleet Street; "Lady Cathrow has lost £30,000 worth of jewellery, if the newspaper accounts are to be trusted."

"They are fairly accurate this time. The robbery differs in few respects from the usual run of country-house robberies. The time chosen, of course, was the dinner-hour, when the family and guests were at table and the servants not on duty were amusing themselves in their own quarters. The fact of its being Christmas Eve would also of necessity add to the business and consequent distraction of the household. The entry to the house, however, in this case was not effected in the usual manner by a ladder to the dressing-room window, but through the window of a room on the ground floor—a small room with one window and two doors, one of which opens into the hall, and the other into a passage that leads by the back stairs to the bedroom floor. It is used, I believe, as a sort of hat and coat room by the gentlemen of the house."

"It was, I suppose, the weak point of the house?"

"Quite so. A very weak point indeed. Craigen Court, the residence of Sir George and Lady Cathrow, is an oddly-built old place, jutting out in all directions, and as this window looked out upon a blank wall, it was filled in with stained glass, kept fastened by a strong brass catch, and never opened, day or night, ventilation being obtained by means of a glass ventilator fitted in the upper panes. It seems absurd to think that this window, being only about four

feet from the ground, should have had neither iron bars nor shutters added to it; such, however, was the case. On the night of the
robbery, some one within the house must have deliberately, and of
intention, unfastened its only protection, the brass catch, and thus
given the thieves easy entrance to the house."

"Your suspicions, I suppose, centre upon the servants?"

"Undoubtedly; and it is in the servants' hall that your services
will be required. The thieves, whoever they were, were perfectly
cognisant of the ways of the house. Lady Cathrow's jewellery was
kept in a safe in her dressing-room, and as the dressing-room was
over the dining-room, Sir George was in the habit of saying that it
was the 'safest' room in the house. (Note the pun, please, Sir George
is rather proud of it.) By his orders the window of the dining-room
immediately under the dressing-room window was always left
unshuttered and without blind during dinner, and as a full stream
of light thus fell through it on to the outside terrace, it would have
been impossible for any one to have placed a ladder there unseen."

"I see from the newspapers that it was Sir George's invariable
custom to fill his house and give a large dinner on Christmas Eve."

"Yes. Sir George and Lady Cathrow are elderly people, with no
family and few relatives, and have consequently a large amount of
time to spend on their friends."

"I suppose the key of the safe was frequently left in the possession of Lady Cathrow's maid?"

"Yes. She is a young French girl, Stephanie Delcroix by name. It
was her duty to clear the dressing-room directly after her mistress
left it; put away any jewellery that might be lying about, lock the safe,
and keep the key till her mistress came up to bed. On the night of the
robbery, however, she admits that, instead of so doing, directly her
mistress left the dressing-room, she ran down to the housekeeper's

room to see if any letters had come for her, and remained chatting with the other servants for some time—she could not say for how long. It was by the half-past seven post that her letters generally arrived from St. Omer, where her home is."

"Oh, then, she was in the habit of thus running down to inquire for her letters, no doubt, and the thieves, who appear to be so thoroughly cognisant of the ways of the house, would know this also."

"Perhaps; though at the present moment I must say things look very black against the girl. Her manner, too, when questioned, is not calculated to remove suspicion. She goes from one fit of hysterics into another; contradicts herself nearly every time she opens her mouth, then lays it to the charge of her ignorance of our language; breaks into voluble French; becomes theatrical in action, and then goes off into hysterics once more."

"All that is quite Français, you know," said Loveday. "Do the authorities at Scotland Yard lay much stress on the safe being left unlocked that night?"

"They do, and they are instituting a keen inquiry as to the possible lovers the girl may have. For this purpose they have sent Bates down to stay in the village and collect all the information he can outside the house. But they want some one within the walls to hob-nob with the maids generally, and to find out if she has taken any of them into her confidence respecting her lovers. So they sent to me to know if I would send down for this purpose one of the shrewdest and most clear-headed of my female detectives. I, in my turn, Miss Brooke, have sent for you—you may take it as a compliment if you like. So please now get out your note-book, and I'll give you sailing orders."

Loveday Brooke, at this period of her career, was a little over thirty years of age, and could be best described in a series of negations.

She was not tall, she was not short; she was not dark, she was not fair; she was neither handsome nor ugly. Her features were altogether nondescript; her one noticeable trait was a habit she had, when absorbed in thought, of dropping her eyelids over her eyes till only a line of eyeball showed, and she appeared to be looking out at the world through a slit, instead of through a window.

Her dress was invariably black, and was almost Quaker-like in its neat primness.

Some five or six years previously, by a jerk of Fortune's wheel, Loveday had been thrown upon the world penniless and all but friendless. Marketable accomplishments she had found she had none, so she had forthwith defied conventions, and had chosen for herself a career that had cut her off sharply from her former associates and her position in society. For five or six years she had drudged away patiently in the lower walks of her profession; then chance, or, to speak more precisely, an intricate criminal case, had introduced her to the notice of the experienced head of the flourishing detective agency in Lynch Court. He quickly enough found out the stuff she was made of, and threw her in the way of better-class work—work, indeed, that brought increase of pay and of reputation alike to him and to Loveday.

Ebenezer Dyer was not as a rule, given to enthusiasm; but he would at times wax eloquent over Miss Brooke's qualifications for the profession she had chosen.

"Too much of a lady, do you say?" he would say to any one who chanced to call in question those qualifications. "I don't care twopence-halfpenny whether she is or is not a lady. I only know she is the most sensible and practical woman I ever met. In the first place, she has the faculty—so rare among women—of carrying out orders to the very letter; in the second place, she has a clear, shrewd brain, unhampered by any hard-and-fast theories; thirdly, and most important item of all, she has so much common sense that it amounts to genius—positively to genius, sir."

But although Loveday and her chief, as a rule, worked together upon an easy and friendly footing, there were occasions on which they were wont, so to speak, to snarl at each other.

Such an occasion was at hand now.

Loveday showed no disposition to take out her note-book and receive her "sailing orders."

"I want to know," she said, "if what I saw in one newspaper is true—that one of the thieves, before leaving, took the trouble to close the safe-door, and to write across it in chalk: 'To be let unfurnished'?"

"Perfectly true; but I do not see that stress need be laid on the fact. The scoundrels often do that sort of thing out of insolence or bravado. In that robbery at Reigate, the other day, they went to a lady's davenport, took a sheet of her notepaper, and wrote their thanks on it for her kindness in not having had the lock of her safe repaired. Now, if you will get out your note-book—"

"Don't be in such a hurry," said Loveday calmly; "I want to know if you have seen this?" She leaned across the writing-table at which they sat, one either side, and handed to him a newspaper cutting which she took from her letter-case.

Mr. Dyer was a tall, powerfully-built man with a large head, benevolent bald forehead, and a genial smile. That smile, however, often proved a trap to the unwary, for he owned a temper so irritable that a child with a chance word might ruffle it.

The genial smile vanished as he took the newspaper cutting from Loveday's hand.

"I would have you to remember, Miss Brooke," he said severely, "that although I am in the habit of using despatch in my business,

I am never known to be in a hurry; hurry in affairs I take to be the especial mark of the slovenly and unpunctual."

Then, as if still further to give a contradiction to her words, he very deliberately unfolded her slip of newspaper and slowly, accentuating each word and syllable, read as follows:—

"SINGULAR DISCOVERY.

"A black leather bag, or portmanteau, was found early yesterday morning by one of Smiths newspaper boys on the doorstep of a house in the road running between Easterbrook and Wreford, and inhabited by an elderly spinster lady. The contents of the bag include a clerical collar and necktie, a Church Service, a book of sermons, a copy of the works of Virgil, a *facsimile* of Magna Charta, with translations, a pair of black kid gloves, a brush and comb, some newspapers, and several small articles suggesting clerical ownership. On the top of the bag the following extraordinary letter, written in pencil on a long slip of paper, was found:

"'The fatal day has arrived. I can exist no longer. I go hence and shall be no more seen. But I would have Coroner and Jury know that I am a sane man, and a verdict of temporary insanity in my case would be an error most gross after this intimation. I care not if it is *felo de se*, as I shall have passed all suffering. Search diligently for my poor lifeless body in the immediate neighbourhood—on the cold heath, the rail, or the river by yonder bridge—a few moments will decide how I shall depart. If I had walked aright I might have been a power in the Church of which I am now an unworthy member and priest; but the damnable sin of gambling got hold of me, and betting has been my ruin, as it has been the ruin of thousands who have preceded me. Young man, shun the bookmaker and the racecourse as you would shun the devil and hell. Farewell, chums of Magdalen. Farewell, and take warning. Though I can claim relationship with a Duke, a Marquess, and a Bishop, and though I am the son of a noble woman, yet am I a tramp and an outcast, verily and indeed. Sweet death, I greet thee! I dare not sign my name. To one and all, farewell. Oh, my poor Marchioness mother, a dying kiss to thee! R. I. P.'

"The police and some of the railway officials have made a 'diligent search' in the neighbourhood of the railway station, but no poor 'lifeless body' has been found. The police authorities are inclined to the belief that the letter is a hoax, though they are still investigating the matter."

In the same deliberate fashion as he had opened and read the cutting, Mr. Dyer folded and returned it to Loveday.

"May I ask," he said sarcastically, "what you see in that silly hoax to waste your and my valuable time over?"

"I wanted to know," said Loveday, in the same level tones as before, "if you saw anything in it that might in some way connect this discovery with the robbery at Craigen Court?"

Mr. Dyer stared at her in utter, blank astonishment.

"When I was a boy," he said sarcastically as before, "I used to play at a game called 'What is my thought like?' Some one would think of something absurd—say the top of the Monument—and some one else would hazard a guess that his thought might be—say the toe of his left boot, and that unfortunate individual would have to show the connection between the toe of his left boot and the top of the Monument. Miss Brooke, I have no wish to repeat the silly game this evening for your benefit and mine."

"Oh, very well," said Loveday calmly; "I fancied you might like to talk it over, that was all. Give me my 'sailing orders,' as you call them, and I'll endeavour to concentrate my attention on the little French maid and her various lovers."

Mr. Dyer grew amiable again.

"That's the point on which I wish you to fix your thoughts," he said; "you had better start for Craigen Court by the first train tomorrow—it's about sixty miles down the Great Eastern line. Huxwell is the station you must land at. There one of the grooms from the Court will meet you, and drive you to the house. I have arranged with the housekeeper there—Mrs. Williams, a very worthy and discreet person—that you shall pass in the house for a niece of hers, on a visit to recruit, after severe study in order to pass board-school teachers' exams. Naturally you have injured your eyes as well as your health with overwork; and so you can wear your blue spectacles. Your name, by the way, will be Jane Smith—better write it down. All your work will lie among the servants of the establishment, and there will be no necessity for you to see either Sir George or Lady Cathrow—in fact, neither of them has been apprised of your intended visit—the fewer we take into our confidence the better. I've no doubt, however, that Bates will hear from Scotland Yard that you are in the house, and will make a point of seeing you."

"Has Bates unearthed anything of importance?"

"Not as yet. He has discovered one of the girl's lovers, a young farmer of the name of Holt; but as he seems to be an honest, respectable young fellow, and entirely above suspicion, the discovery does not count for much."

"I think there's nothing else to ask," said Loveday, rising to take her departure. "Of course, I'll telegraph, should need arise, in our usual cipher."

The first train that left Bishopsgate for Huxwell on the following morning included, among its passengers, Loveday Brooke, dressed in the neat black supposed to be appropriate to servants of the upper class. The only literature with which she had provided herself in order to beguile the tedium of her journey was a small volume bound in paper boards, and entitled, "The Reciter's Treasury." It was published at the low price of one shilling, and seemed specially designed to meet the requirements of third-rate amateur reciters at penny readings.

Miss Brooke appeared to be all-absorbed in the contents of this book during the first half of her journey. During the second, she lay back in the carriage with closed eyes, and motionless, as if asleep or lost in deep thought.

The stopping of the train at Huxwell aroused her, and set her collecting together her wraps.

It was easy to single out the trim groom from Craigen Court from among the country loafers on the platform. Some one else beside the trim groom at the same moment caught her eye—Bates, from Scotland Yard, got up in the style of a commercial traveller, and carrying the orthodox "commercial bag" in his hand. He was a small, wiry man, with red hair and whiskers, and an eager, hungry expression of countenance.

"I am half-frozen with cold," said Loveday, addressing Sir George's groom; "if you'll kindly take charge of my portmanteau, I'd prefer walking to driving to the Court."

The man gave her a few directions as to the road she was to follow, and then drove off with her luggage, leaving her free to indulge Mr. Bates's evident wish for a walk and confidential talk along the country road.

Bates seemed to be in a happy frame of mind that morning.

"Quite a simple affair, this, Miss Brooke," he said; "a walk over the course, I take it, with you working inside the castle walls and I unearthing without. No complications as yet have arisen, and if that girl does not find herself in jail before another week is over her head, my name is not Jeremiah Bates."

"You mean the French maid?"

"Why, yes, of course. I take it there's little doubt but that she performed the double duty of unlocking the safe and the window too. You see I look at it this way, Miss Brooke: all girls have lovers, I say to myself, but a pretty girl like that French maid is bound to have double the number of lovers that the plain ones have. Now, of course, the greater the number of lovers, the greater the chance there is of a criminal being found among them. That's plain as a pikestaff, isn't it?"

"Just as plain."

Bates felt encouraged to proceed.

"Well, then, arguing on the same lines, I say to myself, this girl is only a pretty, silly thing, not an accomplished criminal, or she wouldn't have admitted leaving open the safe door; give her rope enough and she'll hang herself. In a day or two, if we let her alone, she'll be bolting off to join the fellow whose nest she has helped to feather, and we shall catch the pair of them 'twixt here and Dover Straits, and also possibly get a clue that will bring us on the traces of their accomplices. Eh, Miss Brooke, that'll be a thing worth doing?"

"Undoubtedly. Who is this coming along in this buggy at such a good pace?"

The question was added as the sound of wheels behind them made her look round.

Bates turned also. "Oh, this is young Holt; his father farms land about a couple of miles from here. He is one of Stephanie's lovers, and I should imagine about the best of the lot. But he does not appear to be first favourite; from what I hear some one else must have made the running on the sly. Ever since the robbery I'm told the young woman has given him the cold shoulder."

As the young man came nearer in his buggy he slackened pace, and Loveday could not but admire his frank, honest expression of countenance.

"Room for one—can I give you a lift?" he said, as he came alongside of them.

And to the ineffable disgust of Bates, who had counted upon at least an hour's confidential talk with her, Miss Brooke accepted the young farmer's offer, and mounted beside him in his buggy.

As they went swiftly along the country road, Loveday explained to the young man that her destination was Craigen Court, and that as she was a stranger to the place, she must trust to him to put her down at the nearest point to it that he would pass.

At the mention of Craigen Court his face clouded.

"They're in trouble there, and their trouble has brought trouble on others," he said a little bitterly.

"I know," said Loveday sympathetically; "it is often so. In such circumstances as these suspicion frequently fastens on an entirely innocent person."

"That's it! that's it!" he cried excitedly; "if you go into that house you'll hear all sorts of wicked things said of her, and see everything setting in dead against her. But she's innocent. I swear to you she is as innocent as you or I are."

His voice rang out above the clatter of his horse's hoofs. He seemed to forget that he had mentioned no name, and that Loveday, as a stranger, might be at a loss to know to whom he referred.

"Who is guilty Heaven only knows," he went on after a moment's pause; "it isn't for me to give an ill name to any one in that house; but I only say she is innocent, and that I'll stake my life on."

"She is a lucky girl to have found one to believe in her and trust her as you do," said Loveday, even more sympathetically than before.

"Is she? I wish she'd take advantage of her luck, then," he answered bitterly. "Most girls in her position would be glad to have a man to stand by them through thick and thin. But not she! Ever since the night of that accursed robbery she has refused to see me—won't answer my letters—won't even send me a message. And, great Heavens! I'd marry her tomorrow, if I had the chance, and dare the world to say a word against her."

He whipped up his pony. The hedges seemed to fly on either side of them, and before Loveday realised that half her drive was over, he had drawn rein, and was helping her to alight at the servants' entrance to Craigen Court.

"You'll tell her what I've said to you, if you get the opportunity, and beg her to see me, if only for five minutes?" he petitioned before he re-mounted his buggy. And Loveday, as she thanked the young man for his kind attention, promised to make an opportunity to give his message to the girl.

Mrs. Williams, the housekeeper, welcomed Loveday in the servants' hall, and then took her to her own room to pull off her wraps. Mrs. Williams was the widow of a London tradesman, and a little beyond the average housekeeper in speech and manner.

She was a genial, pleasant woman, and readily entered into conversation with Loveday. Tea was brought in, and each seemed to feel at home with the other. Loveday, in the course of this easy, pleasant talk, elicited from her the whole history of the events of the day of the robbery, the number and names of the guests who sat down to dinner that night, together with some other apparently trivial details.

The housekeeper made no attempt to disguise the painful position in which she and every one of the servants of the house felt themselves to be at the present moment.

"We are none of us at our ease with each other now," she said, as she poured out hot tea for Loveday, and piled up a blazing fire. "Every one fancies that every one else is suspecting him or her, and trying to rake up past words or deeds to bring in as evidence. The whole house seems under a cloud. And at this time of year, too; just when everything as a rule is at its merriest!" Here she gave a doleful glance to the big bunch of holly and mistletoe hanging from the ceiling.

"I suppose you are generally very merry downstairs at Christmas time?" said Loveday. "Servants' balls, theatricals, and all that sort of thing?"

"I should think we were! When I think of this time last year and the fun we all had, I can scarcely believe it is the same house. Our ball always follows my lady's ball, and we have permission to ask our friends to it, and we keep it up as late as ever we please. We begin our evening with a concert and recitations in character, then we have a supper, and then we dance right on till morning; but this year!"—she broke off, giving a long, melancholy shake of her head that spoke volumes.

"I suppose," said Loveday, "some of your friends are very clever as musicians or reciters?"

"Very clever indeed. Sir George and my lady are always present during the early part of the evening, and I should like you to have seen Sir George last year laughing fit to kill himself at Harry Emmett, dressed in prison dress with a bit of oakum in his hand, reciting the 'Noble Convict!' Sir George said if the young man had gone on the stage, he would have been bound to make his fortune."

"Half a cup, please," said Loveday, presenting her cup. "Who was this Harry Emmett then—a sweetheart of one of the maids?"

"Oh, he would flirt with them all, but he was sweetheart to none. He was footman to Colonel James, who is a great friend of Sir George's, and Harry was constantly backwards and forwards bringing messages from his master. His father, I think, drove a cab in London, and Harry for a time did so also; then he took it into his head to be a gentleman's servant, and great satisfaction he gave as such. He was always such a bright, handsome young fellow, and so full of fun that every one liked him. But I shall tire you with all this; and you, of course, want to talk about something so different;" and the housekeeper sighed again, as the thought of the dreadful robbery entered her brain once more.

"Not at all. I am greatly interested in you and your festivities. Is Emmett still in the neighbourhood? I should amazingly like to hear him recite myself."

"I'm sorry to say he left Colonel James about six months ago. We all missed him very much at first. He was a good, kind-hearted young man, and I remember he told me he was going away to look after his dear old grandmother, who had a sweetstuff shop some-where or other, but where I can't remember."

Loveday was leaning back in her chair now, with eyelids drooped so low that she literally looked out through "slits" instead of eyes.

Suddenly and abruptly she changed the conversation.

"When will it be convenient for me to see Lady Cathrow's dressing-room?" she asked.

The housekeeper looked at her watch. "Now, at once," she answered; "it's a quarter to five now, and my lady sometimes goes up to her room to rest for half an hour before she dresses for dinner."

"Is Stephanie still in attendance on Lady Cathrow?" Miss Brooke asked as she followed the housekeeper up the back stairs to the bedroom floor.

"Yes. Sir George and my lady have been goodness itself to us through this trying time; they say we are all innocent till we are proved guilty, and will have it that none of our duties are to be in any way altered."

"Stephanie is scarcely fit to perform hers, I should imagine?"

"Scarcely. She was in hysterics nearly from morning till night for the first two or three days after the detectives came down, but now she has grown sullen, eats nothing, and never speaks a word to any of us except when she is obliged. This is my lady's dressing-room,—walk in, please."

Loveday entered a large, luxuriously furnished room, and naturally made her way straight to the chief point of attraction in it—the iron safe fitted into the wall that separated the dressing-room from the bedroom.

It was a safe of the ordinary description, fitted with a strong iron door and Chubb lock. And across this door was written with chalk, in characters that seemed defiant in their size and boldness, the words: "To be let, unfurnished."

Loveday spent about five minutes in front of this safe, all her attention concentrated upon the big, bold writing.

She took from her pocket-book a narrow strip of tracing-paper and compared the writing on it, letter by letter, with that on the safe door. This done she turned to Mrs. Williams and professed herself ready to follow her to the room below.

Mrs. Williams looked surprised. Her opinion of Miss Brooke's professional capabilities suffered considerable diminution.

"The gentlemen detectives," she said, "spent over an hour in this room; they paced the floor, they measured the candles, they—"

"Mrs. Williams," interrupted Loveday, "I am quite ready to look at the room below." Her manner had changed from gossiping friendliness to that of the business woman hard at work at her profession.

Without another word, Mrs. Williams led the way to the little room which had proved itself to be the "weak point" of the house.

They entered it by the door which opened into a passage leading to the back stairs of the house. Loveday found the room exactly what it had been described to her by Mr. Dyer. It needed no second glance at the window to see the ease with which any one could open it from the outside, and swing themselves into the room, when once the brass catch had been unfastened.

Loveday wasted no time here. In fact, much to Mrs. Williams' surprise and disappointment, she merely walked across the room, in at one door and out at the opposite one, which opened into the large inner hall of the house.

Here, however, she paused to ask a question:—

"Is that chair always placed exactly in that position?" she said, pointing to an oak chair that stood immediately outside the room they had just quitted.

The housekeeper answered in the affirmative. It was a warm corner. "My lady" was particular that every one who came to the house on messages should have a comfortable place to wait in.

"I shall be glad if you will show me to my room now," said Loveday, a little abruptly; "and will you kindly send up to me a county trade directory, if, that is, you have such a thing in the house?"

Mrs. Williams, with an air of offended dignity, led the way to the bedroom quarters once more. The worthy housekeeper felt as if her own dignity had, in some sort, been injured by the want of interest Miss Brooke had evinced in the rooms which, at the present moment, she considered the "show" rooms of the house.

"Shall I send some one to help you unpack?" she asked, a little stiffly, at the door of Loveday's room.

"No, thank you; there will not be much unpacking to do. I must leave here by the first up-train tomorrow morning."

"Tomorrow morning! Why, I have told every one you will be here at least a fortnight!"

"Ah, then you must explain that I have been suddenly summoned home by telegram. I'm sure I can trust you to make excuses for me. Do not, however, make them before supper-time. I shall like to sit down to that meal with you. I suppose I shall see Stephanie then?"

The housekeeper answered in the affirmative, and went her way, wondering over the strange manners of the lady, whom, at first, she had been disposed to consider "such a nice, pleasant, conversable person!"

At supper-time, however, when the upper servants assembled at what was, to them, the pleasantest meal of the day, a great surprise was to greet them.

Stephanie did not take her usual place at table, and a fellow-servant, sent to her room to summon her, returned, saying that the room was empty, and Stephanie was nowhere to be found.

Loveday and Mrs. Williams together went to the girl's bedroom. It bore its usual appearance: no packing had been done in it, and, beyond her hat and jacket, the girl appeared to have taken nothing away with her.

On inquiry, it transpired that Stephanie had, as usual, assisted Lady Cathrow to dress for dinner; but after that not a soul in the house appeared to have seen her.

Mrs. Williams thought the matter of sufficient importance to be at once reported to her master and mistress; and Sir George, in his turn, promptly despatched a messenger to Mr. Bates, at the "King's Head," to summon him to an immediate consultation.

Loveday despatched a messenger in another direction—to young Mr. Holt, at his farm, giving him particulars of the girl's disappearance.

Mr. Bates had a brief interview with Sir George in his study, from which he emerged radiant. He made a point of seeing Loveday before he left the Court, sending a special request to her that she would speak to him for a minute in the outside drive.

Loveday put her hat on, and went out to him. She found him almost dancing for glee.

"Told you so! told you so! Now, didn't I, Miss Brooke?" he exclaimed. "We'll come upon her traces before morning, never fear. I'm quite prepared. I knew what was in her mind all along. I said to myself, when that girl bolts it will be after she has dressed my lady for dinner—when she has two good clear hours all to herself, and her absence from the house won't be noticed, and when, without much difficulty, she can catch a train leaving Huxwell for Wreford. Well, she'll get to Wreford safe enough; but from Wreford she'll be followed every step of the way she goes. Only yesterday I set a man on there—a keen fellow at this sort of thing—and gave him full directions; and he'll hunt her down to her hole properly. Taken nothing with her, do you say? What does that matter? She thinks she'll find all she wants where she's going—'the feathered nest' I spoke to you about this morning. Ha! ha! Well, instead of stepping into it, as she fancies she will, she'll walk straight into a detective's arms, and land her pal there into the bargain. There'll be two of them netted before another forty-eight hours are over our heads, or my name's not Jeremiah Bates."

"What are you going to do now?" asked Loveday, as the man finished his long speech.

"Now! I'm back to the 'King's Head,' to wait for a telegram from my colleague at Wreford. Once he's got her in front of him he'll give me instructions at what point to meet him. You see, Huxwell being such an out-of-the-way place, and only one train leaving between 7.30 and 10.15, makes us really positive that Wreford must be the girl's destination, and relieves my mind from all anxiety on the matter."

"Does it?" answered Loveday gravely. "I can see another possible destination for the girl—the stream that runs through the wood we drove past this morning. Good-night, Mr. Bates, it's cold out here. Of course so soon as you have any news you'll send it up to Sir George."

The household sat up late that night, but no news was received of Stephanie from any quarter. Mr. Bates had impressed upon Sir George the inadvisability of setting up a hue-and-cry after the girl that might possibly reach her ears and scare her from joining the person whom he was pleased to designate as her "pal."

"We want to follow her silently, Sir George, silently as the shadow follows the man," he had said grandiloquently, "and then we shall come upon the two, and I trust upon their booty also."

Sir George in his turn had impressed Mr. Bates's wishes upon his household, and if it had not been for Loveday's message, despatched early in the evening to young Holt, not a soul outside the house would have known of Stephanie's disappearance.

Loveday was stirring early the next morning, and the eight o'clock train for Wreford numbered her among its passengers. Before starting, she despatched a telegram to her chief in Lynch Court. It read rather oddly, as follows:—

"Cracker fired. Am just starting for Wreford. Will wire to you from there. L.B."

Oddly though it might read, Mr. Dyer did not need to refer to his cipher book to interpret it. "Cracker fired" was the easily remembered equivalent for "clue found" in the detective phraseology of the office.

"Well, she has been quick enough about it this time!" he soliloquised, as he speculated in his own mind over what the purport of the next telegram might be.

Half an hour later there came to him a constable from Scotland Yard to tell him of Stephanie's disappearance and the conjectures that were rife on the matter, and he then, not unnaturally, read Loveday's telegram by the light of this information, and concluded that the clue in her hands related to the discovery of Stephanie's whereabouts as well as to that of her guilt.

A telegram received a little later on, however, was to turn this theory upside down. It was, like the former one, worded in the enigmatic language current in the Lynch Court establishment, but as it was a lengthier and more intricate message, it sent Mr. Dyer at once to his cipher book.

"Wonderful! She has cut them all out this time!" was Mr. Dyer's exclamation as he read and interpreted the final word.

In another ten minutes he had given over his office to the charge of his head clerk for the day, and was rattling along the streets in a hansom in the direction of Bishopsgate Station.

There he was lucky enough to catch a train just starting for Wreford.

"The event of the day," he muttered, as he settled himself comfortably in a corner seat, "will be the return journey, when she tells me, bit by bit, how she has worked it all out."

It was not until close upon three o'clock in the afternoon that he arrived at the old-fashioned market town of Wreford. It chanced to be cattle-market day, and the station was crowded with drovers and farmers. Outside the station Loveday was waiting for him, as she had told him in her telegram that she would, in a four-wheeler.

"It's all right," she said to him as he got in; "he can't get away, even if he had an idea that we were after him. Two of the local police are waiting outside the house door with a warrant for his arrest, signed by a magistrate. I did not, however, see why the Lynch Court office should not have the credit of the thing, and so telegraphed to you to conduct the arrest."

They drove through the High Street to the outskirts of the town, where the shops became intermixed with private houses let out in offices. The cab pulled up outside one of these, and two policemen in plain clothes came forward, and touched their hats to Mr. Dyer.

"He's in there now, sir, doing his office work," said one of the men, pointing to a door, just within the entrance, on which was painted in black letters, "The United Kingdom Cab-drivers' Beneficent Association." "I hear, however, that this is the last time he will be found there, as a week ago he gave notice to leave."

As the man finished speaking, a man, evidently of the cab-driving fraternity, came up the steps. He stared curiously at the little group just within the entrance, and then, chinking his money in his hand, passed on to the office as if to pay his subscription.

"Will you be good enough to tell Mr. Emmett in there," said Mr. Dyer, addressing the man, "that a gentleman outside wishes to speak with him?"

The man nodded and passed into the office. As the door opened, it disclosed to view an old gentleman seated at a desk apparently writing receipts for money. A little in his rear, at his right hand, sat a young and decidedly good-looking man, at a table on which were placed various little piles of silver and pence. The get-up of this young man was gentleman-like, and his manner was affable and pleasant as he responded, with a nod and a smile, to the cab-driver's message.

"I sha'n't be a minute," he said to his colleague at the other desk, as he rose and crossed the room towards the door.

But once outside that door it was closed firmly behind him, and he found himself in the centre of three stalwart individuals, one of whom informed him that he held in his hand a warrant for the arrest of Harry Emmett on the charge of complicity in the Craigen Court robbery, and that he had "better come along quietly, for resistance would be useless."

Emmett seemed convinced of the latter fact. He grew deadly white for a moment, then recovered himself.

"Will some one have the kindness to fetch my hat and coat?" he said in a lofty manner. "I don't see why I should be made to catch my death of cold because other people have seen fit to make asses of themselves."

His hat and coat were fetched, and he was handed into the cab between the two officials.

"Let me give you a word of warning, young man," said Mr. Dyer, closing the cab door and looking in for a moment through the window at Emmett. "I don't suppose it's a punishable offence to leave a black bag on an old maid's doorstep, but let me tell you, if it had not been for that black bag you might have got clean off with your spoil."

Emmett, the irrepressible, had his answer ready. He lifted his hat ironically to Mr. Dyer. "You might have put it more neatly, guv'nor," he said; "if I had been in your place I would have said: 'Young man, you are being justly punished for your misdeeds; you have been taking off your fellow-creatures all your life long, and now they are taking off you.'"

Mr. Dyer's duty that day did not end with the depositing of Harry Emmett in the local jail. The search through Emmett's lodgings and effects had to be made, and at this he was naturally present. About a third of the lost jewellery was found there, and from this it was consequently concluded that his accomplices in the crime had considered that he had borne a third of the risk and of the danger of it.

Letters and various memoranda discovered in the rooms eventually led to the detection of those accomplices, and although Lady Cathrow was doomed to lose the greater part of her valuable property, she had ultimately the satisfaction of knowing that each one of the thieves received a sentence proportionate to his crime.

It was not until close upon midnight that Mr. Dyer found himself seated in the train, facing Miss Brooke, and had leisure to ask for the links in the chain of reasoning that had led her in so remarkable a manner to connect the finding of a black bag, with insignificant contents, with an extensive robbery of valuable jewellery.

Loveday explained the whole thing, easily, naturally, step by step, in her usual methodical manner.

"I read," she said, "as I dare say a great many other people did, the account of the two things in the same newspaper, on the same day, and I detected, as I dare say a great many other people did not, a sense of fun in the principal actor in each incident. I notice, while all people are agreed as to the variety of motives that instigate crime, very few allow sufficient margin for variety of character in the criminal. We are apt to imagine that he stalks about the world with a bundle of deadly motives under his arm, and cannot picture him at his work with a twinkle in his eye and a keen sense of fun, such as honest folk have sometimes when at work at their calling."

Here Mr. Dyer gave a little grunt; it might have been either of assent or of dissent.

Loveday went on:

"Of course, the ludicrousness of the diction of the letter found in the bag would be apparent to the most casual reader; to me the high falutin sentences sounded in addition strangely familiar; I had heard or read them somewhere I felt sure, although where I could not at first remember. They rang in my ears, and it was not altogether out of idle curiosity that I went to Scotland Yard to see the bag and its contents, and to copy, with a slip of tracing paper, a line or two of the letter. When I found that the handwriting of this letter was not identical with that of the translations found in the bag, I was confirmed in my impression that the owner of the bag was not the writer of the letter; that possibly the bag and its contents had been appropriated from some railway station for some distinct purpose; and, that purpose accomplished, the appropriator no longer wished to be burthened with it, and disposed of it in the readiest fashion that suggested itself. The letter, it seemed to me, had been begun with the intention of throwing the police off the scent, but the irrepressible spirit of fun that had induced the writer to deposit his clerical adjuncts upon an old maid's doorstep had proved too strong for him here, and had carried him away, and the letter that was intended to be pathetic ended in being comic."

"Very ingenious, so far," murmured Mr. Dyer: "I've no doubt, when the contents of the bag are widely made known through advertisements, a claimant will come forward, and your theory be found correct."

"When I returned from Scotland Yard," Loveday continued, "I found your note, asking me to go round and see you respecting the big jewel robbery. Before I did so I thought it best to read once more the newspaper account of the case, so that I might be well up in its details. When I came to the words that the thief had written across the door of the safe, 'To be Let, Unfurnished,' they at once connected themselves in my mind with the 'dying kiss to my Marchioness mother,' and the solemn warning against the race-course and the bookmaker, of the black-bag letter-writer. Then, all in a flash, the whole thing became clear to me. Some two or three years back my professional duties necessitated my frequent attendance at certain low-class penny-readings, given in the South London slums. At these penny-readings young shop-assistants, and others of their class, glad of an opportunity for exhibiting their accomplishments, declaim with great vigour; and, as a rule, select pieces which their very mixed audience might be supposed to appreciate. During my attendance at these meetings, it seemed to me that one book of selected readings was a great favourite among the reciters, and I took the trouble to buy it. Here it is."

Here Loveday took from her cloak-pocket "The Reciter's Treasury," and handed it to her companion.

"Now," she said, "if you will run your eye down the index column you will find the titles of those pieces to which I wish to draw your attention. The first is 'The Suicide's Farewell;' the second, 'The Noble Convict;' the third 'To be Let, Unfurnished.'"

"By Jove! so it is!" ejaculated Mr. Dyer.

"In the first of these pieces, 'The Suicide's Farewell,' occur the expressions with which the black-bag letter begins—'The fatal day has arrived,' etc., the warnings against gambling, and the allusions to the poor 'lifeless body.' In the second, 'The Noble Convict,' occur the allusions to the aristocratic relations and the 'dying kiss to the Marchioness mother.' The third piece, 'To be Let, Unfurnished,' is a foolish little poem enough, although I dare say it has often raised a laugh in a not too-discriminating audience. It tells how a bachelor, calling at a house to inquire after rooms to be let unfurnished, falls in love with the daughter of the house, and offers her his heart, which, he says, is to be let unfurnished. She declines his offer, and retorts that she thinks his head must be to let unfurnished, too. With these three pieces before me, it was not difficult to see a thread of connection between the writer of the black-bag letter and the thief who wrote across the empty safe at Craigen Court. Following this thread, I unearthed the story of Harry Emmett—footman, reciter, general lover, and scamp. Subsequently I compared the writing on my tracing paper with that on the safe door, and, allowing for the difference between a bit of chalk and a steel nib, came to the conclusion that there could be but little doubt but that both were written by the same hand. Before that, however, I had obtained another, and what I consider the most important, link in my chain of evidence—how Emmett brought his clerical dress into use."

"Ah, how did you find out that now?" asked Mr. Dyer, leaning forward with his elbows on his knees.

"In the course of conversation with Mrs. Williams, whom I found to be a most communicative person, I elicited the names of the guests who had sat down to dinner on Christmas Eve. They were all people of undoubted respectability in the neighbourhood. Just before dinner was announced, she said, a young clergyman had presented himself at the front door, asking to speak with the Rector of the parish. The Rector, it seems, always dines at Craigen

Court on Christmas Eve. The young clergyman's story was that he had been told by a certain clergyman, whose name he mentioned, that a curate was wanted in the parish, and he had travelled down from London to offer his services. He had been, he said, to the Rectory, and had been told by the servants where the Rector was dining, and, fearing to lose his chance of the curacy, had followed him to the Court. Now the Rector had been wanting a curate, and had filled the vacancy only the previous week; he was inclined to be irate at this interruption to the evening's festivities, and told the young man brusquely that he didn't want a curate. When, however, he saw how disappointed the poor young fellow looked—I believe he shed a tear or two—his heart softened; he told him to sit down and rest in the hall before he attempted the walk back to the station, and said he would ask Sir George to send him out a glass of wine. The young man sat down in a chair immediately outside the room by which the thieves entered. Now I need not tell you who that young man was, nor suggest to your mind, I am sure, the idea that while the servant went to fetch him his wine, or, in fact, so soon as he saw the coast clear, he slipped into that little room and pulled back the catch of the window that admitted his confederates, who, no doubt, at that very moment were in hiding in the grounds. The housekeeper did not know whether this meek young curate had a black bag with him. Personally I have no doubt of the fact, nor that it contained the cap, cuffs, collar, and outer garments of Harry Emmett, which were most likely re-donned before he returned to his lodgings at Wreford, where I should say he repacked the bag with its clerical contents, and wrote his serio-comic letter. This bag, I suppose, he must have deposited in the very early morning, before any one was stirring, on the doorstep of the house in the Easterbrook Road."

Mr. Dyer drew a long breath. In his heart was unmitigated admiration for his colleague's skill, which seemed to him to fall little short of inspiration. By-and-by, no doubt, he would sing her praises to the first person who came along with a hearty good will; he had not, however, the slightest intention of so singing them in her own ears—excessive praise was apt to have a bad effect on the rising practitioner.

So he contented himself with saying:

"Yes, very satisfactory. Now tell me how you hunted the fellow down to his diggings?"

"Oh, that was mere ABC work," answered Loveday. "Mrs. Williams told me he had left his place at Colonel James's about six months previously, and had told her he was going to look after his dear old grandmother, who kept a sweetstuff shop; but where she could not remember. Having heard that Emmett's father was a cab-driver, my thoughts at once flew to the cabman's vernacular—you know something of it, no doubt—in which their provident association is designated by the phrase, 'the dear old grandmother,' and the office where they make and receive their payments is styled 'the sweetstuff shop.'"

"Ha, ha, ha! And good Mrs. Williams took it all literally, no doubt?"

"She did; and thought what a dear, kind-hearted fellow the young man was. Naturally I supposed there would be a branch of the association in the nearest market town, and a local trades' directory confirmed my supposition that there was one at Wreford. Bearing in mind where the black bag was found, it was not difficult to believe that young Emmett, possibly through his father's influence and his own prepossessing manners and appearance, had attained to some position of trust in the Wreford branch. I must confess I scarcely expected to find him as I did, on reaching the place, installed as receiver of the weekly moneys. Of course, I immediately put myself in communication with the police there, and the rest I think you know."

Mr. Dyer's enthusiasm refused to be longer restrained.

"It's capital, from first to last," he cried; "you've surpassed yourself this time!"

"The only thing that saddens me," said Loveday, "is the thought of the possible fate of that poor little Stephanie."

Loveday's anxieties on Stephanie's behalf were, however, to be put to flight before another twenty-four hours had passed. The first post on the following morning brought a letter from Mrs. Williams telling how the girl had been found before the night was over, half dead with cold and fright, on the verge of the stream running through Craigen Wood—"found too"—wrote the housekeeper, "by the very person who ought to have found her, young Holt, who was, and is, so desperately in love with her. Thank goodness! at the last moment her courage failed her, and instead of throwing herself into the stream, she sank down, half-fainting, beside it. Holt took her straight home to his mother, and there at the farm she is now, being taken care of and petted generally by every one."

THE HOLE IN THE WALL

G. K. Chesterton

Gilbert Keith Chesterton (1870–1936) created, in Father Brown, one of fiction's Great Detectives. In addition, during the course of an extraordinarily industrious literary career, he wrote a wide range of other stories touching on the crime genre, as well as many articles which reflect his enthusiasm for fictional crime. John Peterson's enjoyable *G. K. Chesterton on Detective Fiction* (2010) is a compilation of the author's writings on the subject which includes his seminal essay "A Defence of Detective Stories" and the characteristically witty and thoughtful "How to Write a Detective Story". Chesterton became the first President of the Detection Club on its formation in 1930 and held that office until his death. Among the many authors whom he influenced was Carter Dickson, whose Great Detective Dr. Gideon Fell bears a physical resemblance to Chesterton.

"The Hole in the Wall" is one of Chesterton's most highly regarded detective stories not to feature Father Brown. It first appeared in *Harper's Monthly Magazine* in October 1921 and was included in *The Man Who Knew Too Much*, published in the following year. Eight stories in the book featured Horne Fisher, the man who knew too much. Fisher was based on Chesterton's friend Maurice Baring, in his day a well-regarded man of letters. The book's title evidently appealed to Alfred Hitchcock, who adopted it for a film he directed in 1934 (and remade in 1956). Although some sources suggest that Hitchcock had acquired the rights to some of the stories in the book, his films had nothing to do with Chesterton's characters.

TWO MEN, THE ONE AN ARCHITECT AND THE OTHER AN archaeologist, met on the steps of the great house at Prior's Park; and their host, Lord Bulmer, in his breezy way, thought it natural to introduce them. It must be confessed that he was hazy as well as breezy, and had no very clear connexion in his mind, beyond the sense that an architect and an archaeologist begin with the same series of letters. The world must remain in a reverent doubt as to whether he would, on the same principles, have presented a diplomatist to a dipsomaniac or a ratiocinator to a ratcatcher. He was a big, fair, bull-necked young man abounding in outward gestures, unconsciously flapping his gloves and flourishing his stick.

"You two ought to have something to talk about," he said cheerfully. "Old buildings and all that sort of thing; this is rather an old building, by the way, though I say it who shouldn't. I must ask you to excuse me a moment; I've got to go and see about the cards for this Christmas romp my sister's arranging. We hope to see you all there, of course. Juliet wants it to be a fancy-dress affair; abbots and crusaders and all that. My ancestors, I suppose, after all."

"I trust the abbot was not an ancestor," said the archaeological gentleman with a smile.

"Only a sort of great-uncle, I imagine," answered the other, laughing. Then his rather rambling eye rolled round the ordered landscape in front of the house; an artificial sheet of water ornamented with an antiquated nymph in the centre and surrounded by a park of tall trees now grey and black and frosty, for it was in the depth of a severe winter.

"It's getting jolly cold," his lordship continued. "My sister hopes we shall have some skating as well as dancing."

"If the crusaders come in full armour," said the other, "you must be careful not to drown your ancestors."

"Oh, there's no fear of that," answered Bulmer; "this precious lake of ours is not two feet deep anywhere."

And with one of his flourishing gestures he stuck his stick into the water to demonstrate its shallowness. They could see the short end bent in the water; so that he seemed for a moment to lean his large weight on a breaking staff.

"The worst you can expect is to see an abbot sit down rather suddenly," he added, turning away. "Well, au revoir; I'll let you know about it later."

The archaeologist and the architect were left on the great stone steps smiling at each other; but whatever their common interests, they presented a considerable personal contrast; and the fanciful might even have found some contradiction in each considered individually. The former, a Mr. James Haddow, came from a drowsy den in the Inns of Court, full of leather and parchment; for the law was his profession and history only his hobby; he was indeed, among other things, the solicitor and agent of the Prior's Park estate. But he himself was far from drowsy and seemed remarkably wide-awake, with shrewd and prominent blue eyes and red hair brushed as neatly as his very neat costume. The latter, whose name was Leonard Crane, came straight from a crude and almost cockney office of builders and house-agents in the neighbouring suburb, sunning itself at the end of a new row of jerry-built houses with plans in very bright colours and notices in very large letters.

But a serious observer, at a second glance, might have seen in his eyes something of that shining sleep that is called vision; and his yellow hair, while not affectedly long, was unaffectedly tidy. It was a manifest if melancholy truth that the architect was an artist. But the artistic temperament was far from explaining him; there was something else about him that was not definable but which some even felt to be dangerous. Despite his dreaminess he would sometimes surprise his friends with arts and even sport apart from his ordinary life, like memories of some previous existence. On this occasion, nevertheless, he hastened to disclaim any authority on the other man's hobby.

"I mustn't appear on false pretences," he said with a smile. "I hardly even know what an archaeologist is; except that a rather rusty remnant of Greek suggests that he is a man who studies old things."

"Yes," replied Haddow grimly. "An archaeologist is a man who studies old things and finds they are new."

Crane looked at him steadily for a moment and then smiled again.

"Dare one suggest," he said, "that some of the things we have been talking about are among the old things that turn out not to be old?"

His companion also was silent for a moment; and the smile on his rugged face was fainter as he replied quietly:

"The wall round the park is really old. The one gate in it is Gothic, and I cannot find any trace of destruction or restoration. But the house and the estate generally—well, the romantic ideas read into these things are often rather recent romances, things almost like fashionable novels. For instance, the very name of this place, Prior's Park, makes everybody think of it as a moonlit mediaeval abbey; I dare say the spiritualists by this time have discovered the ghost of a monk there. But according to the only authoritative study of the matter I can find, the place was simply called Prior's as any rural place is called Podger's. It was the house of a Mr. Prior; a farmhouse probably, that stood here at some time or other and was a local landmark. Oh, there are a great many examples of the same thing, here and everywhere else. This suburb of ours used to be a village, and because some of the people slurred the name and pronounced it Holliwell, many a minor poet indulged in fancies about a Holy Well, with spells and fairies and all the rest of it, filling the suburban drawing-rooms with the Celtic twilight. Whereas anyone acquainted with the facts knows that 'Hollinwall' simply means 'hole in the wall' and probably referred to some quite trivial accident. That's what I mean when I say that we don't so much find old things as we find new ones."

Crane seemed to have grown somewhat inattentive to the little lecture on antiquities and novelties; and the cause of his restlessness was soon apparent and indeed approaching. Lord Bulmer's sister, Juliet Bray, was coming slowly across the lawn, accompanied by one gentleman and followed by two others. The young architect was in the illogical condition of mind in which he preferred three to one.

The man walking with the lady was no other than the eminent Prince Borodino, who was at least as famous as a distinguished diplomatist ought to be, in the interests of what is called secret diplomacy. He had been paying a round of visits at various English country houses; and exactly what he was doing for diplomacy at Prior's Park was as much a secret as any diplomatist could desire. The obvious thing to say of his appearance was that he would have been extremely handsome if he had not been entirely bald. But indeed that would itself be a rather bald way of putting it. Fantastic as it sounds, it would fit the case better to say that people would have been surprised to see hair growing on him; as surprised as if they had found hair growing on the bust of a Roman Emperor. His tall figure was buttoned up in a rather tight-waisted fashion that rather accentuated his potential bulk, and he wore a red flower in his buttonhole. Of the two men walking behind one also was bald, but in a more partial and also a more premature fashion; for his drooping moustache was still yellow, and if his eyes were somewhat heavy it was with languor and not with age. His name was Horne Fisher; and he talked so easily and idly about everything, that nobody had ever discovered his favourite subject. His companion was a more striking and even more sinister figure; and he had the added importance of being Lord Bulmer's oldest and most intimate friend. He was generally known with a severe simplicity as Mr. Brain; but it was understood that he had been a judge and police official in India; and that he had enemies, who had represented his measures against crime as themselves almost criminal. He was a brown skeleton of a man with dark, deep sunken eyes and a black moustache that hid the meaning of his mouth. Though he had the look of one wasted by some tropical disease, his movements were much more alert than those of his lounging companion.

"It's all settled," announced the lady with great animation when they came within hailing distance. "You've all got to put on masquerade things and very likely skates as well; though the Prince says they don't go with it; but we don't care about that. It's freezing already, and we don't often get such a chance in England."

"Even in India we don't exactly skate all the year round," observed Mr. Brain.

"And even Italy is not primarily associated with ice," said the Italian.

"Italy is primarily associated with ices," remarked Mr. Horne Fisher, "I mean with ice-cream men. Most people in this country imagine that Italy is entirely populated with ice-cream men and organ-grinders. There certainly are a lot of them; perhaps they're an invading army in disguise."

"How do you know they are not the secret emissaries of our diplomacy?" asked the Prince with a slightly scornful smile. "An army of organ-grinders might pick up hints, and their monkeys might pick up all sorts of things."

"The organs are organised, in fact," said the flippant Mr. Fisher. "Well, I've known it pretty cold before now in Italy and even in India, up on the Himalayan slopes. The ice on our own little round pond will be quite cosy by comparison."

Juliet Bray was an attractive lady with dark hair and eyebrows and dancing eyes; and there was a geniality and even generosity in her rather imperious ways. In most matters she could command her brother; though that nobleman, like many other men of vague ideas, was not without a touch of the bully when he was at bay. She could certainly command her guests; even to the extent of decking out the most respectable and reluctant of them with her mediaeval masquerade. And it really seemed as if she could command the elements also, like a witch. For the weather steadily hardened and sharpened; that night the ice of the lake, glimmering in the moon-light, was like a marble floor; and they had begun to dance and skate on it before it was dark.

Prior's Park, or more properly the surrounding district of Hollinwall, was a country seat that had become a suburb; having once had only a dependent village at its doors, it now found outside all its doors the signals of the expansion of London. Mr. Haddow, who was engaged in historical researches both in the library and the locality, could find little assistance in the latter. He had already gathered from the documents that Prior's Park had originally been something like Prior's Farm, named after some local figure; but the new social conditions were all against his tracing the story by its traditions. Had any of the real rustics remained, he would probably have found some lingering legend of Mr. Prior however remote he might be. But the new nomadic population of clerks and artisans, constantly shifting their homes from one suburb to another, or their children from one school to another, could have no corporate continuity. They had all that forgetfulness of history that goes everywhere with the extension of education.

Nevertheless when he came out of the library next morning, and saw the wintry trees standing round the frozen pond like a black forest, he felt he might well have been far in the depths of the country. The old wall running round the park kept that enclosure itself still entirely rural and romantic; and one could easily imagine that the depths of that dark forest faded away indefinitely into distant vales and hills. The grey and black and silver of the wintry wood were all the more severe or sombre as a contrast to the coloured carnival groups that already stood on and around the frozen pool. For the house-party had already flung themselves impatiently into fancy-dress; and the lawyer, with his neat black suit and red hair, was the only modern figure left among them.

"Aren't you going to dress up?" asked Juliet indignantly, shaking at him a horned and towering blue headdress of the fourteenth century which framed her face very becomingly, fantastic as it was. "Everybody here has to be in the Middle Ages. Even Mr. Brain has put on a sort of brown dressing-gown and says he's a monk; and Mr. Fisher got hold of some old potato-sacks in the kitchen and sewed them together; he's supposed to be a monk too. As to the Prince, he's perfectly glorious, in great crimson robes, as a cardinal. He looks as if he could poison everybody. You simply must be something."

"I will be something later in the day," he replied; "at present I am nothing but an antiquary and an attorney. I have to see your brother presently, about some legal business and also some local investigations he asked me to make. I must look a little like a steward when I give an account of my stewardship."

"Oh, but my brother has dressed up," cried the girl, "very much so. No end, if I may say so. Why, he's bearing down on you now in all his glory."

The noble lord was indeed marching towards them in a magnificent sixteenth-century costume of purple and gold, with a gold-hilted sword and a plumed cap, and manners to match. Indeed, there was something more than his usual expansiveness of bodily action in his appearance at that moment. It almost seemed, so to speak, that the plumes on his hat had gone to his head. He flapped his great gold-lined cloak like the wings of a fairy king in a pantomime; he even drew his sword with a flourish and waved it about as he did his walking-stick. In the light of after events there seemed to be something monstrous and ominous about that exuberance; something of the spirit that is called *fey*. At the time it merely crossed a few people's minds that he might possibly be drunk.

As he strode towards his sister, the first figure he passed was that of Leonard Crane, clad in Lincoln green with the horn and baldrick and sword appropriate to Robin Hood; for he was standing nearest to the lady, where indeed he might have been found during a disproportionate part of the time. He had displayed one of his buried talents in the matter of skating, and now that the skating was over seemed disposed to prolong the partnership. The boisterous Bulmer playfully made a pass at him with his drawn sword, going forward with the lunge in the proper fencing fashion, and making a somewhat too familiar Shakespearean quotation about a rodent and a Venetian coin.

Probably in Crane also there was a subdued excitement just then; anyhow, in one flash he had drawn his own sword and parried; and then suddenly, to the surprise of everyone, Bulmer's weapon seemed to spring out of his hand into the air and rolled away on the ringing ice.

"Well, I never," said the lady, as if with justifiable indignation, "you never told me you could fence too."

Bulmer put up his sword with an air rather bewildered than annoyed, which increased the impression of something irresponsible in his mood at the moment; then he turned rather abruptly to his lawyer, saying: "We can settle up about the estate after dinner; I've missed nearly all the skating as it is; and I doubt if the ice will hold till tomorrow night. I think I shall get up early and have a spin by myself."

"You won't be disturbed with my company," said Horne Fisher in his weary fashion. "If I have to begin the day with ice, in the American fashion, I prefer it in smaller quantities. But no early hours for me in December. The early bird catches the cold."

"Oh, I shan't die of catching a cold," answered Bulmer, and laughed.

A considerable group of the skating party had consisted of the guests staying at the house; and the rest had tailed off in twos and threes some time before most of the guests began to retire for the night. Neighbours always invited to Prior's Park on such occasions went back to their own houses in motors or on foot; the legal and archaeological gentleman had returned to the Inns of Court by a late train, to get a paper called for during his consultation with his client; and most of the other guests were drifting and lingering at various stages on their way up to bed. Horne Fisher, as if to deprive himself of any excuse for his refusal of early rising, had been the first to retire to his room; but, sleepy as he looked, he could not sleep. He had picked up from a table the book of antiquarian topography, in which Haddow had found his first hints about the origin of the local name; and being a man with a quiet and quaint capacity for being interested in anything, he began to read it steadily, making notes now and then of details on which his previous reading left him with a certain doubt about his present conclusions. His room was the one nearest to the lake in the centre of the woods, and was therefore the quietest; and none of the last echoes of the evening's festivity could reach him. He had followed carefully the argument which established the derivation from Mr. Prior's farm and the hole in the wall, and disposed of any fashionable fancy about monks and magic wells, when he began to be conscious of a noise audible in the frozen silence of the night. It was not a particularly loud noise; but it seemed to consist of a series of thuds or heavy blows, such as might be struck on a wooden door by a man seeking to enter. They were followed by something like a faint creak or crack, as if the obstacle had either been opened or had given way. He opened his own bedroom door and listened; but as he heard talk and laughter all over the lower floors, he had no reason to fear that a summons would be neglected or the house left without protection. He went to his open window, looking out over the frozen pond and the moonlit statue in the middle of their circle of darkling woods, and listened again. But silence had returned to that silent place; and after straining his ears for a considerable time he could hear nothing but the solitary hoot of a distant departing train. Then he reminded himself how many nameless noises can be heard by the wakeful during the most ordinary night; and, shrugging his shoulders, went wearily to bed.

He awoke suddenly and sat up in bed with his ears filled, as with thunder, with the throbbing echoes of a rending cry. He remained rigid for a moment, and then sprang out of bed, throwing on the loose gown of sacking he had worn all day. He went first to the window, which was open but covered with a thick curtain, so that his room was still completely dark; but when he tossed the curtain aside and put his head out, he saw that a grey and silver daybreak had already appeared behind the black woods that surrounded the little lake. And that was all he did see. Though the sound had certainly come in through the open window from this direction, the whole scene was still and empty under the morning light as under the moonlight. Then the long, rather lackadaisical hand he had laid on a window-sill gripped it tighter as if to master a tremor, and his peering blue eyes grew bleak with fear. It may seem that his emotion was exaggerated and needless, considering the effort of common sense by which he had conquered his nervousness about the noise on the previous night. But that had been a very different sort of noise. It might have been made by half a hundred things, from the chopping of wood to the breaking of bottles. There was only one thing in nature from which could come the sound that echoed through that dark house at daybreak. It was the awful articulate voice of man; and it was something worse, for he knew what man.

He knew also that it had been a shout for help. It seemed to him that he had heard the very word; but the word, short as it was, had been swallowed up, as if the man had been stifled or snatched away even as he spoke. Only the mocking reverberations of it remained even in his memory; but he had no doubt of the original voice.

He had no doubt that the great bull's voice of Francis Bray, Baron Bulmer, had been heard for the last time between the darkness and the lifting dawn.

How long he stood there he never knew; but he was startled into life by the first living thing that he saw stirring in that half-frozen landscape. Along the path beside the lake, and immediately under his window, a figure was walking slowly and softly but with great composure; a stately figure in robes of a splendid scarlet; it was the Italian Prince, still in his Cardinal's costume. Most of the company had indeed lived in their costumes for the last day or two, and Fisher himself had assumed his frock of sacking as a convenient dressing-gown; but there seemed nevertheless something unusually finished and formal, in the way of an early bird, about this magnificent red cockatoo. It was as if the early bird had been up all night.

"What is the matter?" he called sharply, leaning out of the window; and the Italian turned up his great yellow face like a mask of brass.

"We had better discuss it downstairs," said Prince Borodino.

Fisher ran downstairs, and encountered the great red-robed figure entering the doorway and blocking the entrance with his bulk.

"Did you hear that cry?" demanded Fisher.

"I heard a noise and I came out," answered the diplomatist, and his face was too dark in the shadow for its expression to be read.

"It was Bulmer's voice," insisted Fisher. "I'll swear it was Bulmer's voice."

"Did you know him well?" asked the other.

The question seemed irrelevant though it was not illogical; and Fisher could only answer in a random fashion that he only knew Lord Bulmer slightly.

"Nobody seems to have known him well," continued the Italian in level tones. "Nobody except that man Brain. Brain is rather older than Bulmer, but I fancy they shared a good many secrets."

Fisher moved abruptly, as if waking from a momentary trance, and said in a new and more vigorous voice: "But look here, hadn't we better get outside and see if anything has happened."

"The ice seems to be thawing," said the other, almost with indifference.

When they emerged from the house, dark stains and stars in the grey field of ice did indeed indicate that the frost was breaking up, as their host had prophesied the day before; and the very memory of yesterday brought back the mystery of today.

"He knew there would be a thaw," observed the Prince. "He went out skating quite early on purpose. Did he call out because he landed in the water, do you think?"

Fisher looked puzzled.

"Bulmer was the last man to bellow like that because he got his boots wet. And that's all he could do here; the water would hardly come up to the calf of a man of his size. You can see the flat weeds on the floor of the lake as if it were through a thin pane of glass. No, if Bulmer had only broken the ice he wouldn't have said much at the moment, though possibly a good deal afterwards. We should have found him stamping and damning up and down this path, and calling for clean boots."

"Let us hope we shall find him as happily employed," remarked the diplomatist. "In that case the voice must have come out of the wood."

"I'll swear it didn't come out of the house," said Fisher; and the two disappeared together into the twilight of wintry trees.

The plantation stood dark against the fiery colours of sunrise; a black fringe having that feathery appearance which makes trees when they are bare the very reverse of rugged. Hours and hours afterwards, when the same dense but delicate margin was dark against the cool greenish colours opposite the sunset, the search thus begun at sunrise had not come to an end. By successive stages, and to slowly gathering groups of the company, it became apparent that the most extraordinary of all gaps had appeared in the party; the guests could find no trace of their host anywhere. The servants reported that his bed had been slept in and his skates and his fancy costume were gone, as if he had risen early for the purpose he had himself avowed. But from the top of the house to the bottom, from the walls round the park to the pond in the centre, there was no trace of Lord Bulmer, dead or alive. Horne Fisher realised that a chilling premonition had already prevented him from expecting to find the man alive. But his bald brow was wrinkled over an entirely new and unnatural problem in not finding the man at all.

He considered the possibility of Bulmer having gone off on his own accord, for some reason; but after fully weighing it he finally dismissed it. It was inconsistent with the unmistakable voice heard at daybreak, and with many other practical obstacles. There was only one gateway in the ancient and lofty wall round the small park; the lodge-keeper kept it locked till late in the morning, and the lodge-keeper had seen no one pass. Fisher was fairly sure that he had before him a mathematical problem in an enclosed space. His instinct had been from the first so attuned to the tragedy that it would have been almost a relief to him to find the corpse. He would have been grieved, but not horrified, to come on the nobleman's body dangling from one of his own trees as from a gibbet, or floating in his own pool like a pallid weed. What horrified him was to find nothing.

He soon became conscious that he was not alone even in his most individual and isolated experiments. He often found a figure following him like his shadow, in silent and almost secret clearings in the plantation or outlying nooks and corners of the old wall. The dark-moustached mouth was as mute as the deep eyes were mobile, darting incessantly hither and thither, but it was clear that Brain of the Indian police had taken up the trail like an old hunter after a tiger. Seeing that he was the only personal friend of the vanished man, this seemed natural enough; and Fisher resolved to deal frankly with him.

"This silence is rather a social strain," he said. "May I break the ice by talking about the weather; which, by the way, has already broken the ice? I know that breaking the ice might be a rather melancholy metaphor in this case."

"I don't think so," replied Brain shortly. "I don't fancy the ice had much to do with it. I don't see how it could."

"What would you propose doing?" asked Fisher.

"Well, we've sent for the authorities, of course, but I hope to find something out before they come," replied the Anglo-Indian. "I can't say I have much hope from police methods in this country. Too much red tape: Habeas Corpus and that sort of thing. What we want is to see that nobody bolts; the nearest we could get to it would be to collect the company and count them, so to speak. Nobody's left lately, except that lawyer who was poking about for antiquities."

"Oh, he's out of it; he left last night," answered the other. "Eight hours after Bulmer's chauffeur saw his lawyer off by the train, I heard Bulmer's own voice as plain as I hear yours now."

"I suppose you don't believe in spirits?" said the man from India. After a pause he added: "There's somebody else I should like to find, before we go after a fellow with an alibi in the Inner Temple. What's become of that fellow in green; the architect dressed up as a forester? I haven't seen him about."

Mr. Brain managed to secure his assembly of all the distracted company before the arrival of the police. But when he first began to comment once more on the young architect's delay in putting in an appearance, he found himself in the presence of a minor mystery, and a psychological development of an entirely unexpected kind.

Juliet Bray had confronted the catastrophe of her brother's disappearance with a sombre stoicism in which there was perhaps more paralysis than pain; but when the other question came to the surface she was both agitated and angry.

"We don't want to jump to any conclusions about anybody," Brain was saying in his staccato style, "but we should like to know a little more about Mr. Crane. Nobody seems to know much about him or where he comes from. And it seems a sort of coincidence that yesterday he actually crossed swords with poor Bulmer, and could have stuck him too, since he showed himself the better swordsman. Of course, that may be an accident, and couldn't possibly be called a case against anybody; but then we haven't the means to make a real case against anybody. Till the police come we are only a pack of very amateur sleuth-hounds."

"And I think you're a pack of snobs," said Juliet. "Because Mr. Crane is a genius who's made his own way, you try to suggest he's a murderer without daring to say so. Because he wore a toy sword, and happened to know how to use it, you want us to believe he used it like a blood-thirsty maniac for no reason in the world. And because he could have hit my brother and didn't, you deduce that he did. That's the sort of way you argue. And as for his having disappeared, you're wrong in that as you are in everything else, for here he comes."

And, indeed, the green figure of the fictitious Robin Hood slowly detached itself from the grey background of the trees and came towards them as she spoke.

He approached the group slowly, but with composure; but he was decidedly pale, and the eyes of Brain and Fisher had already taken in one detail of the green-clad figure more clearly than all the rest. The horn still swung from his baldrick, but the sword was gone.

Rather to the surprise of the company, Brain did not follow up the question thus suggested, but, while retaining an air of leading the inquiry, had also an appearance of changing the subject.

"Now we're all assembled," he observed quietly, "there is a question I want to ask to begin with. Did anybody here actually see Lord Bulmer this morning?"

Leonard Crane turned his pale face round the circle of faces till he came to Juliet's: then he compressed his lips a little and said: "Yes, I saw him."

"Was he alive and well?" asked Brain quickly. "How was he dressed?"

"He appeared exceedingly well," replied Crane, with a curious intonation. "He was dressed as he was yesterday, in that purple costume copied from the portrait of his ancestor in the sixteenth century. He had his skates in his hand."

"And his sword at his side, I suppose," added the questioner. "Where is your own sword, Mr. Crane?"

"I threw it away."

In the singular silence that ensued the train of thought in many minds became involuntarily a series of coloured pictures. They had grown used to their fanciful garments looking more gay and gorgeous against the dark grey and streaky silver of the frost, so that the moving figures glowed like stained-glass saints walking. The effect had been more fitting because so many of them had idly parodied pontifical or monastic dress. But the most arresting attitude that remained in their memories had been anything but merely monastic: that of the moment when the figure in bright green and the other in vivid violet had for a moment made a silver cross of their crossing swords. Even when it was a jest it had been something of a drama; and it was a strange and sinister thought that, in the grey daybreak, the same figures in the same posture might have been repeated as a tragedy.

"Did you quarrel with him?" asked Brain suddenly.

"Yes," replied the immovable man in green. "Or he quarrelled with me."

"Why did he quarrel with you?" asked the investigator; and Leonard Crane made no reply.

Horne Fisher, curiously enough, had only given half his attention to this crucial cross-examination. His heavy-lidded eyes had languidly followed the figure of Prince Borodino, who at this stage had strolled away towards the fringe of the wood and, after a pause as of meditation, had disappeared into the darkness of the trees.

He was recalled from his irrelevance by the voice of Juliet Bray, which rang out with an altogether new note of decision:

"If that is the difficulty, it had best be cleared up. I am engaged to Mr. Crane; and when we told my brother, he did not approve of it, that is all."

Neither Brain nor Fisher exhibited any surprise, but the former added quietly:

"Except, I suppose, that he and your brother went off into the wood to discuss it—where Mr. Crane mislaid his sword, not to mention his companion."

"And may I ask," inquired Crane, with a certain flicker of mockery passing over his pallid features, "what I am supposed to have done with either of them? Let us adopt the cheerful thesis that I am a murderer. It has yet to be shown that I am a magician. If I ran your unfortunate friend through the body, what did I do with the body? Did I have it carried away by seven flying dragons, or was it merely a trifling matter of turning it into a milk-white hind?"

"It is no occasion for sneering," said the Anglo-Indian judge with abrupt authority. "It doesn't make it look better for you that you can joke about the loss."

Fisher's dreamy and even dreary eye was still on the edge of the wood behind, and he became conscious of masses of dark red, like a stormy sunset cloud, glowing through the grey network of the thin trees; and the Prince, in his cardinal's robes, re-emerged on to the pathway. Brain had had half a notion that the Prince might have gone to look for the lost rapier, but when he reappeared he was carrying in his hand, not a sword, but an axe.

The incongruity between the masquerade and the mystery had created a curious psychological atmosphere. At first they had all felt horribly ashamed at being caught in the foolish disguises of a festival by an event that had only too much the character of a funeral. Many of them would have already gone back and dressed in clothes that were more funereal, or at least more formal. But somehow at the moment this seemed like a second masquerade, more artificial and frivolous than the first. And as they reconciled themselves to their ridiculous trappings a curious sensation had come over some of them, notably over the more sensitive, like Crane and Fisher and

Juliet, but in some degree over everybody except the practical Mr.
Brain. It was almost as if they were the ghosts of their own ancestors haunting that dark wood and dismal lake, and playing some
old part that they only half remembered. The movements of those
coloured figures seemed to mean something that had been settled
long before, like a silent heraldry. Acts, attitudes, external objects,
were accepted as an allegory even without the key; and they knew
when a crisis had come, when they did not know what it was. And
somehow they knew subconsciously that the whole tale had taken
a new and terrible turn when they saw the Prince stand in the gap
of the gaunt trees, in his robes of angry crimson and with his lowering face of bronze, bearing in his hand a new shape of death. They
could not have named a reason; but the two swords seemed indeed
to have become toy swords, and the whole tale of them broken and
tossed away like a toy. Borodino looked like the old-world heads-
man, clad in terrible red, and carrying the axe for the execution of
the criminal. And the criminal was not Crane.

Mr. Brain, of the Indian police, was glaring at the new object,
and it was a moment or two before he spoke, harshly and almost
hoarsely.

"What are you doing with that?" he asked. "Seems to be a
woodsman's chopper."

"A natural association of ideas," observed Horne Fisher. "If
you meet a cat in a wood, you think it's a wild cat, though it may
have just strolled from the drawing-room sofa. As a matter of
fact, I happen to know that is not the woodman's chopper. It's the
kitchen chopper, or meat axe or something like that, that somebody has thrown away in the wood. I saw it in the kitchen myself
when I was getting the potato sacks with which I reconstructed a
mediaeval hermit."

"All the same, it is not without interest," remarked the Prince, holding out the instrument to Fisher, who took it and examined it carefully. "A butcher's cleaver that has done butcher's work."

"It was certainly the instrument of the crime," assented Fisher in a low voice.

Brain was staring at the dull blue gleam of the axe-head with fierce and fascinated eyes.

"I don't understand you," he said; "there is no—there are no marks on it."

"It has shed no blood," answered Fisher, "but for all that it has committed a crime. This is as near as the criminal came to the crime when he committed it."

"What do you mean?"

"He was not there when he did it," explained Fisher. "It's a poor sort of murderer who can't murder people when he isn't there."

"You seem to be talking merely for the sake of mystification," said Brain. "If you have any practical advice to give, you might as well make it intelligible."

"The only practical advice I can suggest," said Fisher thoughtfully, "is a little research into local topography and nomenclature. They say there used to be a Mr. Prior, who had a farm in this neighbourhood. I think some details about the domestic life of the late Mr. Prior would throw a light on this terrible business."

"And you have nothing more immediate than your topography to offer," said Brain, with a sneer, "to help me to avenge my friend."

"Well," said Fisher, "I should find out the truth about the Hole in the Wall."

That night, at the close of a stormy twilight and under a strong west wind that followed the breaking of the frost, Leonard Crane was wending his way in a wild rotatory walk round and round the high continuous wall that enclosed the little wood. He was driven by a desperate idea of solving for himself the riddle that had clouded his reputation and already even threatened his liberty. The police authorities, now in charge of the inquiry, had not arrested him; but he knew well enough that if he tried to move far afield he would be instantly arrested. Horne Fisher's fragmentary hints, though he had refused to expand them as yet, had stirred the artistic temperament of the architect to a sort of wild analysis, and he was resolved to read the hieroglyph upside down and every way until it made sense. If it was something connected with a hole in the wall, he would find the hole in the wall; but as a matter of fact he was unable to find the faintest crack in the wall. His professional knowledge told him that the masonry was all of one workmanship and one date; and except for the regular entrance, which threw no light on the mystery, he found nothing suggesting any sort of hiding-place or means of escape. Walking a narrow path between the windy wall and the wild eastward bend and sweep of the grey and feathery trees, seeing shifting gleams of a lost sunset winking almost like lightning as the clouds of tempest scudded across the sky and mingling with the first faint blue light from a slowly strengthened moon behind him, he began to feel his head going round as his heels were going round and round the blind recurrent barrier. He had thoughts on the border of thought, fancies about a fourth dimension which was itself a hole to hide anything, of seeing everything from a new angle out of a new window in the senses, or of some mystical light and transparency, like the new rays of chemistry, in which he could see Bulmer's body, horrible and glaring, floating in a lurid halo over the woods and the wall. He was haunted also with the hint, which somehow seemed to be equally horrifying, that it all had something to do with Mr. Prior. There seemed even to be something creepy in the fact that he was always respectfully referred to as Mr. Prior, and that it was in the domestic life of the dead farmer that he had been bidden to seek the seed of these dreadful things. As a matter of fact, he had found that no local inquiries had revealed anything at all about the Prior family. He dimly imagined Mr. Prior in an old top-hat, perhaps with a chin-beard or whiskers. But he had no face.

The moonlight had broadened and brightened, the wind had driven off the clouds and itself died fitfully away, when he came round again to the artificial lake in front of the house. For some reason it looked a very artificial lake; indeed, the whole scene was like a classical landscape with a touch of Watteau; the Palladian façade of the house pale in the moon, and the same silver touching the very pagan and naked marble nymph in the middle of the pond. Rather to his surprise he found another figure there beside the statue, sitting almost equally motionless; and the same silver pencil traced the wrinkled brow and patient face of Horne Fisher, still dressed as a hermit, and apparently practising something of the solitude of a hermit. Nevertheless he looked up at Leonard Crane and smiled, almost as if he had expected him.

"Look here," said Crane, planting himself in front of him. "Can you tell me anything about this business?"

"I shall soon have to tell everybody everything about it," replied Fisher, "but I've no objection to telling you something first. But, to begin with, will you tell me something? What really happened when you met Bulmer this morning? You did throw away your sword, but you didn't kill him."

"I didn't kill him because I threw away my sword," said the other. "I did it on purpose, or I'm not sure what might have happened."

After a pause he went on quietly:

"The late Lord Bulmer was a very breezy gentleman, extremely breezy. He was very genial with his inferiors, and would have his lawyer and his architect staying in his house for all sorts of holidays and amusements. But there was another side to him, which they found out when they tried to be his equals. When I told him that his sister and I were engaged, something happened which I simply can't and won't describe. It seemed to me like some monstrous upheaval of madness. But I suppose the truth is painfully simple. There is such a thing as the coarseness of a gentleman. And it is the most horrible thing in humanity."

"I know," said Fisher. "The Renascence nobles of the Tudor time were like that."

"It is odd that you should say that," Crane went on, "for while we were talking there came on me a curious feeling that we were repeating some scene of the past, and that I was really some outlaw, found in the woods like Robin Hood, and that he had really stepped, in all his plumes and purple, out of the picture-frame of the ancestral portrait. Anyhow, he was the man in possession, and he neither feared God nor regarded man. I defied him, of course, and walked away. I might really have killed him if I had not walked away."

"Yes," said Fisher, nodding, "his ancestor was in possession and he was in possession; and this is the end of the story. It all fits in."

"Fits in with what?" cried his companion, with sudden impatience; "I can't make head or tail of it. You tell me to look for the secret in the hole in the wall, but I can't find any hole in the wall."

"There isn't any," said Fisher. "That's the secret."

After reflecting a moment, he added:

"Unless you call it a hole in the wall of the world. Look here, I'll tell you, if you like, but I'm afraid it involves an introduction.

You've got to understand one of the tricks of the modern mind, a tendency that most people obey without noticing it.

"In the village or suburb outside there's an inn with the sign of St. George and the Dragon. Now suppose I went about telling everybody that this was only a corruption of King George and the Dragoon. Scores of people would believe it, without any inquiry, from a vague feeling that it's probable because it's prosaic. It turns something romantic and legendary into something recent and ordinary. And that somehow makes it sound rational, though it is unsupported by reason. Of course, some people would have the sense to remember having seen St. George in old Italian pictures and French romances; but a good many wouldn't think about it at all. They would just swallow the scepticism because it was scepticism. Modern intelligence won't accept anything on authority. But it will accept anything without authority. That's exactly what has happened here.

"When some critic or other chose to say that Prior's Park was not a priory, but was named after some quite modern man named Prior, nobody really tested the theory at all. It never occurred to anybody repeating the story to ask if there *was* any Mr. Prior, if anybody had ever seen him or heard of him. As a matter of fact, it was a priory, and shared the fate of most priories; that is, the Tudor gentleman with the plumes simply stole it by brute force and turned it into his own private house; he did worse things, as you shall hear. But the point here is that this is how the trick works; and the trick works in the same way in the other part of the tale. The name of this district is printed Holinwall in all the best maps produced by the scholars, and they allude lightly, not without a smile, to the fact that it was pronounced Holiwell by the most ignorant and old-fashioned of the poor. But it is spelt wrong and pronounced right."

"Do you mean to say," asked Crane quickly, "that there really was a well?"

"There is a well," said Fisher, "and the truth lies at the bottom of it."

As he spoke he stretched out his hand and pointed towards a sheet of water in front of him.

"The well is under that water somewhere," he said, "and this is not the first tragedy connected with it. The founder of this house did something which his fellow-ruffians very seldom did, something that had to be hushed up even in the anarchy of the pillage of the monasteries. The well was connected with the miracles of some saint, and the last prior that guarded it was something like a saint himself; certainly he was something very like a martyr. He defied the new owner and dared him to pollute the place, till the noble, in a fury, stabbed him and flung his body into the well; whither after four hundred years it has been followed by an heir of the usurper, clad in the same purple and walking the world with the same pride."

"But how did it happen," demanded Crane, "that for the first time Bulmer fell in at that particular spot?"

"Because the ice was only loosened at that particular spot by the only man who knew it," answered Horne Fisher. "It was cracked deliberately with the kitchen chopper at that special place, and I myself heard the hammering and did not understand it. The place had been covered with an artificial lake, if only because the whole truth had to be covered with an artificial legend. But don't you see that it is exactly what those pagan nobles would have done, to desecrate it with a sort of heathen goddess, as the Roman Emperor built a temple to Venus on the Holy Sepulchre? But the truth could still be traced out by any scholarly man determined to trace it. And this man was determined to trace it."

"What man?" asked the other, with a shadow of the answer in his mind.

"The only man who has an alibi," replied Fisher. "James Haddow, the antiquarian lawyer, left the night before the fatality, but he left that black star of death on the ice. He left abruptly, having previously proposed to stay; probably, I think, after an ugly scene with Bulmer at their legal interview. As you know yourself, Bulmer could make a man feel pretty murderous; and I rather fancy the lawyer had himself irregularities to confess, and was in danger of exposure by his client. But it's my reading of human nature that a man will cheat in his trade but not in his hobby. Haddow may have been a dishonest lawyer, but he couldn't help being an honest antiquary. When he got on the track of the truth about the Holy Well, he had to follow it up; he was not to be bamboozled with newspaper anecdotes about Mr. Prior and a hole in the wall; he found out everything, even to the exact location of the well, and he was rewarded, if being a successful assassin can be regarded as a reward."

"And how did you get on the track of all this hidden history?" asked the young architect.

A cloud came across the brow of Horne Fisher.

"I knew only too much about it already," he said, "and, after all, it's shameful for me to be speaking lightly of poor Bulmer, who has paid his penalty, when the rest of us haven't. I dare say every cigar I smoke and every liqueur I drink comes directly or indirectly from the harrying of the holy places and the persecution of the poor. After all, it needs very little poking about in the past to find that hole in the wall; that great breach in the defences of English history. It lies just under the surface of a thin sheet of sham information and instruction, just as the black and bloodstained well lies just under the floor of shallow water and flat weeds. Oh, the ice is thin, but it bears; it is strong enough to support us when we dress up as monks and dance on it in mockery of the dear quaint old Middle Ages. They told me I must put on fancy dress; so I did put on fancy dress, according to my own taste and fancy. You see I do know a little about our national and imperial history, our prosperity and our progress, our commerce and our colonies, our centuries of success or splendour. So I did put on an antiquated sort of costume, when I was asked to do so. I put on the only costume I think fit for a man who has inherited the position of a gentleman and yet has not entirely lost the feelings of one."

In answer to a look of inquiry he rose with a sweeping and downward gesture.

"Sackcloth," he said, "and I would wear the ashes as well, if they would stay on my bald head when I put them there."

DEATH ON THE AIR

Ngaio Marsh

Ngaio Marsh (1895–1982) was a cultured all-rounder, an accomplished artist and a theatre director of distinction, but she is best remembered today for her mystery fiction. She was born in Christchurch, New Zealand, and also died there, but for all her lifelong devotion to her home country, she was a leading exponent of the classic English detective story and became a proud member of the Detection Club. Her detective Roderick Alleyn of Scotland Yard is a suave, gentlemanly figure whose first recorded case was a country house mystery, *A Man Lay Dead* (1934). He enjoyed a career that lasted almost half a century before taking his final bow in *Light Thickens* (1982).

As the crime genre expert Douglas Greene said when introducing a collection of her short fiction, Marsh "brought to her writing the clear-sightedness of an outsider—an outsider who could view a scene as a painter and plot with the dramatic sense of a playwright". "Death on the Air" first appeared in *The Grand Magazine* in 1937. Greene describes it as "a typical closed-circle detective story of the period with a clever murder device and a cleverly hidden murderer". On first appearance, the story was co-credited to Marsh's fellow New Zealander, Archibald Drummond Sharpe, but in its subsequent appearances Marsh has been treated as the author. Sharpe wrote no other fiction and it seems almost certain that he contributed technical information and expertise, but that Marsh alone did the writing.

O N THE 25TH OF DECEMBER AT 7.30 A.M. MR. SEPTIMUS TONKS was found dead beside his wireless set.

It was Emily Parks, an under-housemaid, who discovered him. She butted open the door and entered, carrying mop, duster, and carpet-sweeper. At that precise moment she was greatly startled by a voice that spoke out of the darkness.

"Good morning, everybody," said the voice in superbly inflected syllables, "and a Merry Christmas!"

Emily yelped, but not loudly, as she immediately realised what had happened. Mr. Tonks had omitted to turn off his wireless before going to bed. She drew back the curtains, revealing a kind of pale murk which was a London Christmas dawn, switched on the light, and saw Septimus.

He was seated in front of the radio. It was a small but expensive set, specially built for him; Septimus sat in an armchair, his back to Emily and his body tilted towards the wireless.

His hands, the fingers curiously bunched, were on the ledge of the cabinet under the tuning and volume knobs. His chest rested against the shelf below and his head leaned on the front panel.

He looked rather as though he was listening intently to the interior secrets of the wireless. His head was bent so that Emily could see the bald top with its trail of oiled hairs. He did not move.

"Beg pardon, sir," gasped Emily. She was again greatly startled. Mr. Tonks' enthusiasm for radio had never before induced him to tune in at seven thirty in the morning.

"Special Christmas service," the cultured voice was saying. Mr. Tonks sat very still. Emily, in common with the other servants, was terrified of her master. She did not know whether to go or to stay. She gazed wildly at Septimus and realised that he wore a dinner-jacket. The room was now filled with the clamour of pealing bells.

Emily opened her mouth as wide as it would go and screamed and screamed and screamed...

Chase, the butler, was the first to arrive. He was a pale, flabby man but authoritative. He said: "What's the meaning of this out-rage?" and then saw Septimus. He went to the armchair, bent down, and looked into his master's face.

He did not lose his head, but said in a loud voice: "My Gawd!" And then to Emily: "Shut your face." By this vulgarism he betrayed his agitation. He seized Emily by the shoulders and thrust her towards the door, where they were met by Mr. Hislop, the secretary, in his dressing-gown.

Mr. Hislop said: "Good heavens, Chase, what is the meaning—" and then his voice too was drowned in the clamour of bells and renewed screams.

Chase put his fat white hand over Emily's mouth.

"In the study if you please, sir. An accident. Go to your room, will you, and stop that noise or I'll give you something to make you." This to Emily, who bolted down the hall, where she was received by the rest of the staff who had congregated there.

Chase returned to the study with Mr. Hislop and locked the door. They both looked down at the body of Septimus Tonks. The secretary was the first to speak.

"But—but—he's dead," said little Mr. Hislop.

"I suppose there can't be any doubt," whispered Chase.

"Look at the face. Any doubt! My God!"

Mr. Hislop put out a delicate hand towards the bent head and then drew it back. Chase, less fastidious, touched one of the hard wrists, gripped, and then lifted it. The body at once tipped backwards as if it was made of wood. One of the hands knocked against the butler's face. He sprang back with an oath.

There lay Septimus, his knees and his hands in the air, his terrible face turned up to the light. Chase pointed to the right hand. Two fingers and the thumb were slightly blackened.

Ding, dong, dang, ding.

"For God's sake stop those bells," cried Mr. Hislop. Chase turned off the wall switch. Into the sudden silence came the sound of the door handle being rattled and Guy Tonks' voice on the other side.

"Hislop! Mr. Hislop! Chase! What's the matter?"

"Just a moment, Mr. Guy." Chase looked at the secretary. "You go, sir."

So it was left to Mr. Hislop to break the news to the family. They listened to his stammering revelation in stupefied silence. It was not until Guy, the eldest of the three children, stood in the study that any practical suggestion was made.

"What has killed him?" asked Guy.

"It's extraordinary," burbled Hislop. "Extraordinary. He looks as if he'd been—"

"Galvanised," said Guy.

"We ought to send for a doctor," suggested Hislop timidly.

"Of course. Will you, Mr. Hislop? Dr. Meadows."

Hislop went to the telephone and Guy returned to his family. Dr. Meadows lived on the other side of the square and arrived in five minutes. He examined the body without moving it. He questioned Chase and Hislop. Chase was very voluble about the burns on the hand. He uttered the word "electrocution" over and over again.

"I had a cousin, sir, that was struck by lightning. As soon as I saw the hand—"

"Yes, yes," said Dr. Meadows. "So you said. I can see the burns for myself."

"Electrocution," repeated Chase. "There'll have to be an inquest."

Dr. Meadows snapped at him, summoned Emily, and then saw the rest of the family—Guy, Arthur, Phillipa, and their mother. They were clustered round a cold grate in the drawing room. Phillipa was on her knees, trying to light the fire.

"What was it?" asked Arthur as soon as the doctor came in.

"Looks like electric shock. Guy, I'll have a word with you if you please. Phillipa, look after your mother, there's a good child. Coffee with a dash of brandy. Where are those damn maids? Come on, Guy."

Alone with Guy, he said they'd have to send for the police.

"The police!" Guy's dark face turned very pale. "Why? What's it got to do with them?"

"Nothing, as like as not, but they'll have to be notified. I can't give a certificate as things are. If it's electrocution, how did it happen?"

"But the police!" said Guy. "That's simply ghastly. Dr. Meadows, for God's sake couldn't you—?"

"No," said Dr. Meadows, "I couldn't. Sorry, Guy, but there it is."

"But can't we wait a moment? Look at him again. You haven't examined him properly."

"I don't want to move him, that's why. Pull yourself together, boy. Look here. I've got a pal in the CID—Alleyn. He's a gentleman and all that. He'll curse me like a fury, but he'll come if he's in London, and he'll make things easier for you. Go back to your mother. I'll ring Alleyn up."

That was how it came about that Chief Detective Inspector Roderick Alleyn spent his Christmas Day in harness. As a matter of fact he was on duty, and as he pointed out to Dr. Meadows, would have had to turn out and visit his miserable Tonkses in any case. When he did arrive it was with his usual air of remote courtesy. He was accompanied by a tall, thickset officer—Inspector Fox—and by the divisional police surgeon. Dr. Meadows took them into the study. Alleyn, in his turn, looked at the horror that had been Septimus.

"Was he like this when he was found?"

"No. I understand he was leaning forward with his hands on the ledge of the cabinet. He must have slumped forward and been propped up by the chair arms and the cabinet."

"Who moved him?"

"Chase, the butler. He said he only meant to raise the arm. *Rigor* is well established."

Alleyn put his hand behind the rigid neck and pushed. The body fell forward into its original position.

"There you are, Curtis," said Alleyn to the divisional surgeon. He turned to Fox. "Get the camera man, will you, Fox?"

The photographer took four shots and departed. Alleyn marked the position of the hands and feet with chalk, made a careful plan of the room and then turned to the doctors.

"Is it electrocution, do you think?"

"Looks like it," said Curtis. "Have to be a p.m. of course."

"Of course. Still, look at the hands. Burns. Thumb and two fingers bunched together and exactly the distance between the two knobs apart. He'd been tuning his hurdy-gurdy."

"By gum," said Inspector Fox, speaking for the first time.

"D'you mean he got a lethal shock from his radio?" asked Dr. Meadows.

"I don't know. I merely conclude he had his hands on the knobs when he died."

"It was still going when the housemaid found him. Chase turned it off and got no shock."

"Yours, partner," said Alleyn, turning to Fox. Fox stooped down to the wall switch.

"Careful," said Alleyn.

"I've got rubber soles," said Fox, and switched it on. The radio hummed, gathered volume, and found itself.

"No-oel, No-o-el," it roared. Fox cut it off and pulled out the wall plug.

"I'd like to have a look inside this set," he said.

"So you shall, old boy, so you shall," rejoined Alleyn. "Before you begin, I think we'd better move the body. Will you see to that, Meadows? Fox, get Bailey, will you? He's out in the car."

Curtis, Hislop, and Meadows carried Septimus Tonks into a spare downstairs room. It was a difficult and horrible business with that contorted body. Dr. Meadows came back alone, mopping his brow, to find Detective-Sergeant Bailey, a fingerprint expert, at work on the wireless cabinet.

"What's all this?" asked Dr. Meadows. "Do you want to find out if he'd been fooling round with the innards?"

"He," said Alleyn, "or—somebody else."

"Umph!" Dr. Meadows looked at the Inspector. "You agree with me, it seems. Do you suspect—?"

"Suspect? I'm the least suspicious man alive. I'm merely being tidy. Well, Bailey?"

"I've got a good one off the chair arm. That'll be the deceased's, won't it, sir?"

"No doubt. We'll check up later. What about the wireless?"

Fox, wearing a glove, pulled off the knob of the volume control.

"Seems to be OK," said Bailey. "It's a sweet bit of work. Not too bad at all, sir." He turned his torch into the back of the radio, undid a couple of screws underneath the set, and lifted out the works.

"What's the little hole for?" asked Alleyn.

"What's that, sir?" said Fox.

"There's a hole bored through the panel above the knob. About an eighth of an inch in diameter. The rim of the knob hides it. One might easily miss it. Move your torch, Bailey. Yes. There, do you see?"

Fox bent down and uttered a bass growl. A fine needle of light came through the front of the radio.

"That's peculiar, sir," said Bailey from the other side. "I don't get the idea at all."

Alleyn pulled out the tuning knob.

"There's another one there," he murmured. "Yes. Nice clean little holes. Newly bored. Unusual, I take it?"

"Unusual's the word, sir," said Fox.

"Run away, Meadows," said Alleyn.

"Why the devil?" asked Dr. Meadows indignantly. "What are you driving at? Why shouldn't I be here?"

"You ought to be with the sorrowing relatives. Where's your corpse-side manner?"

"I've settled them. What are you up to?"

"Who's being suspicious now?" asked Alleyn mildly. "You may stay for a moment. Tell me about the Tonkses. Who are they? What are they? What sort of a man was Septimus?"

"If you must know, he was a damned unpleasant sort of a man."

"Tell me about him."

Dr. Meadows sat down and lit a cigarette.

"He was a self-made bloke," he said, "as hard as nails and—well, coarse rather than vulgar."

"Like Dr. Johnson perhaps?"

"Not in the least. Don't interrupt. I've known him for twenty-five years. His wife was a neighbour of ours in Dorset. Isabel Foreston. I brought the children into this vale of tears and, by Jove, in many ways it's been one for them. It's an extraordinary household. For the last ten years Isabel's condition has been the sort that sends these psycho jokers dizzy with rapture. I'm only an out of date GP, and I'd just say she is in an advanced stage of hysterical neurosis. Frightened into fits of her husband."

"I can't understand these holes," grumbled Fox to Bailey.

"Go on, Meadows," said Alleyn.

"I tackled Sep about her eighteen months ago. Told him the trouble was in her mind. He eyed me with a sort of grin on his face and said: 'I'm surprised to learn that my wife has enough mentality to—' But look here, Alleyn, I can't talk about my patients like this. What the devil am I thinking about."

"You know perfectly well it'll go no further unless—"

"Unless what?"

"Unless it has to. Do go on."

But Dr. Meadows hurriedly withdrew behind his professional rectitude. All he would say was that Mr. Tonks had suffered from high blood pressure and a weak heart, that Guy was in his father's city office, that Arthur had wanted to study art and had been told to read for law, and that Phillipa wanted to go on the stage and had been told to do nothing of the sort.

"Bullied his children," commented Alleyn.

"Find out for yourself. I'm off." Dr. Meadows got as far as the door and came back.

"Look here," he said, "I'll tell you one thing. There was a row here last night. I'd asked Hislop, who's a sensible little beggar, to let me know if anything happened to upset Mrs. Sep. Upset her badly, you know. To be indiscreet again, I said he'd better let me know if Sep cut up rough because Isabel and the young had had about as much of that as they could stand. He was drinking pretty heavily. Hislop rang me up at ten twenty last night to say there'd been a hell of a row; Sep bullying Phips—Phillipa, you know; always call her Phips—in her room. He said Isabel—Mrs. Sep—had gone to bed. I'd had a big day and I didn't want to turn out. I told him to ring again in half an hour if things hadn't quieted down. I told him to keep out of Sep's way and stay in his own room, which is next to Phips', and see if she was all right when Sep cleared out. Hislop was involved. I won't tell you how. The servants were all out. I said that if I didn't hear from him in half an hour I'd ring again and if there was no answer I'd know they were all in bed and quiet. I did ring, got no answer, and went to bed myself. That's all. I'm off. Curtis knows where to find me. You'll want me for the inquest, I suppose. Goodbye."

When he had gone Alleyn embarked on a systematic prowl round the room. Fox and Bailey were still deeply engrossed with the wireless.

"I don't see how the gentleman could have got a bump-off from the instrument," grumbled Fox. "These control knobs are quite in order. Everything's as it should be. Look here, sir."

He turned on the wall switch and tuned in. There was a prolonged humming.

"... concludes the programme of Christmas carols," said the radio.

"A very nice tone," said Fox approvingly.

"Here's something, sir," announced Bailey suddenly.

"Found the sawdust, have you?" said Alleyn.

"Got it in one," said the startled Bailey.

Alleyn peered into the instrument, using the torch. He scooped up two tiny traces of sawdust from under the holes.

"Vantage number one," said Alleyn. He bent down to the wall plug. "Hullo! A two-way adapter. Serves the radio and the radiator. Thought they were illegal. This is a rum business. Let's have another look at those knobs."

He had his look. They were the usual wireless fitments, bakelite knobs fitting snugly to the steel shafts that projected from the front panel.

"As you say," he murmured, "quite in order. Wait a bit." He produced a pocket lens and squinted at one of the shafts. "Ye-es. Do they ever wrap blotting paper round these objects, Fox?"

"Blotting paper!" ejaculated Fox. "They do not."

Alleyn scraped at both the shafts with his penknife, holding an envelope underneath. He rose, groaning, and crossed to the desk. "A corner torn off the bottom bit of blotch," he said presently. "No prints on the wireless, I think you said, Bailey?"

"That's right," agreed Bailey morosely.

"There'll be none, or too many, on the blotter, but try, Bailey, try," said Alleyn. He wandered about the room, his eyes on the floor; got as far as the window and stopped.

"Fox!" he said. "A clue. A very palpable clue."

"What is it?" asked Fox.

"The odd wisp of blotting paper, no less." Alleyn's gaze travelled up the side of the window curtain. "Can I believe my eyes?"

He got a chair, stood on the seat, and with his gloved hand pulled the buttons from the ends of the curtain rod.

"Look at this." He turned to the radio, detached the control knobs, and laid them beside the ones he had removed from the curtain rod.

★

Ten minutes later Inspector Fox knocked on the drawing-room door and was admitted by Guy Tonks. Phillipa had got the fire going and the family was gathered round it. They looked as though they had not moved or spoken to one another for a long time.

It was Phillipa who spoke first to Fox. "Do you want one of us?" she asked.

"If you please, miss," said Fox. "Inspector Alleyn would like to see Mr. Guy Tonks for a moment, if convenient."

"I'll come," said Guy, and led the way to the study. At the door he paused. "Is he—my father—still—?"

"No, no, sir," said Fox comfortably. "It's all ship-shape in there again."

With a lift of his chin Guy opened the door and went in, followed by Fox. Alleyn was alone, seated at the desk. He rose to his feet.

"You want to speak to me?" asked Guy.

"Yes, if I may. This has all been a great shock to you, of course. Won't you sit down?"

Guy sat in the chair farthest away from the radio.

"What killed my father? Was it a stroke?"

"The doctors are not quite certain. There will have to be a postmortem."

"Good God! And an inquest?"

"I'm afraid so."

"Horrible!" said Guy violently. "What do they think was the matter? Why the devil do these quacks have to be so mysterious? What killed him?"

"They think an electric shock."

"How did it happen?"

"We don't know. It looks as if he got it from the wireless."

"Surely that's impossible. I thought they were foolproof."

"I believe they are, if left to themselves."

For a second undoubtedly Guy was startled. Then a look of relief came into his eyes. He seemed to relax all over.

"Of course," he said, "he was always monkeying about with it. What had he done?"

"Nothing."

"But you said—if it killed him he must have done something to it."

"If anyone interfered with the set it was put right afterwards."

Guy's lips parted but he did not speak. He had gone very white.

"So you see," said Alleyn, "that your father could not have done anything."

"Then it was not the radio that killed him."

"That we hope will be determined by the postmortem."

"I don't know anything about wireless," said Guy suddenly. "I don't understand. This doesn't seem to make sense. Nobody ever touched the thing except my father. He was most particular about it. Nobody went near the wireless."

"I see. He was an enthusiast?"

"Yes, it was his only enthusiasm except—except his business."

"One of my men is a bit of an expert," Alleyn said. "He says this is a remarkably good set. You are not an expert, you say. Is there anyone in the house who is?"

"My young brother was interested at one time. He's given it up. My father wouldn't allow another radio in the house."

"Perhaps he may be able to suggest something."

"But if the thing's all right now—"

"We've got to explore every possibility."

"You speak as if—as—if—"

"I speak as I am bound to speak before there has been an inquest," said Alleyn. "Had anyone a grudge against your father, Mr. Tonks?"

Up went Guy's chin again. He looked Alleyn squarely in the eyes.

"Almost everyone who knew him," said Guy.

"Is that an exaggeration?"

"No. You think he was murdered, don't you?"

Alleyn suddenly pointed to the desk beside him.

"Have you ever seen those before?" he asked abruptly. Guy stared at two black knobs that lay side by side on an ashtray.

"Those?" he said. "No. What are they?"

"I believe they are the agents of your father's death."

The study door opened and Arthur Tonks came in.

"Guy," he said, "what's happening? We can't stay cooped up together all day. I can't stand it. For God's sake, what happened to him?"

"They think those things killed him," said Guy.

"Those?" For a split second Arthur's glance slewed to the curtain rods. Then, with a characteristic flicker of his eyelids, he looked away again.

"What do you mean?" he asked Alleyn.

"Will you try one of those knobs on the shaft of the volume control?"

"But," said Arthur, "they're metal."

"It's disconnected," said Alleyn.

Arthur picked one of the knobs from the tray, turned to the radio, and fitted the knob over one of the exposed shafts.

"It's too loose," he said quickly, "it would fall off."

"Not if it was packed—with blotting paper, for instance."

"Where did you find these things?" demanded Arthur.

"I think you recognised them, didn't you? I saw you glance at the curtain rod."

"Of course I recognised them. I did a portrait of Phillipa against those curtains when—he—was away last year. I've painted the damn things."

"Look here," interrupted Guy, "exactly what are you driving at, Mr. Alleyn? If you mean to suggest that my brother—"

"I!" cried Arthur. "What's it got to do with me? Why should you suppose—"

"I found traces of blotting paper on the shafts and inside the metal knobs," said Alleyn. "It suggested a substitution of the metal knobs for the bakelite ones. It is remarkable, don't you think, that they should so closely resemble one another? If you examine them, of course, you find they are not identical. Still, the difference is scarcely perceptible."

Arthur did not answer this. He was still looking at the wireless.

"I've always wanted to have a look at this set," he said surprisingly.

"You are free to do so now," said Alleyn politely. "We have finished with it for the time being."

"Look here," said Arthur suddenly, "suppose metal knobs were substituted for bakelite ones, it couldn't kill him. He wouldn't get a shock at all. Both the controls are grounded."

"Have you noticed those very small holes drilled through the panel?" asked Alleyn. "Should they be there, do you think?"

Arthur peered at the little steel shafts. "By God, he's right, Guy," he said. "That's how it was done."

"Inspector Fox," said Alleyn, "tells me those holes could be used for conducting wires and that a lead could be taken from the—the transformer, is it?—to one of the knobs."

"And the other connected to earth," said Fox. "It's a job for an expert. He could get three hundred volts or so that way."

"That's not good enough," said Arthur quickly; "there wouldn't be enough current to do any damage—only a few hundredths of an amp."

"I'm not an expert," said Alleyn, "but I'm sure you're right. Why were the holes drilled then? Do you imagine someone wanted to play a practical joke on your father?"

"A practical joke? On *him*?" Arthur gave an unpleasant screech of laughter. "Do you hear that, Guy?"

"Shut up," said Guy. "After all, he is dead."

"It seems almost too good to be true, doesn't it?"

"Don't be a bloody fool, Arthur. Pull yourself together. Can't you see what this means? They think he's been murdered."

"Murdered! They're wrong. None of us had the nerve for that, Mr. Inspector. Look at me. My hands are so shaky they told me I'd never be able to paint. That dates from when I was a kid and he shut me up in the cellars for a night. Look at me. Look at Guy. He's not so vulnerable, but he caved in like the rest of us. We were conditioned to surrender. Do you know—"

"Wait a moment," said Alleyn quietly. "Your brother is quite right, you know. You'd better think before you speak. This may be a case of homicide."

"Thank you, sir," said Guy quickly. "That's extraordinarily decent of you. Arthur's a bit above himself. It's a shock."

"The relief, you mean," said Arthur. "Don't be such an ass. I didn't kill him and they'll find it out soon enough. Nobody killed him. There must be some explanation."

"I suggest that you listen to me," said Alleyn. "I'm going to put several questions to both of you. You need not answer them, but it will be more sensible to do so. I understand no one but your father touched this radio. Did any of you ever come into this room while it was in use?"

"Not unless he wanted to vary the programme with a little bullying," said Arthur.

Alleyn turned to Guy, who was glaring at his brother.

"I want to know exactly what happened in this house last night. As far as the doctors can tell us, your father died not less than three and not more than eight hours before he was found. We must try to fix the time as accurately as possible."

"I saw him at about a quarter to nine," began Guy slowly. "I was going out to a supper party at the Savoy and had come downstairs. He was crossing the hall from the drawing room to his room."

"Did you see him after a quarter to nine, Mr. Arthur?"

"No. I heard him, though. He was working in here with Hislop. Hislop had asked to go away for Christmas. Quite enough. My father discovered some urgent correspondence. Really, Guy, you know, he was pathological. I'm sure Dr. Meadows thinks so."

"When did you hear him?" asked Alleyn.

"Some time after Guy had gone. I was working on a drawing in my room upstairs. It's above his. I heard him bawling at little Hislop. It must have been before ten o'clock, because I went out to a studio party at ten. I heard him bawling as I crossed the hall."

"And when," said Alleyn, "did you both return?"

"I came home at about twenty past twelve," said Guy immediately. "I can fix the time because we had gone on to Chez Carlo, and they had a midnight stunt there. We left immediately afterwards. I came home in a taxi. The radio was on full blast."

"You heard no voices?"

"None. Just the wireless."

"And you, Mr. Arthur?"

"Lord knows when I got in. After one. The house was in darkness. Not a sound."

"You had your own key?"

"Yes," said Guy. "Each of us has one. They're always left on a hook in the lobby. When I came in I noticed Arthur's was gone."

"What about the others? How did you know it was his?"

"Mother hasn't got one and Phips lost hers weeks ago. Anyway, I knew they were staying in and that it must be Arthur who was out."

"Thank you," said Arthur ironically.

"You didn't look in the study when you came in," Alleyn asked him.

"Good Lord, no," said Arthur as if the suggestion was fantastic. "I say," he said suddenly, "I suppose he was sitting here—dead. That's a queer thought." He laughed nervously. "Just sitting here, behind the door in the dark."

"How do you know it was in the dark?"

"What d'you mean? Of course it was. There was no light under the door."

"I see. Now do you two mind joining your mother again? Perhaps your sister will be kind enough to come in here for a moment. Fox, ask her, will you?"

Fox returned to the drawing room with Guy and Arthur and remained there, blandly unconscious of any embarrassment his presence might cause the Tonkses. Bailey was already there, ostensibly examining the electric points.

Phillipa went to the study at once. Her first remark was characteristic. "Can I be of any help?" asked Phillipa.

"It's extremely nice of you to put it like that," said Alleyn. "I don't want to worry you for long. I'm sure this discovery has been a shock to you."

"Probably," said Phillipa. Alleyn glanced quickly at her. "I mean," she explained, "that I suppose I must be shocked but I can't feel anything much. I just want to get it all over as soon as possible. And then think. Please tell me what has happened."

Alleyn told her they believed her father had been electrocuted and that the circumstances were unusual and puzzling. He said nothing to suggest that the police suspected murder.

"I don't think I'll be much help," said Phillipa, "but go ahead."

"I want to try to discover who was the last person to see your father or speak to him."

"I should think very likely I was," said Phillipa composedly. "I had a row with him before I went to bed."

"What about?"

"I don't see that it matters."

Alleyn considered this. When he spoke again it was with deliberation.

"Look here," he said, "I think there is very little doubt that your father was killed by an electric shock from his wireless set. As far as I know the circumstances are unique. Radios are normally incapable of giving a lethal shock to anyone. We have examined the cabinet and are inclined to think that its internal arrangements were disturbed last night. Very radically disturbed. Your father may have experimented with it. If anything happened to interrupt or upset him, it is possible that in the excitement of the moment he made some dangerous readjustment."

"You don't believe that, do you?" asked Phillipa calmly.

"Since you ask me," said Alleyn, "no."

"I see," said Phillipa; "you think he was murdered, but you're not sure." She had gone very white, but she spoke crisply. "Naturally you want to find out about my row."

"About everything that happened last evening," amended Alleyn.

"What happened was this," said Phillipa; "I came into the hall some time after ten. I'd heard Arthur go out and had looked at the clock at five past. I ran into my father's secretary, Richard Hislop. He turned aside, but not before I saw... not quickly enough. I blurted out: 'You're crying.' We looked at each other. I asked him why he stood it. None of the other secretaries could. He said he had to. He's a widower with two children. There have been doctor's bills and things. I needn't tell you about his... about his damnable servitude to my father nor about the refinements of cruelty he'd had to put up with. I think my father was mad, really mad, I mean. Richard gabbled it all out to me higgledy-piggledy in a sort of horrified whisper. He's been here two years, but I'd never realised until that moment that we... that..." A faint flush came into her cheeks. "He's such a funny little man. Not at all the sort I've always thought... not good-looking or exciting or anything."

She stopped, looking bewildered.

"Yes?" said Alleyn.

"Well, you see—I suddenly realised I was in love with him. He realised it too. He said: 'Of course, it's quite hopeless, you know. Us, I mean. Laughable, almost.' Then I put my arms round his neck and kissed him. It was very odd, but it seemed quite natural. The point is my father came out of this room into the hall and saw us."

"That was bad luck," said Alleyn.

"Yes, it was. My father really seemed delighted. He almost licked his lips. Richard's efficiency had irritated my father for a long time. It was difficult to find excuses for being beastly to him. Now, of course... He ordered Richard to the study and me to my room. He followed me upstairs. Richard tried to come too, but I asked him not to. My father... I needn't tell you what he said. He put the worst possible construction on what he'd seen. He was absolutely foul, screaming at me like a madman. He was insane. Perhaps it was DTs. He drank terribly, you know. I dare say it's silly of me to tell you all this."

"No," said Alleyn.

"I can't feel anything at all. Not even relief. The boys are frankly relieved. I can't feel afraid either." She stared meditatively at Alleyn. "Innocent people needn't feel afraid, need they?"

"It's an axiom of police investigation," said Alleyn and wondered if indeed she was innocent.

"It just *can't* be murder," said Phillipa. "We were all too much afraid to kill him. I believe he'd win even if you murdered him. He'd hit back somehow." She put her hands to her eyes. "I'm all muddled," she said.

"I think you are more upset than you realise. I'll be as quick as I can. Your father made this scene in your room. You say he screamed. Did anyone hear him?"

"Yes. Mummy did. She came in."

"What happened?"

"I said: 'Go away, darling, it's all right.' I didn't want her to be involved. He nearly killed her with the things he did. Sometimes he'd... we never knew what happened between them. It was all secret, like a door shutting quietly as you walk along a passage."

"Did she go away?"

"Not at once. He told her he'd found out that Richard and I were lovers. He said... it doesn't matter. I don't want to tell you. She was terrified. He was stabbing at her in some way I couldn't understand. Then, quite suddenly, he told her to go to her own room. She went at once and he followed her. He locked me in. That's the last I saw of him, but I heard him go downstairs later."

"Were you locked in all night?"

"No. Richard Hislop's room is next to mine. He came up and spoke through the wall to me. He wanted to unlock the door, but I said better not in case—he—came back. Then, much later, Guy came home. As he passed my door I tapped on it. The key was in the lock and he turned it."

"Did you tell him what had happened?"

"Just that there'd been a row. He only stayed a moment."

"Can you hear the radio from your room?"

She seemed surprised.

"The wireless? Why, yes. Faintly."

"Did you hear it after your father returned to the study?"

"I don't remember."

"Think. While you lay awake all that long time until your brother came home?"

"I'll try. When he came out and found Richard and me, it was not going. They had been working, you see. No, I can't remember hearing it at all unless—wait a moment. Yes. After he had gone back to the study from mother's room I remember there was a loud crash of static. Very loud. Then I think it was quiet for some time. I fancy I heard it again later. Oh, I've remembered something else. After the static my bedside radiator went out. I suppose there was something wrong with the electric supply. That would account for both, wouldn't it? The heater went on again about ten minutes later."

"And did the radio begin again then, do you think?"

"I don't know. I'm very vague about that. It started again sometime before I went to sleep."

"Thank you very much indeed. I won't bother you any longer now."

"All right," said Phillipa calmly, and went away.

Alleyn sent for Chase and questioned him about the rest of the staff and about the discovery of the body. Emily was summoned and dealt with. When she departed, awe-struck but complacent, Alleyn turned to the butler.

"Chase," he said, "had your master any peculiar habits?"

"Yes, sir."

"In regard to his use of the wireless?"

"I beg your pardon, sir. I thought you meant generally speaking."

"Well, then, generally speaking."

"If I may say so, sir, he was a mass of them."

"How long have you been with him?"

"Two months, sir, and due to leave at the end of this week."

"Oh. Why are you leaving?"

Chase produced the classic remark of his kind.

"There are some things," he said, "that flesh and blood will not stand, sir. One of them's being spoke to like Mr. Tonks spoke to his staff."

"Ah. His peculiar habits, in fact?"

"It's my opinion, sir, he was mad. Stark, staring."

"With regard to the radio. Did he tinker with it?"

"I can't say I've ever noticed, sir. I believe he knew quite a lot about wireless."

"When he tuned the thing, had he any particular method? Any characteristic attitude or gesture?"

"I don't think so, sir. I never noticed, and yet I've often come into the room when he was at it. I can seem to see him now, sir."

"Yes, yes," said Alleyn swiftly. "That's what we want. A clear mental picture. How was it now? Like this?"

In a moment he was across the room and seated in Septimus's chair. He swung round to the cabinet and raised his right hand to the tuning control.

"Like this?"

"No, sir," said Chase promptly, "that's not him at all. Both hands it should be."

"Ah." Up went Alleyn's left hand to the volume control. "More like this?"

"Yes, sir," said Chase slowly. "But there's something else and I can't recollect what it was. Something he was always doing. It's in the back of my head. You know, sir. Just on the edge of my memory, as you might say."

"I know."

"It's a kind—something—to do with irritation," said Chase slowly.

"Irritation? His?"

"No. It's no good, sir. I can't get it."

"Perhaps later. Now look here, Chase, what happened to all of you last night? All the servants, I mean."

"We were all out, sir. It being Christmas Eve. The mistress sent for me yesterday morning. She said we could take the evening off as soon as I had taken in Mr. Tonks' grog-tray at nine o'clock. So we went," ended Chase simply.

"When?"

"The rest of the staff got away about nine. I left at ten past, sir, and returned about eleven twenty. The others were back then, and all in bed. I went straight to bed myself, sir."

"You came in by a back door, I suppose?"

"Yes, sir. We've been talking it over. None of us noticed anything unusual."

"Can you hear the wireless in your part of the house?"

"No, sir."

"Well," said Alleyn, looking up from his notes, "that'll do, thank you."

Before Chase reached the door Fox came in.

"Beg pardon, sir," said Fox, "I just want to take a look at the *Radio Times* on the desk."

He bent over the paper, wetted a gigantic thumb, and turned a page.

"That's it, sir," shouted Chase suddenly. "That's what I tried to think of. That's what he was always doing."

"But what?"

"Licking his fingers, sir. It was a habit," said Chase. "That's what he always did when he sat down to the radio. I heard Mr. Hislop tell the doctor it nearly drove him demented, the way the master couldn't touch a thing without first licking his fingers."

"Quite so," said Alleyn. "In about ten minutes, ask Mr. Hislop if he will be good enough to come in for a moment. That will be all, thank you, Chase."

"Well, sir," remarked Fox when Chase had gone, "if that's the case and what I think's right, it'd certainly make matters worse."

"Good heavens, Fox, what an elaborate remark. What does it mean?"

"If metal knobs were substituted for bakelite ones and fine wires brought through those holes to make contact, then he'd get a bigger bump if he tuned in with *damp* fingers."

"Yes. And he always used both hands. Fox!"

"Sir."

"Approach the Tonkses again. You haven't left them alone, of course?"

"Bailey's in there making out he's interested in the light switches. He's found the main switchboard under the stairs. There's signs of a blown fuse having been fixed recently. In a cupboard underneath there are odd lengths of flex and so on. Same brand as this on the wireless and the heater."

"Ah, yes. Could the cord from the adapter to the radiator be brought into play?"

"By gum," said Fox, "you're right! That's how it was done, Chief. The heavier flex was cut away from the radiator and shoved through. There was a fire, so he wouldn't want the radiator and wouldn't notice."

"It might have been done that way, certainly, but there's little to prove it. Return to the bereaved Tonkses, my Fox, and ask prettily if any of them remember Septimus's peculiarities when tuning his wireless."

Fox met little Mr. Hislop at the door and left him alone with Alleyn. Phillipa had been right, reflected the Inspector, when she said Richard Hislop was not a noticeable man. He was nondescript. Grey eyes, drab hair; rather pale, rather short, rather insignificant; and yet last night there had flashed up between those two the realisation of love. Romantic but rum, thought Alleyn.

"Do sit down," he said. "I want you, if you will, to tell me what happened between you and Mr. Tonks last evening."

"What happened?"

"Yes. You all dined at eight, I understand. Then you and Mr. Tonks came in here?"

"Yes."

"What did you do?"

"He dictated several letters."

"Anything unusual take place?"

"Oh, no."

"Why did you quarrel?"

"Quarrel!" The quiet voice jumped a tone. "We did not quarrel, Mr. Alleyn."

"Perhaps that was the wrong word. What upset you?"

"Phillipa has told you?"

"Yes. She was wise to do so. What was the matter, Mr. Hislop?"

"Apart from the… what she told you… Mr. Tonks was a difficult man to please. I often irritated him. I did so last night."

"In what way?"

"In almost every way. He shouted at me. I was startled and nervous, clumsy with papers, and making mistakes. I wasn't well. I blundered and then… I… I broke down. I have always irritated him. My very mannerisms—"

"Had he no irritating mannerisms, himself?"

"He! My God!"

"What were they?"

"I can't think of anything in particular. It doesn't matter does it?"

"Anything to do with the wireless, for instance?"

There was a short silence.

"No," said Hislop.

"Was the radio on in here last night, after dinner?"

"For a little while. Not after—after the incident in the hall. At least, I don't think so. I don't remember."

"What did you do after Miss Phillipa and her father had gone upstairs?"

"I followed and listened outside the door for a moment." He had gone very white and had backed away from the desk.

"And then?"

"I heard someone coming. I remembered Dr. Meadows had told me to ring him up if there was one of the scenes. I returned here and rang him up. He told me to go to my room and listen. If things got any worse I was to telephone again. Otherwise I was to stay in my room. It is next to hers."

"And you did this?" He nodded. "Could you hear what Mr. Tonks said to her?"

"A—a good deal of it."

"What did you hear?"

"He insulted her. Mrs. Tonks was there. I was just thinking of ringing Dr. Meadows up again when she and Mr. Tonks came out and went along the passage. I stayed in my room."

"You did not try to speak to Miss Phillipa?"

"We spoke through the wall. She asked me not to ring Dr. Meadows, but to stay in my room. In a little while, perhaps it was as much as twenty minutes—I really don't know—I heard him come back and go downstairs. I again spoke to Phillipa. She implored me not to do anything and said that she herself would speak to Dr. Meadows in the morning. So I waited a little longer and then went to bed."

"And to sleep?"

"My God, no!"

"Did you hear the wireless again?"

"Yes. At least I heard static."

"Are you an expert on wireless?"

"No. I know the ordinary things. Nothing much."

"How did you come to take this job, Mr. Hislop?"

"I answered an advertisement."

"You are sure you don't remember any particular mannerism of Mr. Tonks's in connection with the radio?"

"No."

"Will you please ask Mrs. Tonks if she will be kind enough to speak to me for a moment?"

"Certainly," said Hislop, and went away.

Septimus's wife came in looking like death. Alleyn got her to sit down and asked her about her movements on the preceding evening. She said she was feeling unwell and dined in her room. She went to bed immediately afterwards. She heard Septimus yelling at Phillipa and went to Phillipa's room. Septimus accused Mr. Hislop and her daughter of "terrible things". She got as far as this and then broke down quietly. Alleyn was very gentle with her. After a little while he learned that Septimus had gone to her room with her and had continued to speak of "terrible things".

"What sort of things?" asked Alleyn.

"He was not responsible," said Isabel. "He did not know what he was saying. I think he had been drinking."

She thought he had remained with her for perhaps a quarter of an hour. Possibly longer. He left her abruptly and she heard him go along the passage, past Phillipa's door, and presumably downstairs. She had stayed awake for a long time. The wireless could not be heard from her room. Alleyn showed her the curtain knobs, but she seemed quite unable to take in their significance. He let her go, summoned Fox, and went over the whole case.

"What's your idea on the show?" he asked when he had finished.

"Well sir," said Fox, in his stolid way, "on the face of it the young gentlemen have got alibis. We'll have to check them up, of course, and I don't see we can go much further until we have done so."

"For the moment," said Alleyn, "let us suppose Masters Guy and Arthur to be safely established behind cast-iron alibis. What then?"

"Then we've got the young lady, the old lady, the secretary, and the servants."

"Let us parade them. But first let us go over the wireless game. You'll have to watch me here. I gather that the only way in which the radio could be fixed to give Mr. Tonks his quietus is like this: Control knobs removed. Holes bored in front panel with fine drill. Metal knobs substituted and packed with blotting paper to insulate them from metal shafts and make them stay put. Heavier flex from adapter to radiator cut and the ends of the wires pushed through the drilled holes to make contact with the new knobs. Thus we have a positive and negative pole. Mr. Tonks bridges the gap, gets a mighty wallop as the current passes through him to the earth. The switchboard fuse is blown almost immediately. All this is rigged by murderer while Sep was upstairs bullying wife and daughter. Sep revisited study some time after ten twenty. Whole thing was made ready between ten, when Arthur went out, and the time Sep returned—say, about ten forty five. The murderer reappeared, connected radiator with flex, removed wires, changed back knobs, and left the thing tuned in. Now I take it that the burst of static described by Phillipa and Hislop would be caused by the short-circuit that killed our Septimus?"

"That's right."

"It also affected all the heaters in the house. *Vide* Miss Tonks's radiator."

"Yes. He put all that right again. It would be a simple enough matter for anyone who knew how. He'd just have to fix the fuse on the main switchboard."

"How long do you say it would take to—what's the horrible word?—to recondition the whole show?"

"M'm," said Fox deeply. "At a guess, sir, fifteen minutes. He'd have to be nippy."

"Yes," agreed Alleyn. "He or she."

"I don't see a female making a success of it," grunted Fox. "Look here, Chief, you know what I'm thinking. Why did Mr. Hislop lie about deceased's habit of licking his thumbs? You say Hislop told you he remembered nothing and Chase says he overheard him saying the trick nearly drove him dippy."

"Exactly," said Alleyn. He was silent for so long that Fox felt moved to utter a discreet cough.

"Eh?" said Alleyn. "Yes, Fox, yes. It'll have to be done." He consulted the telephone directory and dialled a number.

"May I speak to Dr. Meadows? Oh, it's you, is it? Do you remember Mr. Hislop telling you that Septimus Tonks's trick of wetting his fingers nearly drove Hislop demented. Are you there? You don't? Sure? All right. All right. Hislop rang you up at ten twenty, you said? And you telephoned him? At eleven. Sure of the times? I see. I'd be glad if you'd come round. Can you? Well, do if you can."

He hung up the receiver.

"Get Chase again, will you, Fox?"

Chase, recalled, was most insistent that Mr. Hislop had spoken about it to Dr. Meadows.

"It was when Mr. Hislop had flu, sir. I went up with the doctor. Mr. Hislop had a high temperature and was talking very excited. He kept on and on, saying the master had guessed his ways had driven him crazy and that the master kept on purposely to aggravate. He said if it went on much longer he'd... he didn't know what he was talking about, sir, really."

"What did he say he'd do?"

"Well, sir, he said he'd—he'd do something desperate to the master. But it was only his rambling, sir. I dare say he wouldn't remember anything about it."

"No," said Alleyn, "I dare say he wouldn't." When Chase had gone he said to Fox: "Go and find out about those boys and their alibis. See if they can put you on to a quick means of checking up. Get Master Guy to corroborate Miss Phillipa's statement that she was locked in her room."

Fox had been gone for some time and Alleyn was still busy with his notes when the study door burst open and in came Dr. Meadows.

"Look here, my giddy sleuth-hound," he shouted, "what's all this about Hislop? Who says he disliked Sep's abominable habits?"

"Chase does. And don't bawl at me like that. I'm worried."

"So am I, blast you. What are you driving at? You can't imagine that… that poor little broken-down hack is capable of electrocuting anybody, let alone Sep?"

"I have no imagination," said Alleyn wearily.

"I wish to God I hadn't called you in. If the wireless killed Sep, it was because he'd monkeyed with it."

"And put it right after it had killed him?"

Dr. Meadows stared at Alleyn in silence.

"Now," said Alleyn, "you've got to give me a straight answer, Meadows. Did Hislop, while he was semi-delirious, say that this habit of Tonks's made him feel like murdering him?"

"I'd forgotten Chase was there," said Dr. Meadows.

"Yes, you'd forgotten that."

"But even if he did talk wildly, Alleyn, what of it? Damn it, you can't arrest a man on the strength of a remark made in delirium."

"I don't propose to do so. Another motive has come to light."

"You mean—Phips—last night?"

"Did he tell you about that?"

"She whispered something to me this morning. I'm very fond of Phips. My God, are you sure of your grounds?"

"Yes," said Alleyn. "I'm sorry. I think you'd better go, Meadows."

"Are you going to arrest him?"

"I have to do my job."

There was a long silence.

"Yes," said Dr. Meadows at last. "You have to do your job. Goodbye, Alleyn."

Fox returned to say that Guy and Arthur had never left their parties. He had got hold of two of their friends. Guy and Mrs. Tonks confirmed the story of the locked door.

"It's a process of elimination," said Fox. "It must be the secretary. He fixed the radio while deceased was upstairs. He must have dodged back to whisper through the door to Miss Tonks. I suppose he waited somewhere down here until he heard deceased blow himself to blazes and then put everything straight again, leaving the radio turned on."

Alleyn was silent.

"What do we do now, sir?" asked Fox.

"I want to see the hook inside the front door where they hang their keys."

Fox, looking dazed, followed his superior to the little entrance hall.

"Yes, there they are," said Alleyn. He pointed to a hook with two latchkeys hanging from it. "You could scarcely miss them. Come on, Fox."

Back in the study they found Hislop with Bailey in attendance. Hislop looked from one Yard man to another.

"I want to know if it's murder."

"We think so," said Alleyn.

"I want you to realise that Phillipa—Miss Tonks—was locked in her room all last night."

"Until her brother came home and unlocked the door," said Alleyn.

"That was too late. He was dead by then."

"How do you know when he died?"

"It must have been when there was that crash of static."

"Mr. Hislop," said Alleyn, "why would you not tell me how much that trick of licking his fingers exasperated you?"

"But—how do you know! I never told anyone."

"You told Dr. Meadows when you were ill."

"I don't remember." He stopped short. His lips trembled. Then, suddenly he began to speak.

"Very well. It's true. For two years he's tortured me. You see, he knew something about me. Two years ago when my wife was dying, I took money from the cash-box in that desk. I paid it back and thought he hadn't noticed. He knew all the time. From then on he had me where he wanted me. He used to sit there like a spider. I'd hand him a paper. He'd wet his thumbs with a clicking noise and a sort of complacent grimace. Click, click. Then he'd thumb the papers. He knew it drove me crazy. He'd look at me and then... click, click. And then he'd say something about the cash. He never quite accused me, just hinted. And I was impotent. You think I'm insane. I'm not. I could have murdered him. Often and often I've thought how I'd do it. Now you think I've done it. I haven't. There's the joke of it. I hadn't the pluck. And last night when Phillipa showed me she cared, it was like Heaven—unbelievable. For the first time since I've been here I *didn't* feel like killing him. And last night someone else *did*!"

He stood there trembling and vehement. Fox and Bailey, who had watched him with bewildered concern, turned to Alleyn. He was about to speak when Chase came in. "A note for you, sir," he said to Alleyn. "It came by hand."

Alleyn opened it and glanced at the first few words. He looked up.

"You may go, Mr. Hislop. Now I've got what I expected—what I fished for."

When Hislop had gone they read the letter.

Dear Alleyn,

Don't arrest Hislop. I did it. Let him go at once if you've arrested him and don't tell Phips you ever suspected him. I was in love with Isabel before she met Sep. I've tried to get her to divorce him, but she wouldn't because of the kids. Damned nonsense, but there's no time to discuss it now. I've got to be quick. He suspected us. He reduced her to a nervous wreck. I was afraid she'd go under altogether. I thought it all out. Some weeks ago I took Phips's key from the hook inside the front door. I had the tools and the flex and wire all ready. I knew where the main switchboard was and the cupboard. I meant to wait until they all went away at the New Year, but last night when Hislop rang me I made up my mind to act at once. He said the boys and servants were out and Phips locked in her room. I told him to stay in his room and to ring me up in half an hour if things hadn't quieted down. He didn't ring up. I did. No answer, so I knew Sep wasn't in his study.

I came round, let myself in, and listened. All quiet upstairs, but the lamp still on in the study, so I knew he would come down again. He'd said he wanted to get the midnight broadcast from somewhere.

I locked myself in and got to work. When Sep was away last year, Arthur did one of his modern monstrosities of paintings in the study. He talked about the knobs making good pattern. I noticed then that they were very like the ones on the radio and later on I tried one and saw that it would fit if I packed it up a bit. Well, I did the job just as you worked it out, and it only took twelve minutes. Then I went into the drawing room and waited.

He came down from Isabel's room and evidently went straight to the radio. I hadn't thought it would make such a row, and half expected someone would come down. No one came. I went back, switched off the wireless, mended the fuse in the main switchboard, using my torch. Then I put everything right in the study.

There was no particular hurry. No one would come in while he was there, and I got the radio going as soon as possible to suggest he was at it. I knew I'd be called in when they found him. My idea was to tell them he had died of a stroke. I'd been warning Isabel it might happen at any time. As soon as I saw the burned hand I knew that cat wouldn't jump. I'd have tried to get away with it if Chase hadn't gone round bleating about electrocution and burned fingers. Hislop saw the hand. I daren't do anything but report the case to the police, but I thought you'd never twig the knobs. One up to you.

I might have bluffed through if you hadn't suspected Hislop. Can't let you hang the blighter. I'm enclosing a note to Isabel, who won't forgive me, and an official one for you to use. You'll find me in my bedroom upstairs. I'm using cyanide. It's quick.

I'm sorry, Alleyn. I think you knew, didn't you? I've bungled the whole game, but if you will be a super-sleuth… Goodbye.

Henry Meadows

PERSONS OR THINGS UNKNOWN

Carter Dickson

Carter Dickson was the principal pen-name of John Dickson Carr (1906–1977), who also wrote as Carr Dickson and Roger Fairbairn. He was an American who spent much of his life in Britain, and like Ngaio Marsh he achieved lasting eminence as a result of creating English detectives in the classic tradition—notably Dr. Gideon Fell and Sir Henry Merrivale. Carr was also one of a small number of American-born writers to have earned election to the Detection Club, and for several years he served as Club Secretary. His forte was the locked room mystery, and his novels include some of the finest examples of this challenging form of fiction.

"Persons or Things Unknown" first appeared in the Christmas number of *The Sketch* in 1938. Subsequently it was included in *The Department of Queer Complaints* (1940), although unlike the majority of the stories in the book it did not feature Colonel March of Scotland Yard. This mystery is a historical romance dating back to the days of King Charles II, and is an early example of Carr's enthusiasm for combining history with mystery—which was much less common in his hey-day than it is now. In the post-war era, as he fell out of sympathy with the contemporary world, Carr concentrated increasingly on stories set in the past. Here he blends historical atmosphere with a pleasing locked room mystery in the form of an "inverted detective story" of the kind first popularised by R. Austin Freeman.

"AFTER ALL," SAID OUR HOST, "IT'S CHRISTMAS. WHY NOT let the skeleton out of the bag?"

"Or the cat out of the closet," said the historian, who likes to be precise even about *clichés*. "Are you serious?"

"Yes," said our host. "I want to know whether it's safe for anyone to sleep in that little room at the head of the stairs."

He had just bought the place. This party was in the nature of a house-warming; and I had already decided privately that the place needed one. It was a long, damp, high-windowed house, hidden behind a hill in Sussex. The drawing-room, where a group of us had gathered round the fire after dinner, was much too long and much too draughty. It had fine panelling—a rich brown where the firelight was always finding new gleams—and a hundred little reflections trembled down its length, as in so many small gloomy mirrors. But it remained draughty.

Of course, we all liked the house. It had the most modern of lighting and heating arrangements, though the plumbing sent ghostly noises and clanks far down into its interior whenever you turned on a tap. But the smell of the past was in it; and you could not get over the idea that somebody was following you about. Now, at the host's flat mention of a certain possibility, we all looked at our wives.

"But you never told us," said the historian's wife, rather shocked, "you never told us you had a ghost here!"

"I don't know that I have," replied our host quite seriously. "All I have is a bundle of evidence about something queer that once happened. It's all right; I haven't put anyone in that little room at the head of the stairs. So we can drop the discussion, if you'd rather."

"You know we can't," said the inspector: who, as a matter of strict fact, is an Assistant Commissioner of the Metropolitan Police. He smoked a large cigar, and contemplated ghosts with satisfaction. "This is exactly the time and place to hear about it. What is it?"

"It's rather in your line," our host told him slowly. Then he looked at the historian. "And in your line, too. It's a historical story. I suppose you'd call it a historical romance."

"I probably should. What is the date?"

"The date is the year sixteen hundred and sixty."

"That's Charles the Second, isn't it, Will?" demanded the historian's wife; she annoys him sometimes by asking these questions. "I'm terribly fond of them. I hope it has lots of big names in it. You know: Charles the Second and Buckingham and the rest of them. I remember, when I was a little girl, going to see"—she mentioned a great actor—"play David Garrick. I was looking forward to it. I expected to see the programme and the cast of characters positively bristling with people like Dr. Johnson and Goldsmith, and Burke and Gibbon and Reynolds, going in and out every minute. There wasn't a single one of them in it, and I felt swindled before the play had begun."

The trouble was that she spoke without conviction. The historian looked sceptically over his pince-nez.

"I warn you," he said, "if this is something you claim to have found in a drawer, in a crabbed old handwriting and all the rest of it, I'm going to be all over you professionally. Let me hear one anachronism—"

But he spoke without conviction, too. Our host was so serious that there was a slight, uneasy silence, in the group.

"No. I didn't find it in a drawer; the parson gave it to me. And the handwriting isn't particularly crabbed. I can't show it to you, because it's being typed, but it's a diary: a great, hefty mass of stuff. Most of it is rather dull, though I'm steeped in the seventeenth century, and I confess I enjoy it. The diary was begun in the summer of '60—just after the Restoration—and goes on to the end of '64. It was kept by Mr. Everard Poynter, who owned Manfred Manor (that's six or seven miles from here) when it was a farm.

"I know that fellow," he added, looking thoughtfully at the fire. "I know about him and his sciatica and his views on mutton and politics. I know why he went up to London to dance on Oliver Cromwell's grave, and I can guess who stole the two sacks of malt out of his brew-house while he was away. I see him as half a Hat; the old boy had a beaver hat he wore on his wedding day, and I'll bet he wore it to his death. It's out of all this that I got the details about people. The actual facts I got from the report of the coroner's inquest, which the parson lent me."

"Hold on!" said the Inspector, sitting up straight. "Did this fellow Poynter see the ghost and die?"

"No, no. Nothing like that. But he was one of the witnesses. He saw a man hacked to death, with thirteen stab-wounds in his body, from a hand that wasn't there and a weapon that didn't exist."

There was a silence.

"A murder?" asked the Inspector.

"A murder."

"Where?"

"In that little room at the head of the stairs. It used to be called the Ladies' Withdrawing Room."

Now, it is all very well to sit in your well-lighted flat in town and say we were hypnotised by an atmosphere. You can hear motor-cars

crashing their gears, or curse somebody's wireless. You did not sit in
that house, with a great wind rushing up off the downs, and a wall
of darkness built up for three miles around you: knowing that at
a certain hour you would have to retire to your room and put out
the light, completing the wall.

"I regret to say," went on our host, "that there are no great
names. These people were no more concerned with the Court of
Charles the Second—with one exception—than we are concerned
with the Court of George the Sixth. They lived in a little, busy, possibly ignorant world. They were fierce, fire-eating Royalists, most
of them, who cut the Stuart arms over their chimney-pieces again
and only made a gala trip to town to see the regicides executed
in October of '60. Poynter's diary is crowded with them. Among
others there is Squire Radlow, who owned this house then and was
a great friend of Poynter. There was Squire Radlow's wife, Martha,
and his daughter Mary.

"Mistress Mary Radlow was seventeen years old. She was not one
of your fainting girls. Poynter—used to giving details—records that
she was five feet tall, and thirty-two inches round the bust. 'Pretty
and delicate,' Poynter says, with hazel eyes and a small mouth.
But she could spin flax against any woman in the county; she once
drained a pint of wine at a draught, for a wager; and she took eager
pleasure in any good spectacle, like a bear-baiting or a hanging. I
don't say that flippantly, but as a plain matter of fact. She was also
fond of fine clothes, and danced well.

"In the summer of '60 Mistress Mary was engaged to be married
to Richard Oakley, of Rawndene. Nobody seems to have known
much about Oakley. There are any number of references to him in
the diary, but Poynter gives up trying to make him out. Oakley was
older than the girl; of genial disposition, though he wore his hair

like a Puritan; and a great reader of books. He had a good estate at Rawndene, which he managed well, but his candle burned late over his books; and he wandered abroad in all weathers, summer or frost, in as black a study as the Black Man.

"You might have thought that Mistress Mary would have preferred somebody livelier. But Oakley was good enough company, by all accounts, and he suited her exactly—they tell me that wives understand this.

"And here is where the trouble enters. At the Restoration, Oakley was looking a little white. Not that his loyalty was exactly suspect; but he had bought his estate under the Commonwealth. If sales made under the Commonwealth were now declared null and void by the new Government, it meant ruin for Oakley; and also, under the business-like standards of the time, it meant the end of his prospective marriage to Mistress Mary.

"Then Gerald Vanning appeared.

"Hoy, what a blaze he must have made! He was fresh and oiled from Versailles, from Cologne, from Bruges, from Brussels, from Breda, from everywhere he had gone in the train of the formerly exiled king. Vanning was one of those 'confident young men' about whom we hear so much complaint from old-style Cavaliers in the early years of the Restoration. His family had been very powerful in Kent before the Civil Wars. Everybody knew he would be well rewarded, as he was.

"If this were a romance, I could now tell you how Mistress Mary fell in love with the handsome young Cavalier, and forgot about Oakley. But the truth seems to be that she never liked Vanning. Vanning disgusted Poynter by a habit of bowing and curvetting, with a superior smile, every time he made a remark. It is probable that Mistress Mary understood him no better than Poynter did.

"There is a description in the diary of a dinner Squire Radlow gave to welcome him here at this house. Vanning came over in a coach, despite the appalling state of the roads, with a dozen lackeys in attendance. This helped to impress the Squire, though nothing had as yet been settled on him by the new regime. Vanning already wore his hair long, whereas the others were just growing theirs. They must have looked odd and patchy, like men beginning to grow beards, and rustic enough to amuse him.

"But Mistress Mary was there. Vanning took one look at her, clapped his hand on the back of a chair, bowed, rolled up his eyes, and began to lay siege to her in the full-dress style of the French king taking a town. He slid *bons mots* on his tongue like sweetmeats; he hiccoughed; he strutted; he directed killing ogles. Squire Radlow and his wife were enraptured. They liked Oakley of Rawndene—but it was possible that Oakley might be penniless in a month. Whereas Vanning was to be heaped with preferments, a matter of which he made no secret. Throughout this dinner Richard Oakley looked unhappy, and 'shifted his eyes.'

"When the men got drunk after dinner, Vanning spoke frankly to Squire Radlow. Oakley staggered out to get some air under the apple-trees; what between liquor and crowding misfortunes, he did not feel well. Together among the fumes, Vanning and Squire Radlow shouted friendship at each other, and wept. Vanning swore he would never wed anybody but Mistress Mary, not if his soul rotted deep in hell as Oliver's. The Squire was stern, but not too stern. 'Sir,' said the Squire, 'you abuse my hospitality; my daughter is pledged to the gentleman who has just left us; but it may be that we must speak of this presently.' Poynter, though he saw the justice of the argument, went home disturbed.

"Now, Gerald Vanning was not a fool. I have seen his portrait, painted a few years later when periwigs came into fashion. It is a shiny, shrewd, razorish kind of face. He had some genuine classical learning, and a smattering of scientific monkey-tricks, the new toy of the time. But, above all, he had foresight. In the first place, he was genuinely smitten with hazel eyes and other charms. In the second place, Mistress Mary Radlow was a catch. When awarding bounty to the faithful, doubtless the King and Sir Edward Hyde would not forget Vanning of Mallingford; on the other hand, it was just possible they might.

"During the next three weeks it was almost taken for granted that Vanning should eventually become the Squire's son-in-law. Nothing was said or done, of course. But Vanning dined a dozen times here, drank with the Squire, and gave to the Squire's wife a brooch once owned by Charles the First. Mistress Mary spoke of it furiously to Poynter.

"Then the unexpected news came.

"Oakley was safe in his house and lands. An Act had been passed to confirm all sales and leases of property since the Civil Wars. It meant that Oakley was once more the well-to-do son-in-law; and the Squire could no longer object to his bargain.

"I have here an account of how this news was received at the manor. I did not get it from Poynter's diary. I got it from the records of the coroner's inquest. What astonishes us when we read these chronicles is the blunt directness, the violence, like a wind, or a pistol clapped to the head, with which people set about getting what they wanted. For, just two months afterwards, there was murder done."

★

Our host paused. The room was full of the reflections of firelight. He glanced at the ceiling; what we heard up there was merely the sound of a servant walking overhead.

"Vanning," he went on, "seems to have taken the fact quietly enough. He was here at the manor when Oakley arrived with the news. It was five or six o'clock in the afternoon. Mistress Mary, the Squire, the Squire's wife, and Vanning were sitting in the Ladies' Withdrawing Room. This was (and is) the room at the head of the stairs—a little square place, with two 'panel' windows that would not open. It was furnished with chairs of oak and brocade; a needlework-frame; and a sideboard chastely bearing a plate of oranges, a glass jug of water, and some glasses.

"There was only one candle burning, at some distance from Vanning, so that nobody had a good view of his face. He sat in his riding-coat, with his sword across his lap. When Oakley came in with the news, he was observed to put his hand on his sword; but afterwards he 'made a leg' and left without more words.

"The wedding had originally been set for the end of November; both Oakley and Mistress Mary still claimed this date. It was accepted with all the more cheerfulness by the Squire, since, in the intervening months, Vanning had not yet received any dazzling benefits. True, he had been awarded £500 a year by the Healing and Blessed Parliament. But he was little better off than Oakley; a bargain was a bargain, said the Squire, and Oakley was his own dear son. Nobody seems to know what Vanning did in the interim, except that he settled down quietly at Mallingford.

"But from this time curious rumours began to go about the countryside. They all centred round Richard Oakley. Poynter records some of them, at first evidently not even realising their direction.

They were as light as dandelion-clocks blown off, but they floated and settled.

"Who was Oakley? What did anybody know about him, except that he had come here and bought land under Oliver? He had vast learning, and above a hundred books in his house; what need did he have of that? What had he been? A parson? A doctor of letters of physic? Or letters of a more unnatural kind? Why did he go for long walks in the wood, particularly after dusk?

"Oakley, if questioned, said that this was his nature. But an honest man, meaning an ordinary man, could understand no such nature. A wood was thick; you could not tell what might be in it after nightfall; an honest man preferred the tavern. Such whispers were all the more rapid-moving because of the troubled times. The broken bones of a Revolution are not easily healed. Then there was the unnatural state of the weather. In winter there was no cold at all: the roads dusty; a swarm of flies; and the rose-bushes full of leaves into the following January.

"Oakley heard none of the rumours, or pretended to hear none. It was Jamy Achen, a lad of weak mind and therefore afraid of noth- ing, who saw something following Richard Oakley through Gallows Copse. The boy said he had not got a good look at it, since the time was after dusk. But he heard it rustle behind the trees, peering out at intervals after Mr. Oakley. He said that it seemed human, but that he was not sure it was alive.

"On the night of Friday, the 26th November, Gerald Vanning rode over to this house alone. It was seven o'clock, a late hour for the country. He was admitted to the lower hall by Kitts, the Squire's steward, and he asked for Mr. Oakley. Kitts told him that Mr. Oakley was above-stairs with Mistress Mary, and that the Squire was asleep over supper with Mr. Poynter.

"It is certain that Vanning was wearing no sword. Kitts held the candle high and looked at him narrowly, for he seemed on a wire of apprehension and kept glancing over his shoulder as he pulled off his gloves. He wore jack-boots, a riding-coat half-buttoned, a lace band at the neck, and a flat-crowned beaver hat with a gold band. Under his sharp nose there was a little edge of moustache, and he was sweating.

"'Mr. Oakley has brought a friend with him, I think,' says Vanning.

"'No, sir,' says Kitts, 'he is alone.'

"'But I am sure his friend has followed him,' says Vanning, again twitching his head round and looking over his shoulder. He also jumped as though something had touched him, and kept turning round and round and looking sharply into corners as though he were playing hide-and-seek.

"'Well!' says Mr. Vanning, with a whistle of breath through his nose. 'Take me to Mistress Mary. Stop! First fetch two or three brisk lads from the kitchen, and you shall go with me.'

"The steward was alarmed, and asked what was the matter. Vanning would not tell him, but instructed him to see that the servants carried cudgels and lights. Four of them went above-stairs. Vanning knocked at the door of the Withdrawing Room, and was bidden to enter. The servants remained outside, and both the lights and the cudgels trembled in their hands: later they did not know why.

"As the door opened and closed, Kitts caught a glimpse of Mistress Mary sitting by the table in the rose-brocade dress she reserved usually for Sundays, and Oakley sitting on the edge of the table beside her. Both looked round as though surprised.

"Presently Kitts heard voices talking, but so low he could not make out what was said. The voices spoke more rapidly; then there was a sound of moving about. The next thing to which Kitts could testify was a noise as though a candlestick had been knocked over. There was a thud; a high-pitched kind of noise; muffled breathing sounds and a sort of thrashing on the floor; and Mistress Mary suddenly beginning to scream over it.

"Kitts and his three followers laid hold of the door, but someone had bolted it. They attacked the door in a way that roused the Squire in the dining-room below, but it held. Inside, after a silence, someone was heard to stumble and grope towards the door. Squire Radlow and Mr. Poynter came running up the stairs just as the door was unbolted from inside.

"Mistress Mary was standing there, panting, with her eyes wide and staring. She was holding up one edge of her full skirt, where it was stained with blood as though someone had scoured and polished a weapon there. She cried to them to bring lights; and one of the servants held up a lantern in the doorway.

"Vanning was half-lying, half-crouching over against the far wall, with a face like oiled paper as he lifted round his head to look at them. But they were looking at Oakley, or what was left of Oakley. He had fallen near the table, with the candle smashed beside him. They could not tell how many wounds there were in Oakley's neck and body; above a dozen, Poynter thought, and he was right. Vanning stumbled over and tried to lift him up, but of course, it was too late. Now listen to Poynter's own words:

"'Mr. Radlow ran to Mr. Vanning and laid hold of him, crying: "You are a murderer! You have murdered him!" Mr. Vanning cried to him: "By God and His mercy, I have not touched him! I have no sword or dagger by me!" And indeed, this was true. For he was flung down on the floor by this bloody work, and ordered to be searched, but not so much as a pin was there in his clothes.

"'I had observed by the nature of the wide, gaping wounds that some such blade as a broad knife had inflicted them, or the like. But what had done this was a puzzle, for every inch of the room did we search, high, low and turnover; and still not so much as a pin in crack or crevice.

"'Mr. Vanning deposed that as he was speaking with Mr. Oakley, something struck out the light, and overthrew Mr. Oakley, and knelt on his chest. But who or what this was, or where it had gone when the light was brought, he could not say.'"

Bending close to the firelight, our host finished reading the notes from the sheet of paper in his hands. He folded up the paper, put it back in his pocket, and looked at us.

The historian's wife, who had drawn closer to her husband, shifted uneasily. "I wish you wouldn't tell us these things," she complained. "But tell us, anyway. I still don't understand. What was the man killed with, then?"

"That," said our host, lighting his pipe, "is the question. If you accept natural laws as governing this world, there wasn't anything that could have killed him. Look here a moment!"

(For we were all looking at the ceiling.)

"The Squire begged Mistress Mary to tell him what had happened. First she began to whimper a little, and for the first time in her life she fainted. The Squire wanted to throw some water over her, but Vanning carried her downstairs and they forced brandy between her teeth. When she recovered she was a trifle wandering, with no story at all.

"Something had put out the light. There had been a sound like a fall and a scuffling. Then the noise of moving about, and the smell of blood in a close, confined room. Something seemed to be plucking or pulling at her skirts. She does not appear to have remembered anything more.

"Of course, Vanning was put under restraint, and a magistrate sent for. They gathered in this room, which was a good deal bleaker and barer than it is today; but they pinned Vanning in the chimney-corner of that fireplace. The Squire drew his sword and attempted to run Vanning through: while both of them wept, as the fashion was. But Poynter ordered two of the lads to hold the Squire back, quoting himself later as saying: 'This must be done in good order.'

"Now, what I want to impress on you is that these people were not fools. They had possibly a cruder turn of thought and speech; but they were used to dealing with realities like wood and beef and leather. Here was a reality. Oakley's wounds were six inches deep and an inch wide, from a thick, flat blade that in places had scraped the bone. But there wasn't any such blade, and they knew it.

"Four men stood in the door and held lights while they searched for that knife (if there was such a thing): and they didn't find it. They pulled the room to pieces; and they didn't find it. Nobody could have whisked it out, past the men in the door. The windows didn't open, being set into the wall like panels, so nobody could have got rid of the knife there. There was only one door, outside which the servants had been standing. Something had cut a man to pieces; yet it simply wasn't there.

"Vanning, pale but calmer, repeated his account. Questioned as to why he had come to the house that night, he answered that there had been a matter to settle with Oakley. Asked what it was, he said he had not liked the conditions in his own home for the past month: he would beg Mr. Oakley to mend them. He had done Mr. Oakley no harm, beyond trying to take a bride from him, and therefore he would ask Mr. Oakley to call off his dogs. What dogs?

Vanning explained that he did not precisely mean dogs. He meant something that had got into his bedroom cupboard, but was only there at night; and he had reasons for thinking Mr. Oakley had whistled it there. It had been there only since he had been paying attentions to Mistress Mary.

"These men were only human. Poynter ordered the steward to go up and search the little room again—and the steward wouldn't go.

"That little seed of terror had begun to grow like a mango-tree under a cloth, and push up the cloth and stir out tentacles. It was easy to forget the broad, smiling face of Richard Oakley, and to remember the curious 'shifting' of his eyes. When you recalled that, after all, Oakley was twice Mistress Mary's age, you might begin to wonder just whom you had been entertaining at bread and meat.

"Even Squire Radlow did not care to go upstairs again in his own house. Vanning, sweating and squirming in the chimney-corner, plucked up courage as a confident young man and volunteered to go. They let him. But no sooner had he got into the little room than the door clapped again, and he came out running. It was touch-and-go whether they would desert the house in a body."

Again our host paused. In the silence it was the Inspector who spoke, examining his cigar and speaking with some scepticism. He had a common-sense voice, which restored reasonable values.

"Look here," he said, "are you telling us local bogy-tales, or are you seriously putting this forward as evidence?"

"As evidence given at a coroner's inquest."

"Reliable evidence?"

"I believe so."

"I don't," returned the Inspector, drawing the air through a hollow tooth. "After all, I suppose we've got to admit that a man was murdered, since there was an inquest. But if he died of being hacked or slashed with thirteen wounds, some instrument made those wounds. What happened to that weapon? You say it wasn't in the room; but how do we know that? How do we know it wasn't hidden away somewhere, and they simply couldn't find it?"

"I think I can give you my word," said our host slowly, "that no weapon was hidden there."

"Then what the devil happened to it? A knife at least six inches in the blade, and an inch broad—"

"Yes. But the fact is, nobody could see it."

"It wasn't hidden anywhere, and yet nobody could see it?"

"That's right."

"An invisible weapon?"

"Yes," answered our host, with a curious shining in his eyes. "A quite literally invisible weapon."

"How do you know?" demanded his wife abruptly.

Hitherto she had taken no part in the conversation. But she had been studying him in an odd way, sitting on a hassock; and, as he hesitated, she rose at him in a glory of accusation.

"You villain!" she cried. "Ooh, you unutterable villain! You've been making it all up! Just to make everybody afraid to go to bed, and because I didn't know anything about the place, you've been telling us a pack of lies—"

But he stopped her.

"No. If I had been making it up, I should have told you it was a story." Again he hesitated, almost biting his nails. "I'll admit that I may have been trying to mystify you a bit. That's reasonable, because I honestly don't know the truth myself. I can make a guess at it, that's all. I can make a guess at how those wounds came there. But that isn't the real problem. That isn't what bothers me, don't you see?"

Here the historian intervened. "A wide acquaintance with sensational fiction," he said, "gives me the line on which you're working. I submit that the victim was stabbed with an icicle, as in several tales I could mention. Afterwards the ice melted—and was, in consequence, an invisible weapon."

"No," said our host.

"I mean," he went on, "that it's not feasible. You would hardly find an icicle in such unnaturally warm weather as they were having. And icicles are brittle: you wouldn't get a flat, broad icicle of such steel-strength and sharpness that thirteen stabs could be made and the bone scraped in some of them. And an icicle isn't invisible. Under the circumstances, this knife was invisible—despite its size."

"Bosh!" said the historian's wife. "There isn't any such thing."

"There is if you come to think about it. Of course, it's only an idea of mine, and it may be all wrong. Also, as I say, it's not the real problem, though it's so closely associated with the real problem that—

"But you haven't heard the rest of the story. Shall I conclude it?"

"By all means."

"I am afraid there are no great alarms or sensations," our host went on, "though the very name of Richard Oakley became a nightmare to keep people indoors at night. 'Oakley's friend' became a local synonym for anything that might get you if you didn't look sharp. One or two people saw him walking in the woods afterwards, his head was on one side and the stab-wounds were still there.

"A grand jury of Sussex gentlemen, headed by Sir Benedict Skene, completely exonerated Gerald Vanning. The coroner's jury had already said 'persons or things unknown,' and added words of sympathy with Mistress Mary to the effect that she was luckily quit of a dangerous bargain. It may not surprise you to hear that eighteen months after Oakley's death she married Vanning.

"She was completely docile, though her old vivacity had gone. In those days young ladies did not remain spinsters through choice. She smiled, nodded, and made the proper responses, though it seems probable that she never got over what had happened.

"Matters became settled, even humdrum. Vanning waxed prosperous and respectable. His subsequent career I have had to look up in other sources, since Poynter's diary breaks off at the end of '64. But a grateful Government made him Sir Gerald Vanning, Bart. He became a leading member of the Royal Society, tinkering with the toys of science. His cheeks filled out, the slyness left his eyes, a periwig adorned his head, and four Flanders mares drew his coach to Gresham House. At home he often chose this house to live in when Squire Radlow died; he moved between here and Mallingford with the soberest grace. The little room, once such a cause of terror, he seldom visited; but its door was not locked.

"His wife saw to it that these flagstones were kept scrubbed, and every stick of wood shining. She was a good wife. He for his part was a good husband: he treated her well and drank only for his thirst, though she often pressed him to drink more than he did. It is at this pitch of domesticity that we get the record of another coroner's inquest.

"Vanning's throat was cut on the night of the 5th October, '67.

"On an evening of high winds, he and his wife came here from Mallingford. He was in unusually good spirits, having just done a profitable piece of business. They had supper together, and Vanning drank a great deal. His wife kept him company at it. (Didn't I tell you she once drank off a pint of wine at a draught, for a wager?) She said it would make him sleep soundly; for it seems to be true that he sometimes talked in his sleep. At eight o'clock, she tells us, she went up to bed, leaving him still at the table. At what time he went upstairs we do not know, and neither do the servants. Kitts, the steward, thought he heard him stumbling up that staircase out there at a very late hour. Kitts also thought he heard someone crying out, but a high October gale was blowing and he could not be sure.

"On the morning of the 6th October, a cowherd named Coates was coming round the side of this house in a sodden daybreak from which the storm had just cleared. He was on his way to the west meadow, and stopped to drink at a rain-water barrel under the eaves just below the little room at the head of the stairs. As he was about to drink, he noticed a curious colour in the water. Looking up to find out how it had come there, he saw Sir Gerald Vanning's face looking down at him under the shadow of the yellow trees. Sir Gerald's head was sticking out of the window, and did not move; neither did the eyes. Some of the glass in the window was still intact, though his head had been run through it, and—"

It was at this point that the Inspector uttered an exclamation.

It was an exclamation of enlightenment. Our host looked at him with a certain grimness, and nodded.

"Yes," he said. "You know the truth now, don't you?"

"The truth?" repeated the historian's wife, almost screaming with perplexity. "The truth about what?"

"About the murder of Oakley," said our host. "About the trick Vanning used to murder Oakley seven years before.

"I'm fairly sure he did it," our host went on, nodding reflectively. "Nothing delighted the people of that time so much as tricks and gadgets of that very sort. A clock that ran by rolling bullets down an inclined plane; a diving-bell; a burglar-alarm; the Royal Society played with all of them. And Vanning (study his portrait one day) profited by the monkey-tricks he learned in exile. He invented an invisible knife."

"But see here—!" protested the historian.

"Of course he planned the whole thing against Oakley. Oakley was no more a necromancer or a consorter with devils than I am. All those rumours about him were started with a definite purpose by Vanning himself. A crop of whispers, a weak-minded lad to be bribed, the whole power of suggestion set going; and Vanning was ready for business.

"On the given night he rode over to this house, alone, with a certain kind of knife in his pocket. He made a great show of pretending he was chased by imaginary monsters, and he alarmed the steward. With the servants for witnesses, he went upstairs to see Oakley and Mistress Mary. He bolted the door. He spoke pleasantly to them. When he had managed to distract the girl's attention, he knocked out the light, tripped up Oakley, and set upon him with that certain kind of knife. There had to be many wounds and much blood, so he could later account for blood on himself. The girl was too terrified in the dark to move. He had only to clean his knife on a soft but stiff-brocaded gown, and then put down the knife in full view. Nobody noticed it."

The historian blinked. "Admirable!" he said. "Nobody noticed it, eh? Can you tell me the sort of blade that can be placed in full view without anybody noticing it?"

"Yes," said our host. "A blade made of ordinary plain glass, placed in the large glass jug full of water standing on a sideboard table."

There was a silence.

"I told you about that glass water-jug. It was a familiar fixture. Nobody examines a transparent jug of water. Vanning could have made a glass knife with the crudest of cutting tools; and glass is murderous stuff—strong, flat, sharp-edged, and as sharp-pointed as you want to make it. There was only candle-light, remember. Any minute traces of blood that might be left on the glass knife would sink as sediment in the water, while everybody looked straight at the weapon in the water and never noticed it. But Vanning (you also remember?) prevented Squire Radlow from throwing water on the girl when she fainted. Instead he carried her downstairs. Afterwards he told an admirable series of horror-tales; he found an excuse to go back to the room again alone, slip the knife into his sleeve, and get rid of it in the confusion."

The Inspector frowned thoughtfully. "But the real problem—" he said.

"Yes. If that was the way it was done, did the wife know? Vanning talked in his sleep, remember."

We looked at each other. The historian's wife, after a glance round, asked the question that was in our minds.

"And what was the verdict of *that* inquest?"

"Oh, that was simple," said our host. "Death by misadventure, from falling through a window while drunk and cutting his throat on the glass. Somebody observed that there were marks of heels on the board floor as though he might have been dragged there; but this wasn't insisted on. Mistress Mary lived on in complete happiness, and died at the ripe age of eighty-six, full of benevolence and sleep. These are natural explanations. Everything is natural. There's nothing wrong with that little room at the head of the stairs. It's been turned into a bedroom now; I assure you it's comfortable; and anyone who cares to sleep there is free to do so. But at the same time—"

"Quite," we said.

DEAD MAN'S HAND

E. R. Punshon

Ernest Robertson Punshon (1872–1956) was a prolific author who, after serving a long literary apprenticeship as a novelist of melodrama, specialised in writing detective stories. In 1929, he published the first of half a dozen books which appeared in quick succession and featured the Scotland Yard men Carter and Bell. With *Information Received* (1933), he introduced a well-born junior police officer called Bobby Owen. Owen rose through the ranks during the course of a career that stretched for over twenty years and encompassed thirty-five novels as well as a handful of short stories.

Perhaps because he was so productive, Punshon was a variable writer; one never quite knows whether to expect brilliance or a misfire. In *Twentieth Century Crime and Mystery Writers*, Barry Pike summed up a particular strength of the Owen books: "Beneath the traditional patterns of detective fiction… lies something altogether more disturbing. The series is shot through with an eerie intensity, a manic quality that seizes the author's imagination. He stretches the formal framework of detective fiction to accommodate driven personalities with 'tumultuous, unrestrained passions'. There are no half-measures in Punshon's novels: people don't experience dislike, they seethe with venomous hatred. He draws on the basic emotions, manipulating them to create havoc." "Dead Man's Hand" is a non-series story which first appeared in *MacKill's Mystery Magazine* in March 1953.

OUTSIDE THE SNOW WAS FALLING HEAVILY, STEADILY, AS IT had been falling since teatime. No light showed either in the big house at the end of the drive or in the small lodge at its beginning.

Across the snow-covered scene a man was making a slow, cautious way; and behind him the falling snowflakes obliterated his footsteps as fast as he made them. He was wearing a woman's nightdress that, as he was a small man, covered him entirely, and his head was wrapped in a white shawl.

It would have been almost impossible to see him in that driving snow, even if there had been anyone near. There was no one but he was a cautious man and he had neglected no precaution.

He came to the small lodge. He opened the door and entered. The drifting snow followed and a breath of cold air stirred uneasily the line of washing that hung across the dim, warm, half-lit kitchen.

A woman was sitting before the fire. As the man entered she held out to it trembling, shaking hands. The man stood still in the doorway, stamping to clear the snow from his boots, shaking himself to get rid of the clinging snow. He took off the nightdress and the shawl and flung them on a chair. The woman by the fire said:

"Is it done?"

The man did not answer. He was Jeremy Wells, gardener, chauffeur, general factotum to Colonel Anthony Bennett, up at the big house at the other end of the drive. He came nearer the fire. He was still silent. The woman said once more, without looking round:

"Is it done?"

Jeremy felt in his coat pocket. He took out a paper packet and emptied it carefully on the kitchen table. Even in that dim room, where there was no light save firelight, there came a sparkling and a shining from what he had put down on that rough deal table: He said:

"Diamonds. Worth thousands. Thousands. As no one but me knew he had them, so'll never be missed or sought for and nothing missing they can trace to us. You can't devalue diamonds, Colonel said himself, and that's gospel, so it is."

The woman did not look at them, strangely as they shone there in the half-light from the fire. She was groping for the nightdress and the shawl where he had thrown them down. She said:

"They are wet through, both of them. Anyone could tell you had been out. I had best wash them and hang them on the line to dry with the other things." She put them in a small, old, seldom-used tin bath she fetched from the scullery. The bigger one she generally used was in the outside wash-house. She placed it on the kitchen table near the diamonds. She put out her hands towards them, but did not touch them. She said: "They don't look worth thousands. Why should they be?"

The man said:

"As soon as he saw me he knew, I was holding his revolver. He never said a word. He put up his hand before his face so he shouldn't see, and I fired. Twice I fired. One shot took off his middle finger, clean as if it had been a knife.

"The diamonds were there upon the table. No one knew he had them. No one except me. He didn't even buy them under his own name. No one knew it was Colonel Anthony Bennett buying diamonds. Now they're mine. They'll find him in the morning, and they'll think that it was burglars."

"Best be off to bed," the woman said. She was already busy at the small tin bath, washing the nightdress and the shawl. "There's been nothing got on them, has there?" she asked.

"How could there be?" he said, "seeing that I never went near except to get diamonds where they lay all ready on the table."

"Did no one hear you? Are you sure?" she asked.

"How could they with the wireless going and all," he said, "and both the old women deaf as posts as well you know, the way you have to shout to make them hear."

"No one saw you?" she asked, "you are sure no one saw you?"

"How could they," he said, "and me in all that snow as white as it, what with the nightdress and the shawl, so I could have passed by near enough to touch and no one know it?"

"Best be off to bed then," the woman said. "I'll come as soon as I've finished." She was already wringing out the nightdress which had needed, since it was not soiled, no more than a rinsing in a little warm water. "But put the things away first. Safe. Where they won't be found easy."

"They won't be looked for," he repeated, "for there was none that knew he had them, only me."

She did not answer. She was busy hanging the nightdress on the line of washing stretched across the kitchen. She had to take some of the other things down to make room for it.

He picked up the diamonds, slowly, lovingly, and took them to the bedroom with him. When she followed he was sleeping soundly, the packet of diamonds under his pillow.

★

They were up early. The snow had ceased. All the world was white and calm and peaceful. Neither of them said very much. Jeremy found a hiding place for the diamonds by taking up a floorboard.

"Safe as houses," he told her. "Seeing as what can't be missed won't ever be looked for. All on the Q.T. with him it was, diddling the Government and all. Currency offence, like you read in the papers."

She nodded and went on with her work. She cleared the breakfast table and then got out the ironing board. The nightdress had not dried very well and ironing was not easy. There was neither gas nor electricity in the cottage and so the iron had to be heated at the kitchen fire which this morning was slow and sluggish.

Jeremy went upstairs to look at the newly nailed-down floorboard beneath which lay the diamonds none would ever look for. From the window he saw two men struggling down the avenue from the big house, through the deep, untrodden snow. He went downstairs and said:

"There's two of 'em coming. Police. He's been found and the police sent for. They'll be wanting to know if we heard anything. All you have to do is say 'No' and be shocked and upset like."

The woman nodded and went on with her ironing—or rather with trying to get her iron hot enough for the work.

"They are nearly here," Jeremy said. "It's Higgins from the village and a sergeant with him. Higgins must have rung up to report. There'll be more of 'em at the house."

He went to the door and opened it. The two policemen were only a few yards away.

"Saw you coming," he called cheerfully. "Come along in and let the missus get you a cup of tea. What's brought you out so early?"

It was the sergeant who answered. He said: "Colonel's been murdered."

Mrs. Jeremy screamed. She started so violently that she upset the ironing board, the iron and its stand, the half-ironed nightdress. They all went clattering down together.

Jeremy, also, gave the impression of complete bewilderment and surprise.

"What's that?" he asked. "What do you mean? Colonel? The master? He was all right and well last time I saw him just before the snow began."

"Heard anything in the night?" the sergeant asked.

"No, not a thing," Jeremy answered. "Who would go for to do a thing like that?" he asked. "Was it burglars?"

"That's what it looks like," the sergeant said. "Entrance effected at the back by a window forced open. Front door unbolted though securely fastened last thing last night. That'll be the way they left. The poor gentleman's own revolver used. Taken from the drawer in the hall where it was always kept."

"Every one knew that's where he had it," Jeremy said. "Didn't the ladies hear anything even though deaf as they are?"

"Nothing," the sergeant said. "Wireless seems to have been going, too. Doesn't seem to be anything missing. Seems as if they must have panicked and run soon as they saw what they had done."

"No wonder," Jeremy said. "Reason enough." He sat down and began to put on his boots. "I had best go up to the house and see what I can do," he said. "Eh, it's a bad business, a bad, bad business, and means a move for me and the missus, when we thought we were settled for life."

He paused, one boot on, one in his bands. "Missus," he said, "best pick them things up. That nightdress will be needing washing over again, lying in the grate the way it is."

"You were early on the job, missus," the sergeant said.

"Aye, she's an early worker," Jeremy said. He had his other boot on now and he stood up. "I'll be going up to the house," he said again.

"We thought you might be able to help," the sergeant said, half apologetically. "There's nothing you've seen, no suspicious character, nothing unusual in any way?"

"Not a thing," Jeremy said with conviction. To his wife, still sitting silent, as if stunned by such dreadful, shattering news, he said: "Get on with your work, missus. Take your mind off it."

Mechanically she picked up the nightdress and began to arrange it again upon the ironing board. She began to scream.

"His hand," she cried, "look, it's there, there with the middle finger shot clean away."

They all three stared and looked and looked again, gaping, bewildered, not understanding. For where she pointed they saw nothing, nothing but a few spots of iron mould, probably from the old, seldom-used tin bath the nightdress had been washed in. Nothing more. Only a most fevered, fantastic imagination could see in the faint irregular pattern they made even the most remote resemblance to a human hand.

"Upset she is, proper upset," Jeremy said. "There's nothing there, missus, and how could there be? Only red rust off of that old bath you've been using. Enough to upset any one, being told a thing like that so abrupt and sudden. You did ought to have been more gentle like, sergeant, and not so sudden. Make yourself a cup of tea, missus, and lie down a while."

The sergeant said: "Maybe I should have spoke more gradual like, but how was it she did know there was a finger shot away, for that I never said?"

THE CHRISTMAS EVE GHOST

Ernest Dudley

Ernest Dudley was the professional name of Vivian Ernest Coltman-Allen (1908–2006). In his youth, his father ran the King's Arms public house in Cookham, Berkshire. A next door neighbour was Stanley Spencer, later a renowned artist, whose social circle included Ivor Novello and Jack Buchanan. These men were both famous names in their day, and at the age of seventeen, Ernest was inspired to try his hand on the stage. Although he never became a high-profile actor, he did meet his future wife through the theatre.

In the 1930s, he decided to supplement his earnings on the stage with journalism, and proceeded to enjoy considerable success with a range of literary activities, for instance as a boxing correspondent, crime reporter, jazz critic, and (under the jokey by-line Charles Ton) gossip columnist. His eclectic non-fiction included a book about the life and loves of Lillie Langtry, but he became best known for his detective fiction. Novels, short stories, film scripts, and radio plays poured from his pen, and in 1953 he supported John Creasey's efforts to form the Crime Writers' Association, becoming a founder member of the CWA. "The Christmas Eve Ghost" appeared in *The Private Eye*, a short story collection published in 1948.

S OPHIE FORREST WAS BLUE-EYED AND PRETTY, LIKE A CHINA doll and her face was about as hard. Craig let his gaze run down to her very shapely legs advantageously displayed in sheerest stockings.

She didn't look the type to scare easily and yet here she was leaning across his deck, saying:

"I'm scared and I'm admitting it. I just didn't know who to turn to for help then I thought of you."

Craig was accustomed to this angle but it never ceased to flatter him slightly.

"Have a cigarette," he offered. "Now," he added as they lit up. "You don't really believe in this spook do you?"

"Seeing is believing, isn't it? I've seen it all right—two nights running."

"The ghost of a Burmese Dancing Girl," murmured Craig thoughtfully to himself. He was beginning to be interested, especially as he hadn't expected anything out of the ordinary to come his way on Christmas Eve. He had resigned himself to a series of phone calls asking him to go and guard the family silver at Christmas house-parties.

Sophie Forrest pulled raggedly at her cigarette and managed to smile.

"I know it sounds quite ridiculous to you, Mr. Craig," she said in the voice of one who didn't see anything ridiculous in it at all, "but it does tie up with the old story."

Craig told her:

"Better get the whole thing off your chest. Up to date all I know is that the house is supposed to be haunted by a Burmese dancer and you've seen her. What more?"

She flicked a golden flake of tobacco off her lip with a red-tipped finger before she answered him.

"Years ago it seems, the house was owned by some Eastern prince who kept this dancing girl there and then eventually killed her in a fit of jealous rage. The general idea now, is that she appears every year at Christmas time."

"And how long have you been in the house, Mrs. Forrest?"

She smiled wryly.

"This is my first Christmas—and my last, I'm beginning to think! When my husband and I took the house last summer to convert into an hotel we merely thought it was silly nonsense."

Craig asked:

"And your husband? Has he seen it? What does he think now?"

She hesitated. When she spoke it was slowly and she kept her eyes on the tip of her cigarette. She said:

"Nick—my husband—is dead."

Craig's brows contracted.

"Was it a sudden death, Mrs. Forrest?"

She nodded.

"He was found in the river early one morning two months ago. He'd been shot."

"Naturally, you had the police in."

This was definitely more in his line than the unhappy spirits of Burmese dancing girls.

"They can't find out who did it. I don't believe they ever will."

Craig was remembering newspaper reports of some young Putney hotel proprietor being pulled out of the river. At the time it had sounded to him like a murder job. He said only:

"So you're running the place alone now?"

She shook her head.

"No. My husband's partner is still there. Mr. Craig—"

But he interrupted to ask:

"Has he been scared by the ghost too?"

"He saw it before I did. The next night we waited up together to see if it came again. It did."

"Exactly what sort of a performance does this dancing girl put over?"

"Scoff if you like, Mr. Craig. It isn't so funny once you've seen it. She suddenly appears in the corridor—from nowhere, it seemed to me, but Arthur said he thought she walked right through the wall—then she cries out: 'I'll haunt this house' twice and the second time she adds: 'Until my death be avenged!' It's always the same words. Then she disappears."

Craig remained unimpressed.

"Looks like somebody will have to avenge her death then," he remarked lightly. "If she is indeed a ghost. What does she look like?"

Sophie Forrest shuddered.

"Horrible. Wild, with blood all over her dress and black hair falling about her face."

He regarded her silently for a moment. Then:

"What do you want me to do about it?"

"I thought," and there was a touch of pleading in her voice, "that if you would come down tonight and see for yourself, as an outsider you know, it would help. Then, if it is a ghost, I suppose I shall have to get out. It's scared off everybody in the hotel so there won't be much point in staying anyway."

"How are you going to pass me off? As a ghost-slayer, a guest or just myself?"

She answered him quickly.

"A guest. Pretend you have come to stay over Christmas."

"What is your partner's name besides Arthur?"

"Lennox. Arthur Lennox. He says he is going to shoot at the thing if it shows up again tonight."

"Which, if it is a spook," Craig observed, "won't inconvenience it much. All right, I'll come. It's one way of spending Christmas Eve that I haven't tried yet."

She didn't answer him but stood up, collecting her bag and gloves off the desk.

"I'll be along in time for dinner," said Craig. "I hope your plum-pudding's good."

"It's good," she said.

He wondered if she really hadn't any sense of humour or whether it had all been knocked out of her by the goings-on at Putney.

He saw her politely to the door.

"By the by," he said, "you haven't told anybody about me?"

"Nobody."

"Not even Lennox?"

She stared at him.

"I said nobody, Mr. Craig."

He leant against the doorpost whistling softly to himself as she disappeared down the stairs, then, the whistle still on his lips, he went quickly back to his desk. He sat down and put his feet up in their favourite position. He might as well be comfortable, he had a number of telephone calls to make.

When he hung up finally from his chats with the Putney police and Scotland Yard, he leant thoughtfully back in his chair and gazed intently at the ceiling.

Among other items that interested him quite a lot he had learned that the late Mr. Nick Forrest had a brother.

River View Private Hotel stood dark and dismal in its own grounds, the mist from the river swirling about its gaunt grimness.

"Blimey!" exclaimed the dejected-looking little individual who had clambered out of the taxi at Craig's heels. "Looks okay for all the works and no mistake."

"Setting certainly has atmosphere," Craig agreed.

He turned away from the illuminated meter of the taxi and stood looking up the drive. He laughed light-heartedly.

"Never mind. Mrs. Forrest should have a nice comforting drink ready and waiting."

"Couldn't be any readier than I am," the other retorted.

Their footsteps crunched up the drive, Craig's companion trotting miserably in the rear, muttering:

"Christmas Eve too. Cor!"

The door was flung open as soon as they set foot on the steps and Craig had a shrewd suspicion their approach had been watched by Sophie Forrest from some unlighted window.

"Mr. Craig," she said swiftly, glancing back for a moment over her shoulder. "Come in. Your room is all ready for you."

Her welcoming manner couldn't disguise her nervousness. She caught sight of the other man as he followed Craig into the lighted hall.

"Who is he?"

Craig said easily:

"This is Brown. He wishes to spend Christmas here for want of a better place to go. His wife has just left him." Craig encountered a startled look from the woman. He grinned at her. "I shall want another room," he said firmly.

His voice was loud enough to benefit any inquisitive ears that might be listening.

Later in the evening Craig found Arthur Lennox was the jovial and hearty type. When dinner was over Arthur became the life and soul of the party. Despite the fact that there wasn't anybody in the place with the exception of the three men, Mrs. Forrest and a pudding-faced stolid maid, he was full of a misguided Christmas spirit plus jokes which sounded as if they had come out of a cracker and were about as funny. Unlike Sophie Forrest, who was very silent, the possible appearance of any ghostly visitation did not seem to worry him.

At ten-thirty Craig could take it no longer.

"If you will excuse me, Mrs. Forrest, I think I will go to bed." He included the man he'd called Brown with a movement of his head. "It's been a somewhat exhausting day."

"It's early," Arthur Lennox protested.

"Mr. Brown always goes to bed early," said Craig piously.

The big clock down in the darkened hall had struck half-past eleven when there was a light tap on Craig's door. He opened it without switching on the light.

It was Sophie Forrest.

"I just wanted to make sure you were ready," she whispered.

He answered in a low voice:

"I'll be there when the fun starts."

She nodded, satisfied, and crept silently away. At a few minutes to midnight Craig's door slowly opened again.

"We'll get in the shadow of that doorway," Craig told Brown quietly. The other, who was peering over his shoulder, nodded. Noiselessly they approached the shadows Craig had indicated. Craig glanced at his watch. The luminous dial showed twelve o'clock.

Almost at once a gentle scraping noise broke the quiet of the house and something seemed to emerge from the wall a few yards away.

"'S'trewth," whispered Craig's companion inelegantly. "The ruddy ghost!"

"But *not*," murmured Craig, "of the Burmese dancing girl."

As he spoke Craig became aware of Sophie Forrest and Arthur Lennox waiting in the darkness farther down the passage. The apparition was making straight for them.

A sudden gasp from Sophie shattered the tension.

"Nick! It's Nick!"

"It can't be!"

It was Lennox who cried out, but he shrank farther back as the terrifying figure, looking as if it had climbed out of the river, slowly advanced, stabbing an accusing finger.

Lennox flung out a hand as if to ward it off.

"Go away," he shrieked. "Go away. Don't touch me!"

The figure laughed hollowly, and in deep, sepulchral tones said:

"You know who I am, Arthur Lennox. I am Nick Forrest."

Lennox was gibbering.

"Don't look at me like that—Go away—*go away!*"

"Nick Forrest," repeated the advancing figure relentlessly. "Accusing my murderer!"

Lennox was wild-eyed.

"I didn't mean it, Nick, I didn't mean to kill you. Don't come any nearer." His voice rose to a scream.

The man beside Craig drew a long whistle and Sophie Forrest, crouched against the wall, forgot her terror for a second:

"So it *was* you who did it!"

At the sound of her words something seemed to snap in Lennox's benumbed brain. He pushed her aside and a gun gleamed in his hand.

"Keep away!" he yelled at the approaching figure. "Stand away, I tell you!"

The answer he got was another hollow cackle.

Then a report roared through the house. Another and another as Lennox fired at point-blank range. There was a moment of silence as Lennox realised that the apparition was still moving towards him. The gun clattered from his grasp. He gave a strangled noise in his throat and slid to the floor in a dead faint.

"Very nice," observed Craig coolly as the girl turned and fled down the stairs. Craig and Brown emerged from the doorway.

"All right, Bill."

At Craig's voice the apparition turned and remarked cheerfully:

"Not so bad, eh? Looks like we proved the blighter did kill poor old Nick."

"Never said a truer word." It was the man called Brown speaking in a tone of deep satisfaction as he snapped a pair of handcuffs over Lennox's wrists. He straightened up. "And I don't mind admitting as you gave *me* a bit of a turn once or twice."

Craig chuckled and went downstairs in search of Sophie Forrest.

He found her huddled in a corner of the sofa in the lounge.

"What you need," he told her, "is a good stiff drink. Where do I find you one? And one for my friends?" When he returned she said:

"Please explain. I feel a little weak."

Handing her a glass and grinning:

"Get outside this first."

She took it gratefully and Craig sat down beside her. "Sorry I had to scare you that way," he apologised. "But I wasn't sure if you were in on your husband's murder or not."

She smiled at him wanly over the rim of her glass.

"I had a feeling all along it was Arthur Lennox who killed him but there didn't seem to be any proof."

Craig told her:

"The Putney police had the same feeling too. His aim, of course, was to scare you off, which would have left him with the hotel all to himself. Pretty crude stuff," he reflected, "but he might have got away with it."

She gulped her drink.

"Do you think he's mad?"

"Most people think murderers are mad. It was such an elaborate set-up I would say Lennox may have had some sort of a kink."

She asked:

"You guessed the ghost was phoney from the start, didn't you?"

He nodded.

"When you gave me her little speech," he said, "it didn't sound so very much like Burmese to me."

She began to laugh shakily.

"Why, of course. She wouldn't have spoken in English!"

He grinned at her.

"Exactly. One of his girl friends popping through the secret panel he'd discovered. I knew there must be one if the apparition was flesh and blood, and it was pretty easy to find after you had pointed the spot out to me where it always did its disappearing act. I found the girl friend there this evening and your husband's brother just took her place. Didn't you know about him?"

She shook her head.

"I knew of him but I had never met him."

"He is an actor out of a job, so—I gave him a job."

She looked incredulous.

"And he took it, knowing he risked being shot?"

Craig smiled quietly.

"You told me Lennox was going to take a pot-shot at his dancing-girl," he said, "so I knew he'd be demonstrating with blanks to give the right ghostly effect."

He raised his glass and said:

"Happy Christmas!"

DICK WHITTINGTON'S CAT

Victor Canning

Victor Canning (1911–1986) was a highly successful writer whose work is perhaps less well-remembered today than its quality merits. According to an admirably informative website in his honour created by John Higgins, Canning was responsible for no fewer than sixty-one novels. These included "one travel book, eighteen novels both comic and serious, four historical novels set in Roman and Arthurian Britain, three children's books, two short story collections (plus an abundance of other stories) and thirty-three thrillers". John Higgins argues that the best of those thrillers "are some of the finest ever written in the genre" and several were filmed, including *The Rainbird Pattern*, which Alfred Hitchcock transformed into *Family Plot*.

Canning's first novel, published in 1934, was *Mr. Finchley Discovers His England*. This comic story proved highly successful and was the first of a trilogy. After war service, Canning concentrated on thrillers. *Venetian Bird*, filmed with Richard Todd in the lead, earned the admiration of critics as discerning as Julian Symons and Michael Gilbert, who praised its meticulous construction and sense of place. His books about the private eye Rex Carver and his "Birdcage" espionage series also achieved considerable popularity. The posthumous publication in 2009 of *The Minerva Club* by the independent press Crippen & Landru, highlighted his flair for the short form. "Dick Whittington's Cat", a story of the pantomime, first appeared in the *Evening Standard* on 22 December 1950.

D ICK WHITTINGTON, A SLENDER FIGURE IN GREEN HOSE, scarlet doublet and feather cap, called pleadingly to his cat:

"Dear Puss, 'twill be a bitter blow indeed
If you desert me in my hour of need."

The cat, sadly shaking its head, backed away to the edge of the proscenium arch of the New Gaiety Theatre. A spot flicked on and the tabby fur was streaked gold and black in the light.

The orchestra drifted slowly into a melancholy tune. Dick ran forward, arms outstretched, but the cat turned and with an agile leap reached the sill of the stage box and then using the stucco ornamental swags for feet and handholds climbed rapidly miaowing up to the dress circle while the curtain dropped on the disconsolate Dick.

The audience held its breath as the cat went along the circle. In the centre box was a young woman in a white evening dress, her fair hair caught up with a narrow diamond fillet. The cat blew her a kiss and the audience roared.

The young man sitting with her, his arm along the back of her chair, grinned. He was dark-haired, his face browned, and his body as he slumped back in his chair, his right hand thrust deep into his trouser pocket, was the body of an athlete.

As the cat persisted in its attentions, miaowing at the box of chocolates on the young woman's lap, an embarrassed frown moved across the young man's face.

The girl held up the box and the cat took a chocolate. It hopped a little excitedly on the sill of the box and then reached out its paws and, taking the girl's hand, raised it to its lips in a long kiss.

"You're going to lose your girl, mister!" a husky voice shouted from the gallery. The cat, emboldened by the shouts that now came from the gallery, blew the girl a kiss and waggled his head admiringly at her.

The young man fidgeted nervously and the cat, hopping sideways a little, reached out a paw and patted him on the cheek. Then, mischievously, it flicked the man's dress tie loose.

The cat half rose and reached out again for the girl's hand to kiss it, but as it did so the laughter in the theatre stilled. The cat lost its balance, teetered for a moment and then fell. Its body thudded against the carpet of the stalls gangway twelve feet below.

The young man in the box leapt to his feet and leaned over. The cat tried to sit up and gave a low groan. The young man turned and rushed out of the box.

Then minutes later the pantomime was proceeding smoothly… with a substitute cat. The manager had come on stage and made a little announcement. Mr. Alfred Stainer, who played the part of the cat, had twisted his ankle and an understudy would carry on.

The young man had returned to his box.

Charles Brockhurst leaned across to the girl and said. "Stella, darling. I can see this thing upset you. Would you like to go?"

She turned and nodded, but as he bent to get her wrap, she said abruptly: "Charles—my bracelet! It's gone."

He straightened up quickly and his face was suddenly stiff, almost bitter in its look. "Are you sure? Let me look."

After a while he turned to her and said quietly: "There's some kind of jinx on me. This is the fourth time and I don't like it. It would be a good idea for you to call one of the attendants. It's better if I don't move from here."

"Don't be an ass, Charles—"

"Nevertheless, I'm not moving."

Fifteen minutes later they were in the manager's office. With them in evening dress was Detective Inspector Rawlings of Scotland Yard who had been sitting in the stalls.

"Now, Miss Morton, which wrist was the bracelet on?"

"The left."

"As far as I remember, though I couldn't see very well from the stalls, that was the hand that the cat kissed?"

"Yes, it was."

"What kind of fastening had it?"

"A kind of clip which you pressed. Oh I see what you mean. The cat could have pressed it in his paws when he held my hand?"

"Maybe. I take it that neither of you left the box from the time you last remember having the bracelet until the manager came along and searched it with you?"

"That is so—"

"No, that is not so. I left the box when the cat fell." Charles Brockhurst, his hands in his pockets, was leaning against the wall, his face a little defiant. "Stella and I were holding hands before the cat episode. I could have slipped the bracelet off and got rid of it when I left the box—"

"Charles, please!"

"But I could."

Rawlings nodded slowly. "He's quite right, Miss Morton. Mr. Charles Brockhurst..." He cocked his head towards the young man. "Now I wonder why your name seems familiar to me."

The young man gave a short laugh. "I'll tell you. In the last six months I've been at three house parties where jewellery has disappeared. I was the only person who was present on all the occasions. One or two people have taken the trouble to point it out to me. Also I'm hard up. Young architects have quite a struggle when they take off on their own. And I have rather expensive tastes."

Stella stood up. "Please, Inspector Rawlings, don't take too much notice of him. I'm sure Charles had nothing to do with it."

Rawlings examined the ash on the end of his cigar. "I remember about the jewellery business now, of course. I know how you feel, Miss Morton, but it's no good ignoring facts. Mr. Brockhurst could have taken the bracelet and passed it to someone in the theatre. And our friend the cat could have taken it and done the same."

A little later Rawlings was in the dressing room along with Alfred Stainer. Stainer's right foot was propped on a cushion and wrapped lightly in a bandage.

Rawlings gave him a curt nod.

"Well, Stainer, I see you've got another profession these days."

Stainer groaned. "Always had it as a sideline before. Come from a family of acrobats, as you know, inspector. But cut the cackle and come to the business. What's all the malarkey?"

"Remember the couple in the box from which you took a tumble?"

"I certainly do. Jealous young swine, he was. If ever I meet up with him again, he'll get an old-fashioned on the kisser."

"Why?"

"You don't fink I fell, do you? Not me—don't have that kind of falling in our family. That Brockhurst bloke couldn't take my jokey ways with his gal, and when I was going to leave him he outs with his hand and gives me knee a push and over I goes. Mighta killed me."

"That's very interesting. The young lady he was with has had her diamond bracelet stolen."

"Indeed, and I'm supposed to have taken it, eh? I suppose just because I've got a record you'll hang it on me."

Rawlings was silent for a moment. Then he said: "So, our young friend pushed you."

"Yes. I had me back to the theatre and no one could see him. He was sitting there with his arm on the back of his girl's chair and the next moment he gives me a push. You ain't blind inside them old skins, you know. Saw his hand come out plain as daylight, I did. It's my bet that in all that uproar he swiped the bracelet himself."

A few minutes later the manager showed Miss Morton and Brockhurst into the room. Stainer gave Brockhurst a scowl.

"If it weren't for this 'ere leg, I'd settle up with you now, young feller—"

"That's enough, Stainer. I'll do the talking," Rawlings snapped. "Mr. Brockhurst, Stainer says you pushed him off the edge of the box. Is that true?"

"No, it's a damned lie."

"One of you is lying. The one who is lying almost certainly took the bracelet because whoever it was needed a diversion to cover the loss and to dispose of the bracelet. A fall from the box was good cover. Now which was it—Mr. Brockhurst pushing you or you faking a fall, Stainer?"

"I certainly didn't push him," snapped Brockhurst angrily.

"Go on—pin it on me, just because I got a record," Stainer snarled. "Where's the good of going straight with blokes like you around to twist a feller up. Class war—that's what it is."

Rawlings smiled. "This is common sense, Stainer, not class war. You know you're lying. Before I told you, you knew the man in the box was Mr. Brockhurst. You gave me his name. You knew, I should say, that he had been present when other jewels had disappeared, and as you came to the box and saw Miss Morton's bracelet you worked out a quick plan on the spur of the moment. You always were good at that. It was easy to take the bracelet. All you had to do was to cover the loss just long enough to get rid of it and then trust that suspicion would fall on Mr. Brockhurst. So you fell—though I think you mistimed it and hurt your ankle without meaning to."

"I was pushed."

"You're sure?"

"Yes. Saw his hand come right out at me."

"Which hand?"

Stainer paused. Then he said cunningly, "You don't get me like that. Not the one he had round his girl. The one what was in his pocket. The right."

Rawlings shook his head warningly at Brockhurst. "Leave it to me. After I had left you I remembered why your name was familiar. My son was in your squadron during the war. Show him your right hand, Mr. Brockhurst. The one you pushed him with."

Brockhurst drew his right arm backwards from his pocket and held it out. The sleeve flapped loosely about the wrist.

"Sorry, Stainer," Brockhurst said. "I have a right hand, actually, but the dashed arrangement hurts at times, and I often leave it off."

Rawlings nodded. "I guessed that might be so when I noticed that all this time you haven't once taken it out of your pocket."

For a moment Rawlings thought they were going to have trouble with Stainer. But the pantomime cat thought better of it and with a philosophical shrug made no objection when Rawlings insisted on taking the bandage off his right foot. Underneath was the bracelet.

A SURPRISE FOR CHRISTMAS

Cyril Hare

Cyril Hare was the writing name of Alfred Alexander Gordon Clark (1900–1958). He was born in Surrey and a love of countryside pursuits gained in early life stayed with him; fishing plays a central part in *Death is No Sportsman* (1938) while there are hunting references in his final novel, *He Should Have Died Hereafter*, aka *Untimely Death* (1958). He was called to the Bar in 1924 and enjoyed a successful career in the law. Although crime writing was, for him, a part-time vocation, he soon established himself as an author of high calibre. *Tragedy at Law*, widely regarded as his finest book, appeared in 1942. This unorthodox novel makes excellent use not only of his knowledge of arcane legal rules but also of his experience of life on a judicial circuit.

Hare's literary reputation rests mainly on his novels, but he was also an accomplished exponent of the short story. After his early death, his friend and fellow lawyer Michael Gilbert edited *Best Detective Stories of Cyril Hare* aka *Death Among Friends* (1959), this collection included "A Surprise for Christmas", previously published three years earlier.

THEY HAD HAD THEIR CHRISTMAS DINNER IN THE MIDDLE OF the day because this year there were children in the house. Turkey and plum pudding and all the drinks that rightfully go with them had reduced Jimmy Blenkiron to a pleasant state of somnolence. Lying back in an armchair in front of the library fire, he could just discern the red glow of the logs through his half-shut eyes. His hands still caressed the glass that had held his liqueur brandy. It was half-past three and he was at peace with the world.

Anne Blenkiron came into the room and dropped thankfully on to a sofa beside her husband's chair.

"Thank goodness, there's the washing-up done at last," she said.

"Good for you," said Jimmy approvingly. Always a pattern of consideration where his wife was concerned, he shifted his legs slightly to allow some of the warmth from the fire to reach in her direction.

"Why didn't you get the children to help you?" he asked.

"Oh, they're much too busy on their own affairs. They are preparing a surprise for you at teatime."

"Wonderful they've got the energy to do anything after what they put away at dinner," said Jimmy with a yawn. "What sort of a surprise?"

"That you're not to know. I'm in the secret, of course. But I think you'll like it. It's their own idea entirely."

"Nice kids," commented Jimmy tolerantly.

"You're sure you don't mind having them?"

"Not a bit—so long as they don't bother me, they're welcome. After all, they'd nowhere else to go, poor little devils. It was rotten luck their mother dying just before Christmas. I felt very sorry for them."

Jimmy set down his glass and stretched his legs once more to the blaze.

"Do you know," said Anne after a pause, "I think that Derek has a great look of his father."

"God forbid!" said Jimmy. Then, seeing the look on his wife's face, he added, "After all, Anne, even if he was your brother, you must admit that Billy was no sort of good."

Anne was staring into the fire, and her eyes were moist.

"Poor old Billy," she said. "Always hard up, always in trouble. The black sheep of the family, even when he was a little boy. I was very fond of him, all the same. And when he died—"

"Now, Anne, you're just being maudlin!"

Anne dabbed at her eyes with a handkerchief.

"I'm sorry," she said with a gulp. "I know it's silly of me, but I feel in a way we were responsible."

"Responsible? For a bomb hitting Eastbury Station? That's a new one on me. I'd always thought it was Hitler who was responsible."

"I know, but it was our fault that Billy was there, waiting for his train. He wanted to spend the night, and if we'd only let him—"

"Now look here, Anne," said Jimmy reasonably, "it's no manner of good getting morbid over what's past and done with. We were neither of us responsible. You were in bed with 'flu—don't you remember? I had to go out on Civil Defence duty—why, I was at Eastbury just after the incident and a nice shambles it was. Billy couldn't have stayed the night, even if I'd have had him—which I wouldn't."

"I know," said Anne, miserably, "I know…"

"Well, let's just forget it, shall we?"

"If only you could forget things by just wanting to—" She pulled herself together. "Look at the time! I must go and see about getting tea."

It was with an agreeable feeling of superiority that Jimmy watched her go before he turned back to the fire again. What bundles of nerves women were! Brooding over things that had happened—ten, was it?—no, by Jove, twelve years ago! And all this nonsense about forgetting—you could forget anything if you gave your mind to it, with enough time, and a good digestion and a sensible outlook on life. Anything.

It was a remarkable thing, Jimmy reflected, that until his wife's ill-timed reminiscences had brought it back to his mind he had genuinely forgotten that he had killed his brother-in-law on the night of the raid on Eastbury. And it wasn't just a figure of speech, either. Even with the fellow's son and daughter staying in the house, he had really and truly forgotten what he had done to their father. (Not that it would have made any difference to his treatment of them if he had remembered. It was not their fault, and he bore them no malice.)

He grinned to himself. It *was* pretty extraordinary being able to forget a thing like that. Nobody would believe it if you told them—if you could tell anybody. A pity in a way that you couldn't. It would show some people who always pretended to know everything just how little they knew about human nature. What they didn't understand was that if you had no regrets there was no reason why you should have inconvenient memories. Anne, in her silly fashion, regretted her poor Billy, and that was why she still let her conscience torment her over his death. He had no regrets for that sneaking, blackmailing swine, and consequently no conscience. It was as simple as that.

All the same, thought Jimmy, indulging in the unusual luxury of reminiscence, he had been pretty frightened at the time. But for a marvellous stroke of luck he would never have got away with it. If Jerry hadn't chosen to come over that evening Billy's disappearance would have taken a bit of explaining, and the newly dug patch in the garden looked obvious enough next morning to anyone who cared to make enquiries. But it had all ended happily. Good old Civil Defence! No tiresome inquests in those days. Billy's cigarette case shoved into the pocket of a coat covering a fragment of somebody's carcass had been evidence enough of identity.

As for the other matter, a man could do a lot to a garden in twelve years, with Nature to help him.

In spite of the warmth of the fire, Jimmy found himself shivering. That was what came of remembering things. Now he felt thoroughly upset, all thanks to Anne's stupidity. He picked up his liqueur glass. Empty, of course. Well, there was still time for another drink to set himself up before tea. He made his way to the dining-room.

"Oh, Uncle Jimmy, you oughtn't to have come in!" His niece Tessa looked up at him reproachfully from the floor.

Looking down, Jimmy saw the carpet covered with a mass of shiny objects—silver tinsel, coloured glass balls and miniature wax candles among them.

"What on earth are you up to?" he asked.

"It's your surprise, and now you've spoilt it because it won't be a surprise any more."

"That's all right," said Jimmy kindly. "I'll look the other way, and forget all about it in no time. I'm awfully good at forgetting."

He turned to the sideboard and filled his glass. The warm spirit made him feel better again at once. He toasted himself in the looking-glass. "Here's to forgetting!" he murmured.

He put the glass down, and went through into the kitchen. Anne was buttering slices of bread for tea.

"You oughtn't to have gone in there," she said.

"So Tessa told me. What is it all about?"

"The children wanted to give you a Christmas tree, to thank you for having them to stay. Isn't it sweet of them? Tessa has been getting all the old decorations out of the attic."

"Really? That's jolly decent of them. It shows they appreciate things, doesn't it? They've kept it very dark. Where did they hide the tree? I haven't seen it anywhere."

"I told Derek he could get it out of the garden. You know, that little spruce at the end of the vegetable patch. It's just the right size. You don't mind, do you?"

"D'you mean to say he's cut down the little spruce—?" It was all Jimmy could do not to laugh outright. After what he had been thinking of that afternoon the coincidence seemed irresistibly comic.

"No, dear, not cut down. I knew you wouldn't like that. I told him to dig it up very carefully by the roots, so that we could plant it again. That was all right, wasn't it?"

Jimmy turned and walked out of the room. It was a difficult thing to manage, but he walked. Once out of the house door he ran as he had not run for years. But even as he ran, he knew that it was too late. Fifty yards away he could see the top of the little spruce tremble and sink over to one side, and as he arrived breathless at the spot he saw his nephew standing there, staring incredulously down into the hole where its roots had been.

ON CHRISTMAS DAY IN THE MORNING

Margery Allingham

Margery Allingham (1904–66) was, like Ngaio Marsh, one of those legendary "Queens of Crime" who came to dominate the genre in the 1930s and who remain very popular today. Allingham's present day admirers include J. K. Rowling and the leading American private eye novelist Sara Paretsky, who praised her extraordinary range: "Her characters come from every social milieu, and exhibit every quirk of the human animal... Her characters are vivid and true because she understood their speech... Her description of physical space is every bit as masterful... She writes with equal authority about East Anglian marshes and the East End."

Allingham is best known as a novelist; it is often forgotten that she followed in the footsteps of Sir Arthur Conan Doyle in that her early stories were often published in the famous *Strand Magazine*. When the editor, Reeves Shaw, accepted half a dozen short stories from her in 1936, she was inordinately pleased: "me suddenly getting paid for quality rather than quantity". In her mind, this represented a milestone in her literary progress that was important as it was gratifying. She never looked back, and although health problems plagued her in later years, and she died too young, her achievements as a writer of flavoursome crime fiction were impressive. "On Christmas Day in the Morning", a typically pleasing piece of work, first appeared in the *Evening Standard* on 23 December 1950.

S IR LEO PURSUIVANT, THE CHIEF CONSTABLE, HAD BEEN SITTING in his comfortable study after a magnificent lunch and talking heavily of the sadness of Christmas, while his guest, Mr. Campion, most favoured of his large house-party, had been laughing at him gently.

It was true, the younger man had admitted, his pale eyes sleepy behind his horn-rimmed spectacles, that, however good the organisation, the festival was never quite the same after one was six and a half, but then, what sensible man would expect it to be, and meanwhile, what a truly remarkable bird that had been!

At that point the Superintendent had arrived with his grim little story and the atmosphere was spoiled altogether.

The policeman sat in a highbacked chair, against a panelled wall festooned with holly and tinsel, his round black eyes hard and preoccupied under his short grey hair. Superintendent Pussey was one of those lean and urgent countrymen who never quite lose their innate fondness for a wonder. Despite years of experience the thing that simply could not have happened and yet indubitably *had* retained a place in his cosmos. He was holding forth about the latest example. It had already ruined his Christmas and had kept a great many other people out in the sleet all day, but nothing would induce him to leave it alone even for five minutes. A heap of turkey sandwiches was disappearing as he talked and a glass of scotch and soda stood untasted at his side.

"You can see I had to come at once," he was saying. "I had to. I don't see what happened and that's a fact. It's a sort of miracle. Besides, fancy killing a poor old postman on Christmas morning! That's inhuman isn't it? Unnatural?"

Sir Leo nodded his white head. "Let me get this clear: the dead man appears to have been run down at the Benham cross roads…"

Pussey took a handful of cigarettes from the box at his side and arranged them in a cross on the shining surface of the table.

"Look," he said, "here is the Ashby road with a slight bend in it and here, running at right angles, slap through the curve, is the Benham road. You know as well as I do, sir, they're both good wide main thoroughfares as roads go in these parts. This morning the Benham postman, old Fred Noakes, came along the Benham Road loaded down with mail."

"On a bicycle," murmured Campion.

"Naturally. On a bicycle. He called at the last farm before the cross roads and left just about ten o'clock. We know that because he had a cup of tea there. Then his way led him over the crossing and on towards Benham proper."

He paused and looked up from his cigarettes.

"There was very little traffic early today, terrible weather all the time, and quite a bit of activity later, so we've got no skid marks to help us. Well, no one seems to have seen old Noakes until close on half an hour later. Then the Benham constable, who lives some three hundred yards from the crossing, came out of his house and walked down to his gate. He saw the postman at once, lying in the middle of the road across his machine. He was dead then."

"He had been trying to carry on?"

"Yes. He was walking, pushing the bike, and he'd dropped in his tracks. There was a depressed fracture in the side of his skull where something—say a car mirror—had struck him. I've got the doctor's report. Meanwhile there's something else."

He returned to his second line of cigarettes.

"Just about ten o'clock there were a couple of fellows walking here on the *Ashby* road. They report that they were almost run down by a saloon car which came up behind them. It missed them and careered off out of their sight round the bend towards the crossing.

"A few minutes later, half a mile farther on, on the other side of the cross roads, a police car met and succeeded in stopping, the same saloon. There was a row and the driver, getting the wind up suddenly, started up again, skidded and smashed the vehicle on the nearest telephone pole. The car turned out to be stolen and there were four half-full bottles of gin in the back. The two occupants were both fighting drunk and are now detained."

Mr. Campion took off his spectacles and blinked at the speaker.

"You suggest that there was a connection, do you? Fred and the gin drinkers met at the cross roads, in fact. Any signs on the car?"

Pussey shrugged his shoulders. "Our chaps are at work on that now. The second smash has complicated things a bit but last time I 'phoned they were hopeful."

"But my dear fellow!" Sir Leo was puzzled. "If you can get expert evidence of a collision between the car and the postman, your worries are over. That is, of course, if the medical evidence permits the theory that the unfortunate fellow picked himself up and struggled the three hundred yards towards the constable's house."

Pussey hesitated.

"There's the trouble," he admitted. "If that was all we'd be sitting pretty, but it's not and I'll tell you why. In that three hundred yards of Benham Road, between the crossing and the spot where old Fred died, there is a stile which leads to a footpath. Down the footpath, the best part of a quarter of a mile away, there is one small cottage and at that cottage letters were delivered this morning. The doctor says Noakes might have staggered the three hundred yards up the road leaning on his bike but he puts his foot down and says the other journey, over the stile, would have been plain impossible. I've talked to him. He's the best man in the world on the job and we shan't shake him on that."

"All of which would argue," observed Mr. Campion brightly, "that the postman met the car after he came back from the cottage—between the stile and the policeman's house."

"That's what the constable thought." Pussey's black eyes were snapping. "As soon as he'd telephoned for help he slipped down to the cottage to see if Noakes had called there. When he found he had, he searched the road. He was mystified though because both he and his missus had been at their window for an hour watching for the mail and they hadn't seen a vehicle of any sort go by either way. If a car did hit the postman where he fell it must have turned and gone back afterwards and that's impossible, for the patrol would have seen it."

Leo frowned at him. "What about the other witnesses? Did they see any second car?"

"No." Pussey's face shone with honest wonder. "I made sure of that. Everybody sticks to it that there was no other car or cart about and a good job too, they say, considering the way the saloon was being driven. As I see it, it's a proper mystery, a kind of not very nice miracle, and those two beauties are going to get away with murder on the strength of it. Whatever our fellows find on the car they'll never get past the doctor's evidence."

Mr. Campion got up sadly. The sleet was beating on the windows and from inside the house came the more cheerful sound of teacups. He nodded to the Chief Constable.

"I fear we shall have to see that footpath before it gets utterly dark, you know," he said. "In this weather conditions may have changed by tomorrow."

Leo sighed.

They stopped their freezing journey at the Benham police station to pick up the constable, who proved to be a pleasant youngster who had known and liked the postman and was anxious to serve as their guide.

They inspected the cross roads and the bend and the spot where the saloon had come to grief. By the time they reached the stile the world was grey and dismal and all trace of Christmas had vanished.

Mr. Campion climbed over and the others followed him on to the path which was narrow and slippery. It wound out into the mist before them, apparently without end.

The procession slid and scrambled in silence for what seemed a mile only to encounter yet another stile and a plank bridge over a stream leading to a patch of bog. As he struggled out of it Pussey pushed back his dripping hat and gazed at the constable.

"You're not having a game I suppose?" he enquired briefly.

"No, sir, no. The little house is just here. You can't make it out because it's a little bit low. There it is, sir."

He pointed to a hump in the near distance which they had all taken to be a haystack and which now emerged as the roof of a hovel with its back towards them in the wet waste.

"Good Heavens!" Leo regarded its desolation with dismay. "Does anybody actually live here?"

"Oh yes, sir. An old widow lady. Mrs. Fyson's the name."

"Alone? How old?"

"I don't rightly know, sir. Over seventy-five, must be."

Leo grunted and a silence fell on the company. The scene was so forlorn and so unutterably quiet in its loneliness that the world might have died.

Mr. Campion broke the spell.

"This is definitely no walk for a dying man," he said firmly. "The doctor's evidence is completely convincing, don't you think? Now we're here perhaps we should drop in and see the householder."

"We can't all *get* in," Leo objected. "Perhaps the Superintendent...?"

"No. You and I will go." Mr. Campion was obstinate, and taking the Chief Constable's arm led him firmly round to the front of the cottage. There was a yellow light in the single window on the ground floor and as they slid up a narrow brick path to a very small door, Leo hung back.

"I hate this," he muttered. "Oh—all right, go on. Knock if you must."

Mr. Campion obeyed, stooping so that his head might miss the lintel. There was a movement inside and, at once, the door was opened very wide so that he was startled by the rush of warmth from within.

A little old woman stood before him, peering up without astonishment. He was principally aware of bright eyes.

"Oh dear," she said unexpectedly. "You *are* damp. Come in." And then, looking past him at the skulking Leo. "Two of you! Well, isn't that nice. Mind your poor heads."

The visit became a social occasion before they were well in the room. Her complete lack of surprise or question coupled with the extreme lowness of the ceiling gave her an advantage from which the interview never entirely recovered.

From the first she did her best to put them at their ease.

"You'll have to sit down at once," she said, waving them to two chairs, one on either side of the small black kitchener. "Most people have to. I'm all right, you see, because I'm not tall. This is my chair here. You must undo that," she went on touching Leo's coat, "otherwise you may take cold when you go out. It is so very chilly isn't it? But so seasonable and that's always nice."

Afterwards it was Mr. Campion's belief that neither he nor the Chief Constable had a word to say for themselves for the first five minutes. They were certainly seated and looking round the one downstair room the house contained before anything approaching conversation took place.

It was not a sordid interior yet the walls were discoloured, the furniture old without being in any way antique and the place could hardly have been called neat. But at the moment it was festive. There was holly over the two pictures and on the mantel, above the stove, a crowd of bright Christmas cards.

Their hostess sat between them, near the table. It was set for a small tea party and the oil lamp with the red and white frosted glass shade which stood in the centre of it shed a comfortable light on her serene face.

She was a short plump old person whose white hair was brushed tightly to her little round head. Her clothes were all knitted and of an assortment of colours and with them she wore, most unsuitably, a Maltese silk lace collarette and a heavy gold chain. It was only when they noticed she was blushing that they realised she was shy.

"Oh," she exclaimed at last, making a move which put their dumbness to shame. "I quite forgot to say it before! A Merry Christmas to you. Isn't it wonderful how it keeps coming round? It's such a *happy* time, isn't it?"

Leo took himself in hand.

"I do apologise," he began. "This is an imposition on such a day."

"Not at all," she said. "Visitors are a great treat. Not everybody braves my footpath in the winter."

"But some people do, of course?" ventured Mr. Campion.

"Of course." She shot him her shy smile. "Always once a week. They send down from the village every Friday and only this morning a young man, the policeman to be exact, came all the way over the fields to wish me the compliments of the season and to know if I'd got my post!"

"And you had!" Leo glanced at the array of cards with relief. He was a kindly, sentimental, family man with a horror of loneliness.

She nodded at the brave collection with deep affection.

"It's lovely to see them all up there again, it's one of the real joys of Christmas, isn't it? Messages from people you love and who love you and all so *pretty*, too."

"Did you come down bright and early to meet the postman?" The Chief Constable's question was disarmingly innocent but she looked ashamed and dropped her eyes.

"I wasn't up! Wasn't it dreadful? I was late this morning. In fact, I was only just picking the letters off the mat there when the policeman called. He helped me gather them, the nice boy. There were such a lot. I lay lazily in bed this morning thinking of them instead of moving."

"Still, you knew they were there."

"Oh yes." She sounded content. "I knew they were there. May I offer you a cup of tea? I'm waiting for my Christmas party to arrive, just a woman and her dear greedy little boy; they won't be long. In fact, when I heard your knock I thought they were here already."

Mr. Campion, who had risen to inspect the display of cards on the mantel shelf more closely, helped her to move the kettle so that it should not boil too soon.

The cards were splendid. There were nearly thirty of them in all, and the envelopes which had contained them were packed in a neat bundle and tucked behind the clock.

In design they were mostly conventional. There were robins and firesides, saints and angels, with a secondary line in pictures of gardens in unseasonable bloom, and Scots terriers in tam o'shanter caps. One magnificent affair was entirely in ivorine with a cut-out disclosing a coach and horses surrounded with roses and forget-me-nots. The written messages were all warm and personal—all breathing affection and friendliness and the outspoken joy of the season:

> *"The very best to you Darling from All at the Limes"; "To dear Auntie from Little Phil"; "Love and Memories. Edith and Ted"; "There is no wish like the old wish. Warm regards George"; "For dearest Mother"; "Cheerio. Lots of love. Just off. Writing. Take care of yourself. Sonny"; "For dear little Agnes with love from US ALL".*

Mr. Campion stood before them for a long time but at length he turned away. He had to stoop to avoid the beam and yet he towered over the old woman who stood watching him.

Something had happened. It had suddenly become very still in the house. The gentle hissing of the kettle sounded unnaturally loud. The recollection of their loneliness returned to chill the cosy room.

The old lady had lost her smile and there was wariness in her eyes.

"Tell me," Mr. Campion spoke very gently. "How do you do it? Do you put them all down there on the mat in their envelopes before you go to bed on Christmas Eve?"

While the point of his question was dawning upon Leo, there was complete silence. It was breathless and unbearable until old Mrs. Fyson pierced it with a laugh of genuine naughtiness.

"Well," she said devastatingly, "It does make it more fun, doesn't it?" She glanced back at Leo whose handsome face was growing scarlet.

"Then…" He was having difficulty with his voice.

"Then the postman did *not* call this morning, ma'am?"

"The postman never calls here except when he brings something from the Government," she said pleasantly. "Everybody gets letters from the Government nowadays, don't they? But he doesn't call here with *personal* letters because, you see, I'm the last of us." She paused and frowned very faintly. It rippled like a shadow over the smoothness of her quiet, careless brow. "There's been so many wars," she said.

"But, dear Lady…" Leo was completely overcome.

She patted his arm to comfort him.

"My dear man," she said kindly. "Don't be distressed. This isn't sad. It's Christmas. They sent me their love at Christmas and *I've still got it.* At Christmas I remember them and they remember me I expect—wherever they are." Her eyes strayed to the ivorine card with the coach on it. "I do sometimes wonder about poor *George*," she remarked seriously. "He was my husband's elder brother and he really did have quite a shocking life. But he sent me that remarkable card one year and I kept it with the others… after all, we ought to be charitable, oughtn't we? At Christmas."

As the four men plodded back through the fields, Pussey was jubilant.

"That's done the trick," he said. "Cleared up the mystery and made it all plain sailing. We'll get those two crooks for doing in poor old Noakes. The old girl was just cheering herself up and you fell for it, eh, constable? Oh don't worry, my boy. There's no harm done and it's a thing that might have deceived anybody. Just let it be a lesson to you. I know how it happened. You didn't want to worry the old thing with the tale of a death on Christmas morning so you took the sight of the letters as evidence and didn't go into it. As it turned out, you were wrong. That's life."

He thrust the young man on ahead of him and waited for Campion.

"What beats me is how you cottoned to it," he confided. "What gave you the idea?"

"I merely read it, I'm afraid," Mr. Campion was apologetic. "All the envelopes were there, sticking out from behind the clock. The top one had a ha'penny stamp on it so I looked at the postmark. It was 1914."

Pussey laughed. "Given to you!" he chuckled. "Still I bet you had a job to trust your own eyes."

"Ah." Mr. Campion's voice was thoughtful in the dusk. "That, Super, that was the really difficult bit."

GIVE ME A RING

Anthony Gilbert

Lucy Malleson (1899–1973) published under a variety of names no fewer than sixty-five novels as well as upwards of sixty short stories. At first she called herself J. Kilmeny Keith, and later she adopted the name Anne Meredith for a number of books, including her memoir *Three-a-Penny* and *Portrait of a Murderer*, a title included in the British Library Crime Classics series. She is, however, most widely remembered as Anthony Gilbert. As Gilbert, she created the lawyer-detective Arthur Crook, although he does not appear in *Death in Fancy Dress*, another book given fresh life as a British Library Crime Classic. Crook did feature in *The Woman in Red* (1941) but was excluded from the 1945 film adaptation, *My Name is Julia Ross*.

Until recently, Gilbert's short fiction has received relatively little attention. That has begun to change as a result of the publication of an excellent compilation by John Cooper, *Sequel to Murder: The Cases of Arthur Crook and Other Mysteries* (2017), which included stories written in each decade from the 1920s to the 1970s. "Give Me a Ring" first appeared on 11 November 1955 in the *Illustrated London News*.

I T WAS CHRISTMAS EVE AND NEARLY FIVE OF THE CLOCK, BUT an afternoon less like the traditional ideas of the season would be hard to imagine. True, a little snow had fallen in the early hours, but this was rapidly churned into slush by the relentless London traffic and about mid-day a haze of fog began to spread over the city. As the afternoon deepened the fog thickened, throwing a yellowish curtain over buildings and the traffic that even now streamed remorselessly through the darkening streets. Not that Londoners allowed that to deter them from providing themselves with everything they wanted or could lay hands on for a merry day tomorrow. It was the best Christmas ever, according to the shops. Peace was just round the corner and prosperity was knocking on the door. Scarcity was receding, and even at this hour the stalls in the market, east of the Mansion House, were doing a roaring trade. Men, their work done until after the holiday, joined their wives, haggling for turkeys and geese at lower figures than they'd have fetched a few hours earlier; children lugged fish-baskets full of oranges and apples and nuts; the last shining boxes of crackers, the dates, the tins of sweets, even the flowers found ready customers. All the Christmas trees had been sold already, but branches of fir and sprays of holly and mistletoe, were being offered from the crowded pavements. The nylon-sellers had moved east from Oxford Street and set up their portmanteaux of wares on the corner; coloured streamers in the hands of children became unfolded and shone out orange and blue and green against the darkening skies.

Gillian Hinde, a student nurse, as pretty as any fairy-tale princess, with her fair, smooth hair tied up in a blue scarf and her eyes shining, stood back to watch the happy, surging crowds. For her, too, the Day had arrived. Most of her friends who wouldn't be on duty over Christmas had gone home already; the railway stations—record crowds, declared the radio buoyantly—and the coach stations had been packed all day; north, east, south, the west they had departed. But Gillian envied none of them. No one, she felt, could anticipate a more joyous festival than she. Oh, it was beautiful to be twenty-three and in love, and know that next spring you'd be Mrs. Richard Fyfe. Even now the miracle seemed too good to be true. So many girls in the world, pretty, ardent girls, all eager for love, and out of them all, Richard's choice had fallen upon her. She could still hardly believe it. Richard, who was bound to be a success, whose hopes soared as high as clouds in summer; Richard, the young doctor of whom everyone prophesied great things, and who wanted to marry her out of all the women in the world.

She had come off duty immediately after lunch and sped back to her little flat—one room really, with a kitchen and a bathroom big enough for a sparrow, Richard teased her, but it was all the home she knew since her father died three years before—sped back to put the final touches to the little shining tree, add the last cards to the red ribbon strings she'd hung on the walls, put up the few sprigs of holly (no mistletoe, no house that needs mistletoe will have any use for it, Richard said), and set the table for the first Christmas dinner she would ever share alone with Richard, who was her dear love and in a few months, would be her husband. The duck was prepared, the vegetables ready, the fruit set out in the charming rough-cast bowls she had brought back from Spain this summer, the coffee beans were waiting to be ground in the little mill Richard had given her for her last birthday, there were drinks in the ice-box and a dozen silly bits of nonsense tied up in different coloured papers for Richard's pleasure. She had come east, since the big stores had closed their gates and released their employees at mid-day, to look for the cheeses, the cumquats, the twists of rye bread they both liked. Someone had told her that in this market there was a stall where you could buy a special kind of sweetmeat Richard adored, and once there she'd lingered, delighting in the scene, the colour, the sounds, the mixture of races and tongues that declared the coming of joy into a thousand homes.

The change took place with practically no warning at all. Between half-past five and six o'clock the whole city changed. The fog that had been no more than a gauze curtain, shot with gold lights from the stalls and the shop-fronts and the street lamps, became a curtain of darkness. People were so much astounded they stopped dead, where they stood, as confounded as if they had stepped all in a moment from one world to another. Mothers turned, calling their children. Stall-holders stood aghast, then began to put together anything that was left. Gillian, who had just turned out of the market, her basket on her arm, her purse in her pocket, intending to make for the high road and catch one of the red buses that would bring her close to her own home, stood as still as the rest, bewildered, though not panicking yet, because this was London, where she had lived for five years and where it was impossible to imagine you could ever be lost.

"If ever you're not sure of your way in London," her father had said when she left the country rectory five years ago to start her training at St. Ninian's, "look for a red bus. Where there's a bus in London there's life, and where there's life there's hope." She remembered his kind, infinitely tolerant face, his gentle voice, and calmed her fears.

"I came round a corner when I left the market," she reminded herself. "If I go along this street and turn right I'm bound to get back to the high road."

But somehow her calculations must have gone astray, for when she turned the next corner she found herself in another narrow lane, with no lights anywhere. It was useless to try to discover the name of the road; darkness blotted out every landmark, but since all roads lead somewhere, she forged ahead. She had been walking for some minutes before she had to confess to herself that she was as lost as if she'd walked headlong into the City of Dreadful Night. What was strangest of all was the silence; the voices of children that had pealed all round her a few minutes before were dumb; she could hear no footsteps, no sound of wheels. On either side of her blank walls reared up into the dark. Surely, if there were houses here, some golden gleams should be perceptible between the hastily-drawn curtains, the sound of a radio set should come to her attentive ears. But though she compelled herself to stand still and listen intently, she heard nothing, not even the whine of a dog or the sound of a passing car. Of course, there was a rational explanation. Clearly, she had turned away from the residential quarter into one of those roads that were areas of factories, all closed now for the Christmas holiday. Calming her fears, she attempted to retrace her steps. The market couldn't have shut down in these few minutes; soon she would hear wheels rattling over cobblestones, people calling to each other, all the normal sounds of busy London life. But, though she refused to yield to panic, every step she took seemed to take her further into an uninhabited world.

The sight of a window where a light was still burning, at the end of a ribbon of darkness, gave her heart a sudden lift. Where there were lights there must be people, and where there was even one living soul she would get directions to put her on her homeward road. Walking close against the wall, for the pavements here were narrow and she had no wish to trip over the kerb, she made her way to that welcome golden pane. Rather surprisingly, she found the light came from one of those odd establishments known as marine stores, where every kind of junk was on sale, ropes and lanterns and bits of brass, all the flotsam and jetsam of a sea-going community. She stood staring in at the window, wondering what hope an optimistic dealer had of effecting a sale so late and on such a night. And then she saw it—in the very middle of the window, as if someone had set it there for a bait, something so unexpected, and, to her eyes, so beautiful, that she remained transfixed a moment, while the anxious little man on the other side of the glass watched her as eagerly and secretively as an animal peering from its hiding-place.

The object in question was a ring, a quite ordinary setting containing a blue stone that glowed and sparkled as if it had gathered up all the light the fog had sucked out of the streets and flung it back with an unbelievable radiance. She had no notion what precisely it was, no stone to which she could put a name, neither sapphire nor opal nor turquoise—one of those mysterious stones whose names made a chain of beauty in that chapter she had heard her father read in the church at home, beryl, jacinth and chrysophrase—a semi-precious stone, of no particular value, probably, brought back by some sailor who had turned it in for whatever it would fetch in money or goods. In her bag were five pound notes sent by her Aunt Henrietta in the north. Buy yourself a luxury, she had written, but since they had arrived Gillian had seen nothing that would justify the extravagance of so much money for a single present. But once she'd set eyes on the ring she knew there was nothing else in London she wanted so much.

She had a new dress for tonight, a dress of turquoise-blue wool bought for the occasion, just the colour to bring out the blue tints in her eyes that were neither blue nor grey but a mixture of the two. She had scarcely any jewellery. Richard hadn't given her a ring yet; he wouldn't give her anything second-rate and she wouldn't allow him to spend money he couldn't afford on the sort of ring he would think good enough for her.

"Dear Aunt Henrietta," murmured Gillian to herself, putting out her hand with a sudden pang of apprehension, in case, after all, the light was a will-o'-the-wisp and the shop was already shut. But she needn't have feared. The man behind the counter wouldn't dare put up the shutters, draw down the blind and turn the key until the one he'd been told to expect had put in an appearance.

And when he saw Gillian he supposed that this was the one.

He called himself Mr. Benn now, though that hadn't been his name in far-away Morocco, where he had been born, and that seemed part of another world, when he thought of it, which wasn't often. They'd been poor enough then, all of them living in a room not much better than a cave, opening off a narrow alley, with the donkeys going up and down, led by men in native dress, crying as they went, to warn the unwary to get out of the path. He'd been intended to follow in his father's footsteps, become a player in one of the Moorish cafés, making the music come from a stretched skin, not with a stick as in the West, but with the fingers stiffened or slack to get the appropriate sound. All day long he had sat there cross-legged, while the Moroccans and the foreign soldiers and sometimes the tourists passed through to listen to the music and sip the little glasses of sweetened mint tea. Then, when he was sixteen, everything had changed. There had been a brawl in the café, a man had been killed, and early the next day he had been warned that he was in danger. He hadn't waited, he supposed he had never been particularly brave, but had gone like a breath of dust, and had never returned. At first he used to wonder about his family, the three sisters at the carpet-weaving school, the brothers who were herdsmen and the one who was a teacher—but he forgot them all at last. The pity was that he had lost the East and had never become truly merged with the West. He worked his way down to the port and eventually he reached Europe, a drifter, a man without a purpose. Now he was a tool, a not very efficient tool at that, in a nasty business, without hopes or prospects, only knowing he'd be lucky if he died in his bed. So many of them didn't—Eric, who had been taken out of the dock only a week or so before, and the one they called Big Tom, who had contrived to be in the way of a lorry at a place and time where you wouldn't have expected any lorry to be. He might be the next, or the fourth or the tenth, there was no knowing. He only knew that the boss never forgave mistakes—couldn't afford to, that was about the truth of it.

He had been waiting a long time for someone to push open the door. Ever since he put the ring in the window he had been anticipating this moment. It didn't surprise him that he failed to recognise the girl—why should he? He had never seen her before. But he hadn't somehow expected anyone who looked like this. There were women in the drug-running world, of course, but generally there was something—scarred—about them. This girl looked as young as the morning. He even thought it was just coincidence, that she had lost her way and was coming in to ask how to find it. But as soon as she spoke he knew it was all right, because she said what he had been told she would.

"That ring in your window—the one with the blue stone. How much is it?"

He didn't make any move to show it to her. "What can you offer me for it?"

Make sure you don't mention a figure, he had been warned. And she said, "I've only got five pounds. Would that be enough?" She started to open her bag, with a childlike enthusiasm. He turned then and stooped into the window, conscious of a strange disappointment. Not that it was any concern of his, of course. It was just chance—or good judgment on the boss's part more likely—that she should have that clear, shining look. And why should he care? Innocence was a word he'd forgotten long ago.

The ring looked as beautiful in your hand as it had done in the window, Gillian thought. She slipped it on her finger, turning it this way and that to catch the light from the meagre bulb above the counter. It seemed impossible that anyone should be lost in a fog so long as that existed. It would light you through the darkness of the grave. She came back from her reverie with a blush for her own extravagance.

"Is five pounds right?" she asked, scarcely able to keep the marvel out of her voice.

"That's right." His manner seemed strange—weary, as though it made no difference to him whether he made a sale or not; and yet she was convinced it wasn't because he loved the ring so much himself he didn't want to part with it.

"It's Christmas Eve," she reflected compassionately. "He's tired."

And no doubt he had no such glittering prospect to look forward to as awaited her on her return.

"It's like blue fire, isn't it?" She smiled. But he didn't reply. What was there to say? It was a business transaction, like the kiss of Judas in the Christian story that meant nothing to him. Even his own faith didn't matter any more. He knew he'd never again hear the muezzin ring out from the balcony of a mosque or hear the guns sound for Ramadan.

He picked up the money she'd laid on the counter and put it in the till. She was looking about her with frank interest, but he thought it was all assumed, so that she shouldn't see him take the little packet from under the counter and lay it before her. When she looked back and espied it there she contrived a gesture of quite realistic surprise.

"Oh? What's that? It's not mine, I didn't bring anything..."

"No." He couldn't flog any enthusiasm into his voice.

She leaned nearer. "Mr. Smith, 19, Merriton Square. Oh, is it something to be posted?"

Only it wasn't stamped, and it would be too late for Christmas, anyway.

The little brown man behind the counter began to cough; he coughed as though he couldn't help it, as though his whole life was slipping away from him in those agonised sounds.

"Oh, dear," said Gillian. "You do sound bad. Have you got to take this round tonight? What a shame!"

He said, smoothing his thin brown hands over his face as though to wipe away the last trace of the cough, "It's got to be delivered tonight."

He watched her anxiously. It couldn't be that he was wrong about her after all. A police constable, materialising out of the fog, came to stand by the window. Mr. Benn felt himself turning cold.

At last Gillian looked up. "I could take it for you, if you like," she said. "Merriton Square isn't very far out of my way, and—I'm sure you shouldn't go out again tonight."

The boss trained them well, he thought; if that policeman was watching he'd swear she didn't know a thing.

"I know how it is with a present," she went on. "Even if you know it's coming, it never seems quite the same thing if you don't get it on the day."

He felt the germ of unease stir within him. Acting was all very well, but surely this was overdoing it. But before he could speak again she had opened her bag and slipped the packet in and turned to smile at him. The policeman, who had only been staring in the window, perhaps, because it was the one lighted place in the area, strolled on. His heart settled down. Of course it was all right.

"Is there any message?" she enquired, turning to go.

He shook his head, smiling faintly for the first time. "No. It's expected. They rang up. That's when I promised…" He could do a little acting, too, when he had to.

He moved to indicate that there was nothing more to be said. He told her how to find the main road and watched her go. Now he wanted nothing but to put up the shutters, close the shop and find the only peace left to him, oblivion at the point of a needle. She saw the move and turned to the door.

"You needn't worry," she said. "It'll be all right." And as she went out she threw a "Happy Christmas" over her shoulder. That shook him, made him wonder if, after all… But it was too late now, she'd gone. And anyway, what on earth was she doing here at this hour, a girl like that, if she wasn't part of the scheme? He came round, walking a little lame, and began to put up the shutters.

Gillian came out of the shop and began to make her careful way towards the main road, following Mr. Benn's instructions. As she crossed the street she looked up; the fog had cleared sufficiently for her to be able to make out his name painted above the door. She felt the blue stone under her dark glove and confidence began to return. It was quite a little adventure to tell Richard, and remembering him, she glanced at the watch on her wrist. To her horror she found it was twenty minutes to seven—and Richard was expected at seven o'clock. It was unthinkable that he should arrive and find the flat in darkness, an omen even for the future. She drove the thought away and hurried forward. Perhaps, now it had lightened a little, some of the omnibuses would be running. But, of course, they had stopped some time ago. Sheer suicide and murder to keep them on the roads, drivers and conductors had agreed. The long main street was full of shadows but not much else. All sane people would be under cover by now. She passed a few lighted windows, all closed and curtained, though here and there a wireless sang or shouted through the dusk.

Love came down at Christmas, she heard, and her heart lifted again. She began to hurry. Perhaps there was an Underground station not far off. But she saw no welcoming blue lighted sign and was beginning to despair, when a whisper of wheels reached her ears and, turning, she saw a solitary taxi come chugging up behind her, its flag covered. She stood on the kerb, holding up her hand and shouting, "Gordon Street," in the hope that it might be going that way. The cab stopped and the driver peered out.

"I'm going to Ship Street," he said, "if that's any good."

She jumped in gratefully. She knew Ship Street, it wasn't more than five minutes away from her home. Oh, what good fortune that she should have found this cab. She might just catch Richard after all. All her thoughts were for him and of him; the encounter with Mr. Benn might never have taken place; in her heart she urged the taxi to greater speed, and when it set her down she hurried towards Gordon Street as fast as feet would take her. She didn't give the little packet a thought—not then. If she had, the whole story might have been different for them all.

The telephone was shrilling away as she came up the stairs, and as she thrust her key into the door she thought, "Richard! Something's happened. He can't come tonight. He's ill—changed his mind—dead." Even as she thought this she knew it was nonsense, for how could love die in an hour yet her heart beat wildly as she flung down her bag and gloves, pulled off the blue mackintosh and wrenched the receiver from its rest.

It was Richard, but he sounded exasperated rather than loving.

"At last!" he exclaimed. "This is the third time I've rung. Where on earth have you been?"

"Darling, I was out—shopping."

"At this hour?"

"There were just a few little things—and then the fog came on and I lost my way."

"That's what I thought. Know why I'm going to be late this evening?" He disregarded her protesting wail. "Because some other bright boy thought he'd do a bit of shopping and lost his way in the fog and walked slap into a bus."

"Oh, darling! On Christmas Eve? What wicked luck! Is he...?"

"He'll do," was Richard's grim rejoinder. "Don't expect me to feel sorry for the chap. He's going to do me out of at least half an hour of your company. Oh, yes, he'll be all right, but if anyone was looking to him to lend a hand with the washing-up this Christmas they're going to be disappointed. Now, don't take it into your head, because you've got a little time on your hands, to go out and buy a few more things we don't need."

"Darling, I couldn't. The shops are all shut. Yes, I promise. Oh, darling, I do love you so. I don't want you to neglect your poor casualty, but don't be longer than you can help. I've got so much to tell you. Richard, I've bought a ring."

"You've bought what?"

"With Aunt Henrietta's five pounds. With a lovely blue stone. From a queer old man called Benn in the East End, near the market. It was quite an adventure. I'll tell you…" She stopped suddenly.

"I can't wait," came Richard's dry voice over the line. "Take care of yourself, my darling. Darling, I love you, too."

Gillian hung up the receiver, and looked round the pretty, welcoming room. She switched on the electric fire and its golden glow was reflected in the little coloured balls shining on the tree and the glasses on the table. She had set a little home-made crib along the top of the bookcase and a string of little silver bells rippled into music as the wind touched them. But she wasn't thinking of any of these things. She was remembering the little parcel in her handbag, the parcel she had promised old Mr. Benn faithfully she'd deliver before night.

She looked once more at her watch. Quite apart from her promise to Richard, she couldn't go out again. There wasn't time. He mustn't come and find the door closed. And yet—that unknown Christmas present that she'd accepted as her responsibility lay heavy on her tender heart. She thought desperately. Perhaps she and Richard could deliver it together this evening after dinner. But she knew Richard wouldn't feel much enthusiasm about that. He had probably had a hard day—people seemed to choose the eve of public holidays to get themselves knocked out—and the weather would tempt no one but a man who expected to profit by the cold and the dark. For some reason a rhyme began to jingle through her mind.

Another little job for the undertaker.

Put through a call to the tombstone-maker…

Suddenly she had a better idea. She would deliver the parcel herself next morning, quite early, on her way back from church. It wasn't likely anyone not a child would start opening presents before then. So—her spirits rose like milk bubbling up in a saucepan—she had only to let Mr. Smith know she'd be coming, and all would be well.

There were scores of Smiths in the telephone directory, but she couldn't find one who lived at 19, Merriton Square. She supposed dismally it must be someone spending Christmas in London. She dialled the operator and explained her difficulty.

"The trouble is I don't know the name of the tenant."

"Perhaps the house isn't on the 'phone," suggested the operator, cheerfully.

"Mr. Smith rang up from somewhere trying to trace the parcel," Gillian recalled. "Isn't there any way…?"

"There might be—seeing it's Christmas. Hold on."

She held on for what seemed a very long time. Then the operator's voice said: "It's the Angel. Know it?"

She shook her head before she realised she couldn't be seen. "No. What is it? A pub?"

"More of a road-house," said the voice, a little doubtfully. "Big place on the corner, with a restaurant. Anyway, I'll give you the number."

She scribbled it down on a pad beside the telephone.

"Thank you. You've been very kind. I'm most grateful."

"Don't give it a thought." He rang off, and Gillian depressed the receiver and dialled again.

"Is that Mr. Smith?" Whoever it was must have been sitting beside the telephone.

"Who's that?"

"You won't know my name, but I have a parcel for you—from Mr. Benn. You know who I mean? I gathered you'd left it there this afternoon and he promised to return it."

"Fair enough," murmured Mr. Smith. "Where are you 'phoning from?"

"I'm at home."

The voice deepened a little. "What's up? You haven't lost it?"

"Oh, no, but the truth is I forgot all about leaving it—I was very late, you see, had an appointment myself…"

"And you've still got it? Is that it?" The voice sounded like Nurse Williams in one of her moods and for a moment she felt anger stir in her. Still, this was the season of peace and goodwill, so she smoothed out her voice and said, "I was going to suggest bringing it round in the morning—oh, quite early, before nine. Would that do? If it's a present, I mean?"

"But it isn't a present," exclaimed the voice, sounding dismayed. "It's very urgent. Didn't the old man explain? It's a prescription for my wife; she must have it this evening. Benn rang up to say it was on the way. I couldn't send for it, because I can't leave her—is there no way you can get it here tonight?"

Gillian felt exasperation rise again in her heart. A man hadn't any right to mislay anything so important and then sound outraged because someone else had forgotten too. But she was a nurse and she knew what might happen if a patient didn't get the right treatment at the right time, so she said: "In that case, of course, I must bring it round."

She rang off. She had been horribly disappointed when Richard had said he would be late, even half-an-hour's an age when you are in love, but perhaps it was a good thing, after all. Merriton Square wasn't very far and if she ran all the way there and all the way back she might be home before Richard arrived. Still, it wasn't safe to count on that. Taking up the pencil again she turned over the slip of paper and scribbled:

Darling, don't be angry, I've had to go out, a matter of life and death. I hope I'll be back before you read this, but anyway I won't be long.

Darling, I love you.

She'd pin the note on the door where he couldn't miss it, and leave the flat door open just a crack. The landlord wouldn't like it, but then he need never know, and burglars wouldn't be looking for anything worth their trouble in a house like this. On an impulse, she snatched up the pencil once more and added: "I have gone to the Angel, Merriton Square." She didn't know what impulse made her add that, or what a difference it was going to make to them both.

After Gillian had left the shop Mr. Benn lost no time in putting up the shutters and locking the door. To his surprise, he found he couldn't forget the girl in the blue mackintosh, the girl who was such a good actress that he'd been tempted to think her coming was one of those coincidences which occur in life so much more often than writers of fiction dare ask their readers to believe. He went into a room behind the shop and began making his own preparations for the rest of the evening. When that was done he saw that it was almost seven o'clock, and on an impulse he turned on the news. World affairs didn't interest him, but there might be something... He sat patiently by the little radio-set while a cheerful, competent voice told about record crowds leaving the main London stations and London's sudden blackout, and prophesied better weather for the morning. At the end came the bit he had been waiting for.

Police are continuing their enquiries into the death of the man whose body was found in the dock on Tuesday last. He has been identified as a labourer named Eric Boxer. It is now thought that death was due to collision with a motor vehicle, the body being deposited in the water after this had occurred. Any driver or passer-by who may have witnessed an accident or any suspicious circumstances…

He put out his hand and turned off the radio. So they were on the trail, and the police were like their own dogs, they never gave up. When he had heard he had felt a shudder of apprehension—what Arthur Crook would have called a hunch. The boss had taken the one risk too many. He took off his coat and put on a dressing-gown, eased his feet into slippers, filled the needle… And then he heard it, the knocking at the front door, a steady, quiet rapping of knuckles on glass. He felt himself freeze up. Steady, he thought, it's some child—or p'raps he'd left the light burning in the shop and some officious policeman making his rounds wanted to be sure that all was well. The police were on their toes these days. Eric Boxer had been killed not 500 yards away. No one had told Mr. Benn just what had happened, but though he hadn't had much schooling—just a small school, where you sat in a long row and learned the Koran and nothing else—he could add two and two as well as most people. Not that he could afford it for the girl. If you have any pity to spare, keep it for yourself—that was one of the lessons life had taught him.

The knocking became more insistent. Then the bell started to peal. He knew then he had to go out. He put the needle down and went reluctantly into the shop.

He recognised the man in the doorway. Pug Mayhew, they called him; he was well in with the boss, much better in than poor Mr. Benn would ever be. His big face was scowling.

"What's the idea of the fancy dress?" he demanded, nodding towards the dressing-gown. "More than that, what's the game? Well, come on, out with it." He came into the shop, slamming the door behind him, and caught Mr. Benn by the faded silken lapels. "Sold us up the river, have you? What did they give you? Enough to pay for a fine funeral, I hope. The boss don't pay funeral expenses—in his opinion rats don't deserve as much as a shroud."

Mr. Benn tried to struggle free. "I don't understand you."

"No? How about that ring, then?"

Mr. Benn recovered some of his lost breath. "It's all right; she came half-an-hour ago. The stuff will be delivered by this time."

Pug Mayhew pushed forward, thrusting Mr. Benn back. He closed the door of the shop behind him.

"What's that you're saying? Who's been?"

"The girl. The girl for the ring."

But he had begun to tremble.

Pug nodded casually, as if it didn't really matter much, after all. He let his eyes roam round the walls, examine the junk that filled the room, the bits of brass, the old stone Buddha, the ropes and the lanterns—the whole stock wouldn't fetch £50 at an auction.

"That's very interesting," he said at last, when he'd completed his leisurely survey. "About the girl, I mean. The boss'll want to know a bit more about her."

Mr. Benn was staring at him, the fear undisguised in the brown eyes.

"She came in and asked for the ring, just as I was told she would; she offered five pounds. Five pounds was right, wasn't it? How was I to know? Do you mean that wasn't the right one?"

"I mean the rozzers have laid a trap and you've walked right into it. You old fool!" His voice changed, became savage and menacing.

"Well, you've signed your death-warrant, I suppose you realise that. Didn't you know they were after us, ever since they took Eric out of the water? That's why the boss had to be so careful, couldn't send anyone who might be recognised. They picked up the chap who ought to have come; picked him up this morning on a charge of car-stealing; that's why I'm here."

"I wasn't to blame," stammered Mr. Benn. "She said the right things, didn't she? Anyway, she took the stuff, she'll deliver it. She didn't dream—I swear…" But his voice faltered away into an ago-nised silence.

A good actress, he'd thought; the boss knows how to pick 'em. But it wasn't the boss, it was the authorities; and he remembered the police constable stopping by the window. Wanting to make sure everything was going off all right, that she got the packet. Of course, Smith wouldn't have it; it would be at the station. He felt a surge of impotent rage that a girl who looked so innocent could have cheated him like that. But desperately, in the face of Pug Mayhew's threats, he stuck to his assertion.

"If she wasn't the one, she wasn't in with *them*. She said she'd leave the parcel, and she meant it."

"Did she? You know, Benn, I don't think the boss is going to be pleased when he hears you've given away the address of the head-quarters. Has Smith telephoned to say it's O.K.?"

"No. No, not yet. But—why should he? He…"

Pug Mayhew pushed the little man out of the way as if he'd been an old sack or a broken chair that's only fit for the rubbish-heap, and indeed the analogy was a pretty accurate one. Like his boss, that ruthless criminal who was making his pile out of the weaknesses and the corruption of his fellow-creatures, Pug had no use for people when they ceased to be profitable. He strode into the back room and snatched up the telephone. Mr. Benn watched him from the doorway. He couldn't make a bolt for it, not in a dressing-gown and slippers, and it wouldn't have helped him, anyway. He was pretty sure in that moment he wasn't going to be one of those fortunate enough to die in his own bed.

Pug was talking to Mr. Smith. "How long ago?" he repeated, and looked across to Mr. Benn. "How long ago did this girl leave?"

"About half-an-hour—but there's a fog…"

"Not now, not bad enough for you to lose your way. And don't tell me there are no buses running, because I know it. You could walk to Merriton Square in half the time, supposing you wanted to get there, that is." He hung up the telephone receiver.

"Funny thing," he remarked, and now his tone was almost conversational. "Your lady friend never reached the Angel. And do you know why? Because she never meant to go there. She laid a neat little trap and you walked into it, like a bloody mouse. And you know what happens to mice when they go into traps? Or haven't you even the guts to put them down? Well, I'll tell you. They get their bloody little necks broken. And you're nothing but a mouse, are you, Benn?"

The little brown man shrank back. Keep away from me; his lips formed the words, but they remained inaudible. He knew Mayhew was speaking the truth, that to him this outcast from a foreign country, this landless man, was of no more account than a rat or a mouse on which he'd put his great boot without a second thought.

Pug Mayhew had taken up the telephone again, called another number. When he had finished that conversation he took a knife from his pocket and deliberately cut the wires.

"You won't be needing it any more tonight," he explained. "We're going for a little walk together, you and me. Because, you see, that stuff never reached our friend at the Angel, and any minute now you may get another visitor, an official one this time, and the boss doesn't want to give you the chance to squeal. He don't like squealers, Benn." With a sudden gesture he drew his hand across his throat, sawing at it, and uttered the loud, terrified squeal of a dying pig. "So we think, him and me, it 'ud be a good thing if you weren't here when they come."

He made a last desperate fight for his life, though why, he could hardly have told you, since it was worth so little, even to him.

"That girl was honest," he said. "She'll deliver the goods to the Angel. She must have lost her way."

Pug Mayhew laughed. "Well, it doesn't matter really either road. She'll be taken care of. Smith's got his orders. She's like you, Benn—expendable."

He saw the hypodermic lying on the table, picked it up and tossed it contemptuously into the grate. "O.K. O.K. You won't be wanting that any more, and we oughtn't to put temptation in the way of the innocent." He let out a yelp of laughter. "That 'ud make the Commissioner howl, wouldn't it? An innocent rozzer. Come on. There's a way out by the back, isn't there?"

Mr. Benn shivered. The back way led, eventually, to the river, the same water wherein Eric had been found, and where soon he, too… He thrust the thought away, looking longingly at the shattered syringe. That might have been his way, if he'd had the courage to take it—might have taken it long ago for all the value his life had had all these years.

"Coming?" suggested Mayhew. "Nothing to wait for now." And, hypnotised, helpless, he crossed the floor, passed into the passage, and their feet could be heard ringing on the stone corridor.

★

Back in the Angel Mr. Smith was dialling Benn's shop, but he got nothing but an angry hiss for his pains. When at last he got hold of the operator he was told the number was out of order.

"It wasn't out of order ten minutes ago," he insisted.

"P'raps someone's cut the line," grinned the operator. "Christmas Eve's the time for good, clean fun." He rang off, laughing. Arthur Crook, that black sheep among lawyers, might have reminded him that many a true word is spoken in jest.

Smith sat thoughtful for a moment. He'd wanted to tell Pug that the girl had just telephoned and the stuff was on its way, in spite of the bloomer old man Benn had made. For Smith knew beyond the shadow of a doubt that someone had blundered. This girl hadn't the smallest idea that she was passing dynamite. After a bit, and with some trepidation, he rang another number, one that didn't appear in the book, and made his report. When he heard what the boss had to say he rang off again and became very busy indeed.

When Gillian came out into the street she found the fog was a pale greenish haze in place of the brown blanket it had been an hour before. All the same, there were no buses running.

She sent one beseeching glance up and down the road, but this time there was no cruising taxi, so she set off at a brisk pace in the direction of Merriton Square. From her window on the ground-floor of Gordon Street, old Miss Beachcroft watched her go, and wondered what it felt like to be young and pretty, and so obviously in love, and with so much to do you were in and out like a jack-in-the-box. She was an old woman now and she lived vicariously in the lives of others.

"Gone to meet that young man of hers, I suppose," sighed Miss Beachcroft. She was going to spend Christmas Day alone, as Mr. Benn had planned to do; for her, like a lot of other solitary people, Christmas was just another Sunday, without any newspapers.

Church bells were ringing as the girl hurried through the empty streets. It made her think of childhood, when they'd all been at home together, they who were all scattered now; they used to decorate the church and polish the brass, and Mother had a big sit-down tea for all the helpers, and then they trooped into the church to listen to Daddy reading evensong, with that glow that he never lost right up to the end. When he announced the promise of salvation for mankind it was always with the same throb of incredulous anticipation in his voice. For him the Christmas story never became dulled or blunted; every year the miracle was renewed...

Remembering the past, she reached the Angel before she realised it, had actually walked by the door before the significance of the lights and the traffic and the sound of the wireless came home to her. She turned back, then hesitated, paralysed by shyness. Girls she knew went in and out of bars as readily as they went in and out of shops, but she'd never been like that. She looked about for a private bell, but couldn't see one. Two men were watching her with amused eyes.

"After you, girlie," said one of them, and with the colour rushing into her cheeks she preceded them into the bar.

A good many people were standing or sitting at the counter, exchanging badinage with the girl behind it. Others sat at small tables, with their glasses in front of them. After the foggy streets the interior presented a cheerful, gay picture. But Gillian's mind was filled with a gayer picture still, the room waiting for Richard, decked as eager as a lover. She looked about her uncertainly, then approached the bar. The girl was too busy to take any notice of her at first, and a man she'd never seen before offered her a drink.

"Christmas Eve," he said.

She smiled and moved away; then, catching the barmaid's eye, she asked: "Do you know if Mr. Smith is here?"

There was a sort of chuckle from the girl. "If he said he would be I dare say he is." She looked at the men nearest her, saying: "Any of you gentlemen called Smith?"

One of them said in gallant tones, "I could be, if the little lady doesn't mind."

"It's very important," gulped Gillian. "I telephoned…"

"If he's stood you up, dear, don't you have anything more to do with him," said the girl (she must have been thirty, but we're all girls nowadays). "It's a shame… Look, dear, you sit down and give him five minutes, and then if he doesn't come you go out and find yourself someone more worth the trouble."

"No need to go out," said the man who'd spoken before. He was in the happy stage of drinking, didn't mean her any harm, she had the wit to see that, but, all the same, it was fortunate Richard wasn't here. Richard had a high-flying temper, struck first and looked all round the situation afterwards. She went reluctantly towards a little table, and stared round at the coloured streamers and the balloons that puffed up and down on the smoky air. Anger began to overlay her nervousness. She'd come out at great inconvenience because of a man's carelessness in leaving a parcel in a shop; the least he could do was be waiting for her.

"The very least," she repeated, not aware that she spoke aloud.

"The least shall be first, is that it?" asked a voice so close to her that she jumped. "Did I startle you? Sorry. I believe you may have something for me."

She hadn't even seen the man approach. Somehow he wasn't a bit what she'd anticipated—an anxious, not very young man worried over his wife This one was good-looking in a brash sort of way, good teeth, smiling eyes. "I say, is that what you bought at the old man's?" He looked down at the blue ring. He was wearing rather a showy ring of his own.

"Yes. It was lucky, in a way, that I went in, wasn't it?"

"Nice." He put out a casual hand and touched it. Quickly she produced the little parcel and put it into his hands. "I mustn't stop, I'm expecting someone."

"I'm sure he'll wait. You can't go without a drink."

"Oh, please." She half-rose. "I ought to be back before now."

"O.K. O.K. Matter of fact—where did you say you lived? Oh— Gordon Street? I've got a friend here, got his car, going that way. He'll give you a lift. Yes, of course it'll be all right," as she started to protest. "Pleasure for him."

She subsided; it would be pleasant not to have to walk back.

"What'll it be? A sherry? I'll get it."

She saw him move over to the counter, to return a minute later with two glasses in his hands.

"Happy days!" He lifted his glass and drank. Gillian looked disturbed. This cheerful little character didn't seem to fit in with her notion of a man troubled about his wife's illness. He was ready to hang about the bar and had no sign of anxiety about him. She drank the sherry quickly.

"What took a girl like you down to Benn's place this afternoon?" asked her companion suddenly.

She was so much surprised that she answered the question at once.

"I was told there was a stall in the market where I could get something I specially wanted and couldn't find anywhere else."

"Then I hope you found it," he said heartily. "All the same, Benn's not exactly in the market."

"The fog came on and I missed my way. I found his shop quite by accident, because there was a light in the window."

"That was lucky. Pity I wasn't there to show you the way home."

He must have recognised the flicker of distaste that shadowed her features, for he said in a coaxing way, "Just my fun. Christmas only comes once a year you know. And you're a sweet kid to have fagged out with this." He touched the pocket into which he'd put the little parcel.

Embarrassed, she looked over his head and in the long strip of glass behind the bar she saw the swing-door open a few inches and a face peer in. It hung there for a moment, then caught Mr. Smith's eye and nodded slightly. He nodded back, and the face slid away again.

"I've just had the wigwag that your chariot awaits," said Mr. Smith with sickening facetiousness, "so if you're ready…"

She jumped up so quickly she almost spilled the sherry in his glass.

"I dare say there's someone waiting for you," said Mr. Smith, putting an unnecessary hand on her arm to guide her to the door. A big, red-headed man, with eyebrows like another fellow's moustaches and wearing a suit whose shade would hardly have disgraced a fox, watched them go, with a frown. He hadn't any girls of his own, having never even got around to finding a wife (and what some woman's been spared is more than she can guess, he would acknowledge generously), but if he had had a daughter of that age he wouldn't have cared for her to be knocking about in a bar like the Angel, with that particular chap in tow.

"Still, not my pigeon," acknowledged Arthur Crook.

He'd no idea how soon he was going to have to eat his words.

Outside by the kerb the great black-and-chromium car glistened in the lights from the Angel. Mr. Smith opened the door with a flourish and Gillian stepped inside. It was quite dark and she hadn't realised the car already had an occupant. She started to apologise, but someone invisible said it was quite all right. Then Mr. Smith shut the door and the car drove away. Gillian lay back; she had a headache coming on, due to the smoky air, she supposed, or the sherry perhaps, that had been uncommonly strong. Something bothered her, something that wasn't quite right. They had been travelling several minutes before she realised what it was. No one had asked her for her address. She shifted to lean forward and tell the driver where to go, but before she could speak she blacked out. Someone put an arm round her: a voice said "O.K."

"Never drink with strange men," said the moralists.

And how right they were.

From her vantage-point at her ground-floor window old Miss Beachcroft was intrigued to see the young man, Richard Fyfe, come rushing up the street, "as though the bears were after him," she said afterwards, and jump the steps two at a time. So that pretty creature, Miss Hinde, hadn't gone to meet him, after all.

The eternal triangle, thought Miss Beachcroft, cosily. Say what you like about the crowds and the expense and the loneliness of being an old woman in London, still there remained a lot to be said for living there. Something was always happening. She glued her ancient nose to the window-pane.

Richard had rung three times with no result before apprehension stabbed him. He was about to ring once more when he heard a door close by being pulled open and feet sounded in the hall. The next instant the old witch from the ground floor, whose proper home, in his opinion, was a blasted heath, pulled the front door wide.

"If it's Miss Hinde you want," she ogled him, "she's gone out. She went about half an hour ago, and she's not back yet."

"Oh, I think you must be mistaken," said Richard at once. "I spoke to her on the telephone a little while ago; she's expecting me."

"I dare say she ran out for something she'd forgotten. There are still a few shops open—Christmas Eve, you know. Perhaps you'd like to come in and wait."

He thought if her appearance was anything to go by—old red brocade dressing-grown, fur-edged slippers and a tarnished silver scarf—her room would be as appetising as one of last year's birds'-nests.

"Thanks very much," he said, quickly, "but I'll just go up. She may have left me a message or something."

He caught a glimpse of the room as he went past, and it was just as he'd supposed. A tray of unwashed tea-things, a patience half set out, a pair of corsets on a chair—Jill ought to see that, it would warn her what happened to women who hadn't anyone to keep a home for. The note she had left was pinned on the door and he read it with growing concern. He knew the Angel, knew it wasn't Jill's cup of tea at all. And she hadn't said a word about it when he rang up. If she wanted to buy something to drink she need have gone no further than the very pleasant little pub at the corner. He stood irresolute for a moment—didn't even notice the door was ajar, then, stuffing the note into his pocket, came down again. Miss Beachcroft was standing at the doorway of her room, expectant as a vulture waiting for something to die.

"There was a message," he told her, since it was obvious she wasn't minded to let him go without a word. "I'm going along to meet her."

There were quite a number of girls at the Angel when Richard arrived, but none of them remotely resembled Gillian. He looked about him, perplexed, irritated, more apprehensive than ever. He must have missed her after all, and yet—there had been so few people in the streets and no traffic to speak of, certainly neither buses nor taxis. No, she must have tried to take a short cut, which involved going through a number of narrow back streets, and either she was home now or else she'd irretrievably lost her way. This Christmas that was to have been so perfect—a rehearsal, she had said, for their life together that was going to start so soon—had got off on the wrong foot.

His eye, glancing this way and that, caught the responsive gleam of a bright brown eye belonging to a man who, if you'd never think of comparing him to Adonis, was sufficiently remarkable to hold the attention. He had a big, red face, spiky red brows, red hair, and a red-brown suit. Catching Richard's gaze, he leaned forward to say, "Looking for someone?"

"A girl," Richard acknowledged. "I was to pick her up here."

"You young chaps are a rum lot," said Crook, candidly. "It's not precisely the rendezvous I'd choose—not for a nice girl, as I'm sure yours must be." Then, with no change of voice, he added, "What did she look like?"

Richard tried to describe her, but his best friend must have acknowledged he made rather a hash of it.

"Flashing a handsome blue ring?" asked Crook, sympathetically.

Richard began to say No, and then stopped, recalling Gillian's eager voice on the telephone.

"Well, yes, she may have—a Christmas present. I haven't seen it myself. Do you mean she's here?"

"There was a girl here who could have been yours. Sort of Gainsborough's Blue Girl," he added, brilliantly. "Her first visit, I'd say. I mean, she obviously didn't look on the Angel as a home from home."

"What happened to her?" Crook's heart warmed to the anxiety in the keen young voice.

"She went out with as smooth a Charley as ever I set eyes on. Wearing a sizeable ring, too, very natty. Funny, y'know, I never could fancy a fellow who wore a ring." His voice changed. "If she's your girl you should take more care of her—letting her come to a place like this on her own."

"You've got it wrong," protested Richard. "I didn't even know she'd come till I found her note. She promised me she wouldn't go out again tonight."

"Note?"

"Yes. Pinned on her door. A matter of life and death, she said. I'd just telephoned to say I'd be round in half an hour…"

"And Juliet's proper place is the balcony," Crook approved. "I couldn't agree with you more. Not that I'm much of a balcony hound myself. No mention of Charley in the note, I take it?"

"None." He pulled the bit of paper out of his pocket. "It must have been something quite unexpected. Did you say she left with this chap?"

Crook nodded. "And, unless my ears are missing a beat, in the sort of car no honest man can afford to run these days, unless he gets it on expenses. A *Panther*, big, vulgar affair like a night-club." He spoke with some derision, recalling his own ancient yellow Rolls, that caught every eye and no wonder, he'd tell you, the "Old Superb." He was aware that Richard's anxiety had changed to something much stronger.

"Look here," he said, "I don't know who you are…"

"Crook's the name," said the big, brown man, obligingly. "Arthur Crook, and trouble is my business." He hauled a card out of his pocket. "123, Bloomsbury Street's where I operate, and praise the pigs no one's thought of a closed shop for lawyers, because if anyone put me on to a forty-hour week I'd go off my nut. I work all round the clock when the work's there, and if it ain't I go out and look for it. Same as now," he added.

"I don't get it," said Richard, who wasn't paying much attention to any of this. "What on earth would bring a girl like Jill to this place at a minute's notice?"

"Got the note there?" Crook asked.

Richard pushed it at him. Crook looked at it for a moment, then said politely, "Code? I don't follow. This looks to me like a telephone number."

Richard turned the slip over. Crook read through the note and handed the paper back.

"She could have been a bit more forthcoming," he acknowledged. "Matter of fact, I can tell you one thing; she didn't come empty-handed. She had something with her—don't ask me what it was—but I saw her hand a packet of some sort to this chap. After that they had a drink…"

"It can't have been Jill," Richard broke out, and Crook said easily, "Well that should be simple. I dare say you've got a picture of the young lady somewhere about you."

Blushing in a manner highly unbecoming to a man who meant to have his plate up within the year, Richard drew a photograph out of his wallet.

"That's her," said Crook, with no hesitation at all. "I don't say she's the most beautiful girl I ever saw, but she's got something. That's why I didn't care for the company she was keeping. Now, look, we don't want to make prize idiots of ourselves; it could be it's all on the up-and-up" (though his expression said that pigs might fly, only he'd never seen them do it) "and she may be home by now, wondering what's happened to you. There's a call-box in the passage, and I dare say you don't have to look up her number…"

He hadn't time to finish the sentence before Richard disappeared. He was back a couple of minutes later, his brow as black as the fog.

"I don't like it," he announced abruptly. "In fact, it stinks. Know what this number is?" He indicated the slip of paper he'd taken off Gillian's door. "The number of this pub. What does that add up to to you?"

"That she rang up and made a date," returned Crook, simply. "If someone had rung her, she wouldn't have troubled to write the number down. She came here to hand over a parcel—maybe she brought it home by mistake or something."

"With his name and address on it? Anyhow, if that's the answer, why didn't he come to fetch it at the flat?"

"You wouldn't have liked that any better," was Crook's grim reply. "I'm no young maiden myself, but I'd as soon find a wolf on the doorstep as that catastrophe in human shape she went off with. Well, that's the way it is, son. Question is, where do we go from here?"

"If I could find the chap responsible for this," said Richard, with classic simplicity, "I'd break his ruddy neck for him, and I don't mean maybe."

Gillian opened her eyes to see the unaccustomed snow swirling past the window and to hear the sound of church bells ringing triumphantly to announce one more anniversary of the coming of the Prince of Peace. She lay very still, aware that she had passed through some ordeal of whose nature she was still in doubt, waiting for consciousness to become complete, as on other occasions she had waited to watch the new light struggle into the sky. Glancing cautiously about her, she found herself in an unfamiliar room, lying on an unfamiliar bed. A small coal-fire burned in the hearth, throwing shadows on the ceiling. Somewhere a clock ticked. So far as she could discover, she was quite alone.

After a minute she made a movement to sit up, and realised immediately that whatever had overtaken her the night before had left a physical legacy of languor and discomfort. Her head ached and there seemed loaded balls behind her eyes.

"Where am I?" she wondered aloud, putting one hand to her forehead.

In the corner someone stirred. "Are you feeling any better?" said a voice, and a pleasant-looking middle-aged woman swam into view. "As to where you are, you're in my house. A more pertinent question would be: Who are you? and what on earth were you doing on a bench on the Embankment at ten o'clock last night?"

At the sound of the unexpected voice Gillian turned sharply and a red-hot needle seemed to pierce her temples.

"Now, don't talk till you're ready," advised the stranger. She came over and took the girl's wrist between competent fingers. "You're perfectly safe so long as you stay here."

"Did you say I was on the Embankment?"

"When I found you. It was the merest chance, anyway. I happened to be driving home, and I caught sight of you, and somehow you didn't look the sort of girl who should be sitting there at that hour. Though sitting is rather complimentary. You were all slumped over. I thought at first—well, never mind that. You're all right now, or soon will be, according to the doctor."

"The doctor?"

"I called him in. Well, I felt responsible for you. There was no way of telling who you were or where you lived…"

She made a great effort. "My address was in my bag."

"My dear, you hadn't any bag."

"It was in my hand when I left the Angel."

"The Angel?" The woman's brows creased. "Do you mean the Underground station?"

"No. It's a public-house…"

"Ah! So that's why… My dear, haven't you a mother?"

"She's dead," said the girl rather shortly. "So's my father."

"So you've no one?"

"There's Richard."

"Who's Richard?"

"Oh! A friend." She couldn't discuss Richard with a stranger, no matter how kind. But the woman persisted.

"Was he with you at the Angel?"

"No. I went there to meet someone…"

The woman sighed. "How old are you? You hardly look more than sixteen now. It's the old story, I suppose. You had one and then you had another and—did you know this man?"

"No. I didn't say it was a man," she added.

"Do girls meet each other at public-houses nowadays? What was this Richard of yours doing, letting you run about meeting other men?"

"He didn't know." A fresh thought struck her. "Is it Christmas Day?"

"Of course. Can't you hear the bells?"

She sat up higher against the pillows, fighting against the sickness.

"I must get in touch with him at once. He'll be worried to death."

The woman put out a capable hand and restrained her. "It's no good your meeting him till you've got things straight in your own mind. What happened after you left the Angel?"

"I don't know—I don't remember. Only there was a car. He said he was going to give me a lift home."

"Who was?"

"I don't know. The man called Smith, the one I took the parcel to, said he had a friend going my way."

"What parcel was that?"

"One I'd promised to deliver—for an old man called Benn in a shop near Paxton Market." The mists were dissolving now. "And Smith said it was urgent, a prescription for his wife, and she must have it that night. And when I got to the Angel he made me drink a glass of sherry and said this friend…" She paused. "Wait a minute. There was something wrong. I remember that. But I don't remember what. It was just then everything became swimmy…"

"And all this happened last night?"

"Yes. It must have been about half-past seven. I promised Richard I wouldn't go out again; I told him… Oh, please, I must ring him up."

"You're not fit to ring anyone at the moment. Anyway, the telephone's downstairs. Why not give me his number and I'll ring through? I don't think you told me his other name."

But she didn't like that idea. It seemed of paramount importance she should speak to him herself, making him understand this nightmare as no one else could do.

"Tell me about him," said the woman, gently.

"There isn't anything, really. Just that we're going to be married…" Her voice softened. "He was coming to dinner last night—it was going to be the best Christmas ever, and now, now…"

To her horror she found the tears squeezing between her lids. "You do see what happened, don't you?" she pleaded. "What must have happened? There was something in that sherry. I mean, one glass wouldn't knock me out. And I remember now he made me drink it. And then he said the car was at the door. It was a very big car," she added vaguely. "And there was someone inside already."

"Who was that?"

"I don't know. It's coming back in bits, like a jig-saw puzzle. I have to fit them together. It was a plot, of course."

"Why on earth should anyone want to plot against you?"

"I don't know. It doesn't make sense, does it?"

"And why dump you on the Embankment?"

"Well," protested Gillian, reasonably, "they'd have to leave me somewhere."

"If they'd got the parcel why shouldn't they let you go home?"

"Perhaps because of it, what was in it, I mean. He said it was a prescription for his wife, who was sick, but he didn't look like a man whose wife is ill. I remember thinking that at the time."

"What were you doing in the old man's shop?"

"There was a ring in the window—" Her glance fell automatically to her hand. The next instant she had started up. "It's gone," she cried. "My ring's gone. My beautiful blue ring."

The woman was looking at her oddly. "My dear," she said. "I'm old enough to be your mother. You needn't be afraid of what you tell me. Are you sure that's just what happened? Are you sure you didn't have rather more than one glass of sherry and—well, get just a little tipsy and lose your road home? You might so easily drop down on a bench—or perhaps someone snatched your bag and the ring with it. Was it valuable?"

"I paid five pounds for it. I don't know what it was worth. No, it wasn't valuable, it was just beautiful. I thought Richard would like it as much as I did. Oh, please, let me telephone Richard. If it were the other way round and it was he who was missing, I should be quite, quite mad. With fear, I mean."

"You're very much in love, aren't you?" said the woman gently. She sat by the bed and held Gillian's hand. "The doctor's coming in a minute, and if he says you can get up you shall dress at once." She stroked the girl's cheek. "It'll come out all right in the end, I'm sure it will. Can I trust you to lie quiet for five minutes while I make you a cup of coffee?"

"You're very kind," said Gillian, her voice still trembling.

"My dear, I've got a daughter of my own about your age."

She went out of the room. Before she returned the front-door bell rang and Gillian heard the sound of voices.

"Come in," said the woman clearly. "Yes, she's awake. She remembers quite a lot. I've told her you're coming. She wants to get in touch with someone called Richard."

"So do we," said a man's voice. "We want to find out quite a lot about the young lady."

The door opened and a tall man came in. "Sitting up and taking notice?" he asked, genially. "This isn't precisely how one would choose to start Christmas Day…"

But Gillian said nothing. She lay frozen against the pillows. For this wasn't a stranger, someone she'd never met before; this was a face she had seen hanging in a patch of darkness between the swing-doors of the Angel not much more than twelve hours ago. She hadn't been meant to see it, of course; she'd looked up and there it had been, reflected in the mirror; and the head had nodded and the man who called himself Smith had laughed, and said, "Ready?" and they'd got up—and the horror had begun.

"Aren't you going to wish me a Merry Christmas?" said the voice, and as he spoke the door opened again and the woman came in.

"This is Dr. Belvedere," she announced.

At that Gillian found her voice. "Oh, no," she said. "He isn't a doctor. I know him now. He's the driver of the car that took me away from the Angel last night, and you—of course—you're the one who was in the car—your story about finding me on the Embankment is all a lie. You're in the plot too—oh, isn't there anyone to be on my side?" The tears were shaking her voice, but she fought them back.

The woman came over to the bed and caught her hand. "There's Richard," she said, softly. "You hadn't forgotten him, had you? You're going to ring him up, aren't you? Oh, yes. I think you will. I think you're going to do everything we say. Because, if you don't..."

But she wouldn't, all the same. They were quite angry, quite rough with her before she was able to convince them that she didn't propose to betray Richard. They realised it was hopeless, at last; she wouldn't even tell them how much Richard knew. And when they saw they were wasting their time the woman caught her arm, and the man produced a syringe, and though she struggled, she was no match for the pair of them. She felt the prick, felt her arm tossed roughly down, and almost at once, for the second time in twenty-four hours, she swam away into the dark.

There was to be no rest for Richard this Christmas Eve. Long after he was convinced of the futility of such action, he found himself pulling open the doors of telephone booths, slipping his coppers into the slot and dialling Gillian's number. Every time, as the bell began to ring, his heart pounded in unison, and every time it rang to a despairing silence. On—and on—and on. Yet, though he went back into the street swearing he'd make no further effort, he had but to pass another box to remind his ravaged heart that this night was the anniversary of the greatest miracle the world has ever known, and in he went again, click, click, click, went the pennies—and always with the same result. He even paid another visit to Gordon Street; this time there was no need to ring the bell, for Miss Beachcroft was watching avidly from the window and came scuttling into the hall to assure him there was no news.

"Have you tried the hospitals?" she demanded, twitching her ancient crimson garment round her shapeless form. "Anyone could be knocked down on a night like this."

Richard brushed past her, taking the stairs two at a time, till he reached the third floor. It was then that he discovered the door on the latch and pushed it open. When he saw the brave, gay preparations she had made, the happy tree, the parcels tied with silk ribbons, the cards strung along the wall, he almost forgot his manhood. If he had been tempted for one second to doubt her good faith, this would have reassured him, but, in fact, no such temptation had assailed his tormented heart. He was as sure of her love as he was of his own, had a terrifying glimpse of what loneliness could mean for the un-companioned, the undesired and the bereaved.

There was no further message here, and he came down with a new resolve in his mind. Gillian's disappearance was connected in some way with this fellow Benn, from whom she'd bought the ring. Evidence? Crook might have murmured, and of course there was none. But—what was in the parcel and where had she found it? If she hadn't got it from Benn... but she hadn't spoken of it over the telephone. Perhaps someone had called her up after she'd spoken to him. Perhaps—perhaps. At all events, he couldn't rest and was in the mood of desperation when men snatch at straws. If Benn knew anything he was going to talk. The telephone directory showed quite a number of Benns, but only one who appeared to answer to his requirements. Benn, H., Marine Store Dealer. That would be the fellow. Richard got out his little car and turned east.

Mr. Benn's shop was as shuttered as the ancient tombs of one of his own ancestors; no amount of ringing and knocking called forth any response. There wasn't even anything to indicate that the old man actually lived on the premises, no private door, no card. The rooms over the shop might be used as storerooms—Richard couldn't tell. One thing was obvious, no one was coming down to the door tonight, and though he peered industriously, like some night animal after its prey, he couldn't detect a gleam of light anywhere.

"Probably gone off somewhere for Christmas," Richard supposed, taking stock of his environment. There appeared to be no residential quarters on either side of the shop. A large building with a blank wall, that was probably a factory, stood on one side and a door leading to a workyard on the other; the little shop was sandwiched, like a very thin slice of meat between two hunks of bread, amid these formidable walls. There was a bomb-site opposite, where nothing remained but part of a wall, a basement window-frame, bricks among which the coarse grass flourished and a fair amount of rubbish shot there in defiance of restrictions. The only life he discerned was a thin, young black cat, which streaked off the site, looking like a bit of black velvet with a shining green stone in it, that was her eye. He didn't stop to wonder, as a clod like Arthur Crook would have done, what brought her out so suddenly, and it didn't occur to him to look over the broken wall, and so it was he never saw the shadow moving in that world of shadows, a bit of flotsam in a lost world, who leaned over the smashed brickwork and thoughtfully watched him go.

After that there was nothing for it but to try the hospitals and every other source of information who might know about accidents, fatal and otherwise; every time he got a connection his heart leaped like a fish on a string, and always the reply was the same. He had an uneasy feeling that he was making a prize fool of himself, that whenever a receiver was replaced on its rest someone at the other end was grinning. Another chap taken for a ride, they'd think, and his own heart sickened anew. Oh, if anyone had been taken for a ride, it wasn't he, but Gillian, his dear love, who, by some appalling misfortune, in which he could still scarcely believe, had been whirled away in a car—the sort of car no honest man can afford to run—and was now—where?

Next morning he woke with a start, wondering what was wrong. He hadn't expected to sleep at all, and was rather ashamed that he had been able to do so. Then it all came surging back, and he couldn't believe it at first. Things like this don't happen, he exclaimed, but that was all tommy-rot. Of course they happened; you read about them in the papers five days out of seven. What he meant was, nothing like this had ever happened to him before. He snatched up the telephone and defiantly rang Gillian's number. Perhaps this time someone would lift the receiver, her voice would say, "Hallo, darling..." He felt he would scarcely ask her for an explanation if only he could hear her voice again. But, naturally, nothing of the sort happened. The bell pealed away as heartless as the bright morning light, and at last he gave up and put the receiver back on its rest.

The morning passed somehow; he envied bus conductors and clergymen taking services, and people cooking Christmas dinners, because they had something to do. He had forgotten that, in Gillian's absence, he had nowhere to go on what was known as the family feast; he went into a restaurant where he wasn't likely to see anybody he knew and ate something—it could have been sawdust chips for all he could have told you—and then, because he could stand inaction no longer, he got into his car and once more drove down past Aldgate Pump.

Mr. Benn's shop looked much the same by day as it had done last evening, except that he could see it better; but there was one change. On the step stood a small bottle of milk.

"So the old so-and-so does live here, and seeing he hasn't cancelled his milk order, he hasn't gone away," Richard reflected. "Well, I'll get him this time, if I have to tear the place down, brick by brick."

It looked as though he might be driven even to these lengths, for no amount of knocking or ringing brought the sound of footsteps, or, indeed, any indication of life. He became very cunning, ringing the bell and stepping back into the middle of the road to make sure no one was huddling behind curtains at an upper window. But all the windows were closed.

"But the curtains aren't drawn over them," he told himself. "There must be someone there."

It didn't occur to him that perhaps they'd never been drawn last night.

Realising the impossibility of breaking in through the shutters, Richard now began to explore for an entry by the rear. A narrow lane ran behind the factory and ended in a *cul-de-sac*, with a high wall obviously enclosing the workyard on Mr. Benn's further side. And in the wall behind Mr. Benn's house he found a shabby wooden door that must once have been blue but was so discoloured by time and weather that now it had no colour at all. To his surprise, this opened easily. It never occurred to him that there might be a trap, that other men were at least as intelligent and far-sighted as he; it didn't even pass through his mind that he might have been seen talking to Crook the previous night—and at this stage he'd no idea that in the underworld Crook was as readily recognised as a Sinatra or a Ray by bobby-soxers in a rather different *milieu*. On the further side of the door was a little paved yard and an outside privy. And beyond these was the back door of the shop. He advanced, banging mightily and arousing nothing but local echoes, and was about to make a frenzied attack, when it came into his mind to turn the handle. The door opened under his grasp and he found himself in a narrow stone passage, very dark because there were no windows and no light was burning. He switched on the torch he habitually carried. The passage led past a flight of stone steps, giving, he supposed, on to a storeroom or coal-cellar. He flashed his light on the stairs, and then stood very still, holding his breath. Because there was something at the foot, something dark and unmoving, like an old sack, but, he was convinced, not an old sack. He went down quickly, his breath catching in his throat. It was easy to understand now why Mr. Benn had let the bells ring unchecked and paid no heed to the hammering on the door.

"He must have been dead several hours," reflected Richard, straightening himself at last. "Probably was lying here last night."

But what connection had that bit of human wreckage with happy Gillian Hinde?

"Wonder what he was coming down here for in the dark," Richard reflected, and Crook himself couldn't have experienced a more startling reaction. From the instant of his discovery, he had been uncomfortably convinced that there was something wrong about the scene, something missing, and now he knew what it was. Light. Since Gillian had talked with the old man not earlier than six o'clock, it followed that it must have been quite dark when he started on his downward journey. Yet no light was burning and, search where he might, Richard could find no trace of torch or candle. He bent again above the little, shrivelled face, and a worse fear struck him. This was no accident. A man tripping and falling on those sharp-edged steps would show signs of his fall, there'd be bruises, abrasions, the hands would be outflung to try and save himself; and though there might well be facial injuries, these wouldn't be on the appalling scale the torch revealed when Richard gently turned the body over. He leaned against the wall, feeling pretty sick.

"Someone picked him up and deliberately chucked him down the stairs," he said aloud, and the sound of his own voice was shocking in the half-dark. "Nothing else would account for the fact that the bones of one side of the face were stove in, but there's practically no other surface injury."

Blood was sprinkled profusely on the stones where the dead man lay, but there were no traces of blood on the steps themselves. And then he perceived something else. ("Quite the little Sherlock Holmes," said Crook, drily, when he heard later.) On the stairs the dust lay thick; his own feet had left marks. But there were no other footmarks discernible.

"I shall have to get the police now," he thought. "This is murder."

And, as though that most dreadful of words had opened a door and let in a host of fiends, he understood that in the hands of whoever was responsible for this outrage against human dignity and human rights lay Gillian, whom he loved and who, surely, waited for him to come and save her. Anger, pain and fear all swirled together in his heart. It was like someone banging a knocker in his head. He forgot his pity for the dead man, even forgot about ringing the police—(the police?—the only man likely to help him now was Arthur Crook)—and he came surging out of the back door like a storm-cloud, to be brought up short on the step by an apparition so unexpected that for the moment it seemed a chimera of his overwrought imagination, and he lunged forward as if to walk through it.

The apparition put out a large, powerful arm in a blue sleeve.

"Good afternoon, sir," said the police officer. "Were you looking for someone?"

The shock of discovering poor Mr. Benn and then running slap into a constable seemed to paralyse Richard's natural good sense.

"Where on earth did you spring from?" he demanded. "And what do you want?"

It is very hard to discompose the police. "I was asking you, sir," said P.C. Oliver, his voice still perfectly pleasant, but as unyielding as a Sten gun.

"I came to see someone."

"Yes, sir? Did you come the front way?"

"Of course not. It's locked, presumably from the inside. I got in the same way you did. What made you follow me? Did I leave the gate ajar?"

"As a matter of fact, you did, but that isn't why. Someone telephoned the police that a man had been noticed stealing up the back way, and seeing it was Christmas and the place might be untenanted, they thought we might be interested."

Richard burst into a staccato laugh. "I can't imagine that at the best of times there could be much here worth taking," he remarked.

"No, sir?" Richard sobered suddenly. What an idiotic thing to have said. Why, there could be hundreds of pounds' worth of stuff on the premises for all he knew. "Did you—er—find anyone at home?"

Richard threw his hand up to cover his mouth. There was something so absurdly formal about this chap, asking if he'd found anyone at home, when you realised, in fact, what he had found…

"Yes," he said after a minute. "He's at home all right—you'll find him at the bottom of the stairs. Matter of fact, I was going to call you."

The policeman marched into the house with Richard at his side. "Down there," said the young doctor. "And—he doesn't seem to have left any footprints in the dust."

The policeman turned sharply. "Meaning, sir?"

"Meaning, I don't think it was an accident. I'm a doctor," he added, feeling for his driving licence. "Naturally, you'll get your own police surgeon, but I fancy his opinion will be the same as mine."

P.C. Oliver went sturdily down the stairs; there wasn't really any need to hesitate. No one, thought Richard, could have been more dead.

"Did you say he was a friend of yours?" enquired the constable.

"Living, I never set eyes on him."

"And yet you wanted to see him so badly you came in by the back? But never mind about telling me now, sir. I'll have to let my sergeant know what's happened, and you'll be asked for a statement in due course." He came up the stairs and stood looking left and right. "Where would the telephone be?" he enquired.

"How should I know? I've never been in the house before."

The officer opened a door and revealed the dismembered instrument. For the first time he allowed his dismay to penetrate his official composure.

"Cut!" he observed. "With a knife, I'd say. That's queer."

"Isn't murder generally queer?" Richard demanded.

"Murder? As to that we don't know how the deceased came to his end, not till we have the official report."

"I'll let you into a secret," said Richard, bitterly. "The deceased met his death through being slung down that flight of stairs as if he were a sack of old garbage; his face was smashed, as you saw, by the stone corridor."

"Are you going to offer that as evidence?" asked the policeman.

Richard shrugged. "I haven't any evidence to give, beyond the fact that I found him. At all events, I'm the first person to inform the police."

He found his companion regarding him rather oddly.

Richard coloured. "Well, all right," he said. "I hadn't got round to calling you. Some other fellow got in first. Which reminds me, what happened to him?"

"He didn't stop," said Oliver, stolidly. "It's a funny thing how perfectly respectable people fight shy of the police. Of course, he might have thought there was more than one of you... There's a booth at the corner. I'll call my sergeant from that."

As they came round the side of the factory the policeman jerked his thumb towards Richard's little car.

"That yours, sir?"

"That's right. What of it? You're not trying to run me in for a parking offence, I suppose? Well, then, what's it all about? You aren't by any chance casting me for the murderer? Good Heavens, I never saw him before and, anyway, he's been dead the better part of twenty-four hours, I'd say."

"Quite so, sir. Perhaps I should tell you that a car resembling yours, a *Moonbeam* 8, and the same colour, was seen standing outside this house last night. Perhaps you could tell me where you were, round about ten o'clock. Would that be roughly the hour the gentleman was killed?"

An inspector called Oldfield and a sergeant named Waters took over the case. When the police car arrived Richard felt quite dazed, it seemed as if half the Yard must be tumbling out; but they soon resolved themselves into doctor, fingerprint expert, photographer, etc. The doctor's diagnosis as to cause of death tallied with Richard's.

"Some time last night," he said. "Impossible to be very sure. This passage is like an ice-box. Must have been killed instantly, neck broken. Most likely a man's crime, if you're asking my opinion," he added. "A big chap…" It was just chance, of course, that his eyes rested for a moment on Richard, who stood six foot two in his socks.

"I wonder if you'd care to come along to the station and make a statement," suggested Oldfield. "I'm rather in the dark as to why you were here at all, if the deceased wasn't a friend of yours."

"Do you ever go to the films?" asked Richard.

The Inspector looked pardonably startled. "Sometimes, if my wife wants to see a picture… Why?"

"Because you won't need to go to one for a long while after hearing my story. It begins with a girl…"

After he'd finished speaking, the Inspector said, "But what made you so sure that Benn had anything to do with it?"

"I wasn't. But the trouble started after she bought the ring. And the ring must be mixed up in it somehow, because Crook saw this chap make some reference to it. I don't pretend to understand…" He stopped when he saw the chagrined expression on Oldfield's face.

"Did you say Crook? Would that be…?"

"Arthur Crook. He's a lawyer. I've got his card somewhere. Why? Do you know him?"

"Couldn't you trust him to come muscling in on a job like this?" muttered the Inspector. "Know him? Of course we do. I suppose I shouldn't be surprised to hear he's mixed up in this. One of these days he'll fall out of the skin of the Derby winner. So he saw Miss Hinde at the Angel. A regular haunt of hers?"

"I doubt if she'd ever been there before."

"Did Crook happen to notice if she went out with anyone?"

"I told you, he thinks she was given a lift—since when no one's seen her. That is, no one I've been able to come across. Look here, Inspector, what is all this? You didn't seem surprised when you heard of peculiar doings at the Angel."

"I wasn't," admitted Oldfield. "Dr. Fyfe, how long have you known Miss Hinde?"

"How long? Oh, about eight months. Since I came to the hospital. What on earth's that got to do with it?"

"Do you know her family, by any chance?"

"She hasn't any, not in England. There's a married brother in Germany, and a sister in Scotland. That's all."

"But you know—that is, you have mutual acquaintances?"

"Only at the hospital."

"I see."

"Perhaps," said Richard, holding on to his temper with an effort, "you'd be good enough to tell me what you see."

"I'll be frank with you," said Oldfield. "We've had our eye on a gang of dope-peddlers for quite a while now. We knew the stuff was being passed, and we could put our hands on one or two of the small fry. But that doesn't help. As soon as we show the smallest interest in any of them something happens. You may have seen a mention in the papers of a chap found floating in the dock recently? We've every reason to suppose he was one of them and—well, a chain's as strong as its weakest link, and sometimes your best policy is to shorten the chain and get rid of the faulty link."

"I see," said Richard. "And this chap, Benn, was another link."

"Looks remarkably like it."

"And—oh, no, Inspector, that's crazy. You're not suggesting that Jill... It's fantastic. She's a nurse, she knows what drugs do to people.

Just a slow form of murder instead of the speedy kind. If you'd set eyes on her, you'd know…"

"But I haven't," said the Inspector slowly. "And suppose, just for the sake of argument, you're wrong? Suppose they got hold of her in some way… Now, Dr. Fyfe, I'm only trying to answer your question. What can have happened to her, I mean."

"Then perhaps you can answer this one, too. Why should she leave a note telling me she was going to the Angel?"

"In build-ups like this one there's always danger for the little man, the little woman, too, of course. I mean, the chaps at the top stay put, but the personnel are always changing, just as soon as they stop being assets and start being a danger—to X, I mean."

"Blackmail?" Richard felt his head swim.

"Or conversion. Or just blue funk. The authorities don't look kindly on these dope rings, and no one likes the idea of spending years behind bars. Sometimes, particularly with women, they fall in love, want to cut clear, make a fresh start. They can swear till they're blue in the face that they've put the past behind them, don't remember a thing, but X and his friends aren't going to take a chance like that, and they'd be mugs if they did," he added, candidly. "So, you see…?"

"Eric in the dock, Benn in the basement. What's this leading up to? Gillian on the bomb-site? I keep telling you, she knew nothing."

"She knew where Benn hung out, and she'd told you."

"She didn't tell me," Richard interrupted. "She just said he had a junk shop near the market—and his name. I looked him up in the telephone book."

"And came to see him?"

"He was the last person I could get hold of who had seen her. I don't count the crowd at the Angel, I didn't know who they were.

But if there was anything—wacky—then Benn was probably in it. So I came down, last night, but I couldn't get any answer."

"And you came again today?"

"I had to do something. And he might have been back. When I saw the milk I was pretty sure he was on the premises, and I meant to get some information out of him, if I had to…" He stopped abruptly.

"Break his neck, you were going to say. Dr. Fyfe, when you realised the young lady hadn't come back, why didn't you ring the police?"

"I didn't want to see her name in capitals in every rag in the kingdom, and find my doorstep cluttered up with Press hounds," returned Richard, savagely. "Besides, you'd only have told me it's a free country and if a girl chooses to change her mind about who she'll go out with, I mean, that's no concern of yours."

"You don't do us justice," returned the Inspector drily. "Nothing else occur to you? Then I don't think we need detain you any longer, Dr. Fyfe. You're not thinking of leaving London for the next few days, I take it?"

"I'm a doctor," said Richard, his voice as dry as the Inspector's. "You can't walk out on a crowd of sick people, you know. Anyway, until I've got some information about Miss Hinde, from you or anyone else…"

"If you should get any information about Miss Hinde from any other quarter, I rely on you to pass it on to us at once," said the Inspector in a sharp tone. "And whatever you do, don't try and pull the chestnuts out of the fire yourself. For some reason I've never been able to fathom, amateurs always get the idea they can outwit the professionals."

It wasn't often that Arthur Crook found himself in agreement with the police, but he'd have given them an ungrudging hand on that.

"It wouldn't help us to have you hit over the head," the police-man continued. "We're short-handed as it is…"

"And so's my hospital. Try and get it into your head, Inspector, that I haven't the slightest desire to find myself in the mortuary queue behind Benn and that other chap you found in the water."

The Inspector said politely it was nice they understood each other, but when he found himself alone with his sergeant, he said, "I don't like it; I don't like it a bit. I don't think this young chap's implicated, but say he found out the girl was and came hot-foot to see Benn—he was in the neighbourhood last night, he admits it himself, and Benn was killed some time between six and eleven, as far as Burgess can say."

"He came round again today," his sergeant reminded him.

"They do it. You know that as well as I do. Some can't stand the suspense. Has he been found? Am I suspected? What's happening? Some of them even think it's a smart thing to be the one that finds the body. And he said he was going to telephone us, but when Oliver met him he was coming out of the house and he hadn't tried to ring us—he knew the house was on the 'phone, remember, because he'd looked it up in the book to get the address. If someone hadn't hap-pened to see him sneaking in the back way, should we have learned about Benn's death as early as we did?"

"Ever done a jig-saw puzzle?" Crook enquired cheerfully of his companion. "Ever find a bit that don't seem to fit in anywhere, and say, 'This must belong to something else,' and then you find you've got the bits in wrong and your mystery piece does fit, after all?"

He was talking to Richard Fyfe, who had gone round to see him on the evening of the Bank Holiday.

There was still no news about Gillian.

"Who's your odd bit in this puzzle?" demanded the young doctor, wishing people wouldn't talk in riddles when your head ached like blazes and you were so sick with anxiety you could scarcely distinguish a migraine from a meningitis.

"The chap who gave the alarm. In the police's shoes, I'd have wanted to know quite a lot about him. What was he doing in an empty street on Christmas Day? He didn't live there or he'd have hung around. Why didn't he stop to meet them? And why should he care if a perfect stranger, in broad daylight, mark you, or as broad as we ever get it in this country in December, tries to get into a house by the back if he doesn't get in at the front. More." He wagged an enormous pudgy finger at his audience. "How come he was there two days running and could identify your car? Well? Want to know the answer?"

"You tell me," agreed Richard, feeling rather overwhelmed by Crook's boisterous energy.

"My guess 'ud be he was set to watch the house and report in due course. He saw you come down on Christmas Eve—well, obviously, or he wouldn't have known you were there. You didn't get in, so Bob's your uncle. But the next day you go down and you go for the back way and you don't come out again. Didn't you say the street was a *cul-de-sac*?"

"Yes," agreed Richard, thinking this was perhaps how patients felt when they found themselves confronted by some medical authority of immense reputation—tongue-tied.

"So,"—Crook plodded on, the most pertinacious of elephants— "when you didn't come back he did a bit of arithmetic and guessed you'd got inside. And he knew what you were going to find there. Well, of course he did. Otherwise, why should he care if you got in or not? The police are like rats, you know. They hang on. Someone's going to swing one of these days for Benn, just as they will for that chap they pulled out of the dock, and your shadow didn't see why it shouldn't be you."

"Shadow?" repeated Richard.

"Well," said Crook politely, "you didn't mention you were bringing a friend with you."

"I didn't. I haven't spoken of this to anyone else."

"Just as well," Crook agreed. "It ain't healthy to know too much. If I could persuade chaps of that, the undertakers 'ud have a lot more time on their hands. Now, just drift up alongside and tell me if you've seen that type on the other side of the street before."

He was leaning casually against the window-frame as he spoke. Richard came over, stood an instant glancing up and down the street and turned away.

"No," he said. "Do you think he's there because I'm here?"

"I don't think, I know. Point is—did the rozzers put him on to you or could it be X? Didn't notice if he tailed you home from Aldgate Pump?"

"No. Do you think he could have been the chap who gave the alarm? He wasn't in evidence after the police arrived."

"Would you be, in the circumstances? No, no; depend upon it, he was shut up nice and tight in a telephone booth giving his boss the lowdown on developments. Made your will?"

He shot out the question so suddenly that Richard's eyes bulged. He spun round.

"You don't suppose…"

"My dear chap, do be your age and remember you ain't playing a panel game now. Also that the most bloodstained murderer can't hang twice. If these chaps think you're the slightest danger to them they won't give you time to say your prayers. Take my tip and don't go hanging about dark corners by yourself; if a chap stops you and asks for a light, ask him what's wrong with buying himself a box of matches; and if he wants a lift remind him that Providence equipped him with two feet. And if he should happen to be a one-legged man," he added, "it shows he's a careless type, anyway, and not to be trusted. Don't keep any appointments without checking up that they're with the right dick, and, above all, don't let a stranger stand you a drink."

"In short," suggested Richard, "about the only place where I shall be safe is the churchyard."

Crook looked disgusted. "If you want to play safe I don't know why the hell I'm wasting my time on you," he said.

Richard hadn't been back long when he received a telephone call.

"Dr. Fyfe?" said a voice. "Just thought you'd like to know the little lady's fine, which is how you'd like her to stay, I guess. Well, then, don't go starting anything, will you?"

"If you mean the police, you know as well as I do it's out of my hands." He couldn't really believe he was talking to someone who knew where Gillian was. "Let me speak to her," he exclaimed in sudden fury. "I don't believe you've got her."

"It 'ud be a shame to deprive her of her beauty sleep," said the voice. "And I don't mean the police. The police…" It appeared that the speaker's opinion of them tallied with Crook's. And Crook's was the next name he heard. "Been seeing much of him lately?" asked the voice. "Got a big nose, hasn't he? Might drop him a hint it 'ud be healthier to keep it out of matters that don't concern him."

There was a sharp click as the receiver was replaced. Richard's first impulse was to dial 999. Then his hand dropped to his side. He didn't know much about tapping telephone wires, but he didn't believe this gang would leave much to chance. "Mind you tell us of any developments," the Inspector had said. It's your duty, he'd meant, but what did he, Richard, care about duty if Gillian was the penalty for being a good citizen? Let the police catch their own criminals. Wasn't that what they were for?

He walked over to the window and there was the same fellow hanging about at the corner. He marched down the stairs and across the street.

"Who put you on to watching me?" he demanded.

The man turned, staring. Richard felt a pang of misgiving. Was this the same man? He hadn't really seen him properly.

"Watching you?" said the other. "Why? If you think I've got nothing better to do than hang about on your doorstep you should have your head examined."

He threw away the stub of his cigarette, stuck his hands in his pockets and swaggered off. Richard went into the house again and asked the telephone operator if a recent call could be traced. It couldn't, of course, having been made on the automatic exchange. When he put back the instrument Richard stole across and looked out of the window. There wasn't anyone to be seen; he looked again a little later, but there was still no one there. But when he drew the curtains and turned on the light the watcher came out of his hiding-place and resumed his patient vigil.

In a house whose address she didn't know, Gillian lay on her back and stared at the ceiling.

The little room into which they had now moved her was not much larger than a cell and contained very little more furniture. Each day the woman the men called Lena led her down to the bathroom, and she realised vaguely that this must be quite a large house, her prison being on the top floor. She had never seen her bag again, and though they let her have her powder compact, they withheld the lipstick.

"You're not going anywhere, you don't need lipstick," Lena chaffed her.

"Are you afraid I'd write a message on the bathroom wall?" They hadn't broken her spirit yet, though no one could complain they hadn't tried; in that bare little room, so old-fashioned there wasn't even electric light, just a little gas-jet high in the wall and a rusty little iron grate. They didn't give her a fire, only an oil-stove during the day. At night the door was locked on the outside.

Another man had turned up; they called him Pug, and it was he who did the endless questioning.

"Who's Richard?"

"A friend."

"What's his real name?"

"Just Richard."

"Where does he live?"

"In London. Where am I now?"

"I'm asking the questions. Why did you give him Benn's address?"

"I didn't. I couldn't. I don't know it myself."

"Found your way there all right."

"It was an accident. Because of the fog."

Pug laughed. It wasn't a nice sound. "Too bad."

"Why do you keep me here?"

"Why did you muscle in? Now it's too late."

Too late for what? she wanted to say, but she couldn't speak the words. Sometimes she thought she was really going mad. That was what they wanted her to believe, of course.

There was a tiny window in her room, looking over precisely nothing. All she could tell was that the house was isolated; only a few sounds floated up to her, and no one ever went walking along the waste space that was her view. But once she saw a van going past, and she shouted and screamed and pounded on the glass—she couldn't open the window, it was screwed down. The driver didn't hear her, but the others did. They came bursting in and pulled her away and tied her hands and feet; they put a gag in her mouth and threw her on the bed—they didn't worry about being gentle—and while "Dr. Belvedere" pasted dark paper over the glass, the woman told her what to expect if she tried any more tricks.

"You've got a pretty face," she said. "It would be a pity to get it spoiled." She didn't know what day of the week it was, how long she had been there. Two days, three days, a week, a month? Time had stopped like a clock that had run down. At the back of her mind was the realisation that they couldn't keep her here forever, and how would they ever dare let her go, except to a deeper darkness still?

The woman came in, carrying a tray. "Ready for your dinner?" she said. She brought a box of matches with her, and she lighted the gas-jet. "Eat it up and then I'll give you some news."

Gillian looked at her, perplexed. Her fair, pretty hair was lank and uncombed, her face shadowed—she seemed quite old when she saw herself in the glass.

"What day is it?"

"What does that matter to you?"

"How long have I been here?"

"Not long enough to learn sense, it seems. What a silly girl you are, Gillian Hinde. Living in the dark like a troglodyte. Now eat up and you shall see a newspaper."

Panic flared up in her. "What's happened to him?"

"Happened to who?" Lena's face was cunning.

"Richard." The word was a breath of sound.

"Dr. Fyfe? Oh, yes, we know who he is; so do the police."

"The police?" She was falling back into her silly habit of repeating the last words she'd heard.

"That's right. Eat your dinner and I'll tell you."

Gillian gulped down the unpalatable food. She ached with cold and hunger and the pummelling she'd so recently received.

"That's better. Now—that column. That's right."

Poor Mr. Benn hadn't attracted much attention in life, and in death he didn't rate more than a few lines in a side column.

Police are investigating the death of a marine-store dealer known as Hassan Benn, believed to be of Arab descent, who was found with his neck broken at the foot of a flight of stone stairs behind his shop on Christmas Day. This is the second mysterious death in this area during the past month, the other being that of Eric Boxer, whose body was taken out of the St. Julian Dock less than two weeks ago.

Gillian laid the paper aside. "It doesn't say a word about Richard."

"Ah, but he was there. It so happens a friend of ours was passing and he saw a young man breaking into the house by the back, so he rang the police, and when they came your Dr. Fyfe was beside the body. Now do you understand? You told him where to go and he went and he lost his temper and pushed the old man downstairs. That's murder, Gillian Hinde, and murderers hang. We're doing you a favour really, keeping you hidden, because there's something called accessory before the fact…"

Gillian got up, her eyes wild. "It's all lies. Richard…"

"Why don't you ask him yourself?" insinuated the voice. "You could get him on the telephone."

She closed her lips tight. You could be a coward and shiver in the dark, wondering what your tormentors' next step would be, but, even so, you wouldn't betray your dear love.

"Shall I get his number. It's Pleasance 1948, isn't it? He must be quite anxious about you. Such strange things happen to girls who go where they're not invited, especially after dark."

Gillian learned against the blacked-out window; it was another trick, of course. The trouble was that, sooner or later, they'd catch you off your guard and you'd say the fatal word... Her head swam; what was the fatal word? She didn't even know the answer to her own question.

"Come," said the woman, putting an authoritative arm round her shoulders, "lean on me and we'll go downstairs. The telephone's downstairs. What? You won't come? Very well, if you won't talk to him, I will. I'll leave your door open so you can hear. I'm afraid you don't trust us very far, do you?"

She walked out of the room and down the stairs; light came in from the landing. Gillian stole out and leaned over the bannisters. There was the sound of a telephone dial being spun. She held her breath. Then the woman's voice came pealing up the staircase.

"Dr. Fyfe? That is Dr. Fyfe speaking? Hold the line, please. Miss Hinde would like a word with you."

Richard's voice came quite clearly over the line, though she couldn't hear the words.

"Yes, she's just coming. Gillian!"

She was there, staggering, shaking, her hand outstretched to take the receiver. But it was jerked out of her reach. The man called Pug was there; she didn't know where he'd come from.

"Just remember we can hear everything you say," he warned her, "so don't talk out of line. What you're to tell the boy-friend is, first, not to get on to the police about this call, or it'll be the worse for you, and next, that if he's patient and plays along he can come and see you. If he doesn't play, there'll be danger all round. Got that?"

She nodded. He put the receiver into her hand. "Now, no tricks, mind," he said.

"Gillian!" Richard was clamouring at the other end of the line. "Is it you? I can't believe it..."

"Darling. Oh, Richard..." Her voice failed.

On his side, too, there was a moment of incredulous silence. Then: "Where are you?"

I don't know. Lowering her eyes she saw a number written on the instrument. "That is..."

Something touched her side and she glanced down. The man on the other end of the line heard the long, swift breath she drew.

"Gillie, what is it? What are they doing to you? Gillie!"

She was still staring at the knife. Even now it didn't seem possible it might be driven into your ribs while you stood beside a table, a telephone in your hand. But an inward voice told her not to be silly. Say one word off the record and the knife would move.

"I still can't believe this is us. Richard, I've got a message. Listen carefully. *Don't*—repeat, don't—try and get in touch with the police about this. Come and see me when you get the chance—did you get that? If you don't do what I say, you'll be in great danger—no, I'm not being melodramatic, it's true." Her voice jerked unevenly up and down, giving an odd emphasis to this word and that.

"Gillie, how are they treating you?"

"I'm all right. Richard, don't do anything rash—Darling, I love you. Never forget. I love you, love you..."

The receiver was abruptly twisted out of her hand. "Get that, Dr. Fyfe? If you know what's good for Miss Hinde you'll do like she says. Hang around and I'll ring you again presently and name a rendezvous. And if you're wise you'll come fast."

"Make it now." His words sounded as though they'd been dragged over emery-paper.

"What do you take me for? I'll ring when I'm sure you're not double-crossing me. And don't think we shouldn't know. Of course, if you think it's your duty to get on to that Inspector... How good a citizen are you, Doctor?"

A laugh accompanied the last words.

Richard's voice came through again. "When will you ring?"

"Oh, maybe this afternoon, maybe in an hour. You stand by." He hung up the receiver and turned, grinning, to the shaken girl.

"Don't do anything rash," he gibed. "But he'll come, sweetheart; he'll come. You see, we shall make him understand what might happen to you if he didn't. But I don't think I'll ask you to be present when we ring him next time. To tell you the truth, you cramp my style. Those big, sad eyes of yours—I shall burst out crying soon, really I shall."

When he'd rung off, Richard began walking up and down the room like a man practising for a marathon. Up and down, over and across, up and down... His landlady, Mrs. Lloyd, who occupied the room below, stood it as long as she could and then, when even banging on the ceiling with the handle of a broom made no difference, she decided to come up and find out for herself what was wrong.

Richard hadn't even heard the bumping of the stick. He seemed enmeshed in a nightmare, where your dear love could speak to you and you not have an idea where she was or who were her companions. Her voice, he thought—that had been strange, staccato—perhaps they were using force. He began to repeat her words—Don't tell the police—come and see me—great danger… Light flashed into his darkened mind. Of course, she was using the words as a kind of code. Don't come—great danger—that was what she meant. But danger for whom? For her? Him? For them both, of course, since you couldn't separate them now. Up and down, up and… He was aware of someone banging on the door and when he opened it, there stood Mrs. Lloyd.

"Really, Dr. Fyfe," she said, "if I'd wanted to live in the Lion House I'd have applied for a basement flat in the Zoo."

He stared, not taking anything in, except that she was there and seemed put out about something. She saw that *distrait* look and her manner changed. She could recognise trouble, and young Dr. Fyfe was one of her favourites. A polite, pleasant young man, not given to knocking the furniture about.

"What is it? Something's wrong. Have you had bad news?"

He was thinking fast now. He'd been brooding—what next? Ring the police? Too dangerous. They might have his line tapped; similarly, he shrank from telephoning to Arthur Crook. It wouldn't help anyone for him to wake up in hospital and a gang that didn't draw the line at pitching an old man downstairs and abducting a girl, wouldn't make a thing about hitting Crook over the head. And even Crook, though you'd never get him to say so, was only mortal. But here was a straw at which to grasp, though plump Mrs. Lloyd wouldn't have suggested a straw to most people.

In reply to her question, he said: "Yes. Bad news. That is—I'm waiting for a telephone call. Mrs. Lloyd, you're right. I am in trouble. I need a friend. I know I can trust you…"

Her heart warmed to him; he was like the son she'd never had.

"What is it, then?" she asked, her voice softening. "If I can help…"

"I can't tell you," he said jerkily, "but—if I got in a jam would you ring this number?"

He hauled Crook's card out of his pocket.

"My lawyer," he added quickly. Then he tried to laugh. "I may be riding ahead of the hounds, but—just in case. You understand?"

She understood this was Trouble with a capital T, but she took the card, saying: "I'll do that, Dr. Fyfe. Lawyer?" She glanced down. "That's a funny name for a lawyer to have."

"He's funny sort of lawyer," said Richard. And then the telephone rang and he went quickly back to the room.

But it was only a wrong number. He hung up and looked out of the window. The watchdog was still there. Oh, well—Patience be our watchword, as the old hymn said. He started to prowl again, then remembered Mrs. Lloyd and flung himself down by the telephone. His hands were shaking—like an old drunk, he thought. He picked up a pencil and began to doodle—a cat, the only animal he could draw really, seen in profile, sharp nose, long whiskers, a bow round its neck, and its tail curled neatly round its feet. He hesitated, then added a bell to the bow. He listened; nothing happened, it might be a dead world. It was a Sunday and his off-duty day; everyone seemed asleep or queueing for the pictures. There wasn't much else to do in London on a Sunday. He took up the pencil again and drew a tree and a bird in the tree. What would psychologists make of that? An instinctive expression of danger? But, again—to whom? To the bird? It was safe so long as it stayed in the tree, or until the cat started to climb. Well, if he was the bird, he was going to fly out of the tree the minute he saw the green light.

He looked out of the window once more. Was his shadow still there? You bet. And then he stiffened, rigid, eyes widening. Because he saw the car coming down the street, the long black car with the radio rod and the man in uniform at the wheel. You can't mistake a police car. Still, it had a right to come down the road, hadn't it? Nothing to show it was coming here. It 'ud go right past... The car slowed and stopped at the gate. A man got out, plain-clothes, but that's what you'd expect. He pushed open the gate and walked up the path.

When the knock fell on his door Richard was doodling again.

"Come in! Yes, Mrs. Lloyd?" Had he got the right note of surprise in his voice? And then he saw that didn't matter, saw she was remembering their conversation and thought this was what he meant. Trouble with the police! He didn't know how to correct that impression; assure her it wasn't the police he feared...

The plain-clothes man had come up behind her. It wasn't the Inspector, which proved it wasn't just a casual visit to verify a detail or put a couple of additional questions. Anyway, for that they wouldn't come in a car. Mrs. Lloyd came into the room, her hands clasped in front of her; he saw the broad gold wedding-ring she wore...

"Oh, Dr. Fyfe, someone from the police—he would come up."

"May I come in?"

Richard smiled faintly. "Can I prevent you?"

"We can't come into a private house without being invited. You should know your rights, Dr. Fyfe. Not unless we have a warrant, that is."

"And you haven't? Come in, of course. It's all right, Mrs. Lloyd, I'm assisting the police about an inquest. That's so, isn't it?" he added, as the woman slowly retreated.

"That's so, sir. The Inspector 'ud be glad if you could come along to the station..." The newcomer drew off his gloves and stood there, calm and immovable. The sun came out suddenly, just as though there was something to be triumphant about. It caught the chromium fittings of a great blue and silver car going past the window, driven by a girl who looked as though she'd walked straight out of Hollywood, shone on a bit of glass held over his head by a small boy, caught the light on a broad, handsome ring, on the plump side of a china jug on his own mantelshelf.

"Well, not right away, I'm afraid," said Richard pleasantly. "I'm expecting a telephone call. I'll be along later."

"I'm sorry, sir. About your call, I mean…"

"Look here," exploded Richard, "what are you afraid of? That I shall make a bolt for it? I wouldn't have a hope in hell, not with your watchdog on the corner there?"

"Our what?" The man's voice rose, startled.

"Oh, come, that's enough of play-acting. You mustn't think I'm a fool all along the line. I promise you, as soon as my call comes through…" Airily he picked up the pencil and doodled a bit more. Keep your head, keep calm. He wasn't as good at drawing dogs as cats; this might have passed for a pig at a pinch. His companion crossed to the window.

"I can assure you we haven't had you followed. Why should we?" He turned, his voice suspicious. "What does this mean, Dr. Fyfe? There's no one there."

"Well, there was when you arrived." He rose in his turn and came to the window; the street was empty of everything except the big black car—a *Panther*, trust the police to have the best—and the driver sitting immovable at the wheel. "No," he agreed, gently, "he's gone now. And do you know where? I'd be prepared to bet he's in the nearest telephone box, informing his boss of your arrival. Why on earth did you have to come this afternoon? Couldn't you have telephoned?"

"This is a case of murder, Dr. Fyfe. We're concerned..."

"I'm concerned it shan't be another murder." He heard his voice rise, clenched his hands and went back to his chair. "If you're interested, I'm not particularly concerned with who killed that poor devil, Benn. That's for the police to discover." His pencil moved wildly over the paper. If you're sketching, no one can notice how unsteady your hand is. And Gillian was depending on him, having no one else. He drew a car and a driver, as if nothing else in the world really mattered.

"Quite so, Dr. Fyfe. The police are your best friends, if only you'd recognise it. And they're far more likely to find Miss Hinde than any amateur."

He smothered a savage laugh. "Is that so?"

"If you're holding out on us..."

He threw down the pencil and got up. "All right," he said, "all right. Let's go." He caught sight of the man's face. "Is there something fresh? Good Heavens, you don't mean—Miss Hinde?"

"I can't say anything, Dr. Fyfe, but if you're really concerned for the young lady you'll come with me without any more delay."

Mrs. Lloyd was waiting in the hall and saw them come down; she caught Richard's eye.

"If you should hear my telephone, Mrs. Lloyd, I'd be awfully obliged if you'd take the call. I'm expecting some important news. You needn't say where I am—just that I've been called out. I don't expect to be long."

"Don't you, indeed?" reflected Mrs. Lloyd, watching the black car drive away. She knew a good deal about the police, and in her experience they always meant trouble. She wondered about the card in her pocket. And that bit about the telephone call—was that genuine or meant to be a hint? She did a bit of prowling herself, before she made up her mind, and took the receiver off Richard's telephone. But when she rang the Bloomsbury number there was no reply. It was quite a while before she noticed the second number on the card—what Crook called his emergency number, and tried that.

And this time she was more fortunate.

The black car rolled smoothly through the streets; there wasn't much traffic and what there was made way for the police.

"Step on it, Fred," said Richard's companion. "Dr. Fyfe can't wait to meet his young lady. Isn't that so, Dr. Fyfe?"

He stuffed his gloves into the pocket of his overcoat. The sun came through the window and shone on a handsome ring he was wearing. Crook's voice sounded in Richard's ear. "As smooth a Charley as ever I saw," he said. "Wearing a sizeable ring, too. Funny, I never could take to chaps who wear rings."

And, of course, policemen don't wear rings, not when they're on duty.

"Cat got your tongue?" The man beside him laughed.

"I was thinking," said Richard, "that Chesterton was right. You don't look for a hamadryad in a sideboard. And, of course, when you see a police car and a man in uniform, you expect it to be the police."

"That was the idea."

"It's a very good imitation." His eyes were watching the road; in a minute they'd be held up by lights. There were a few people going up and down the pavement...

"You can thank Fred for that. Fred wore a police uniform once, but—the life didn't offer enough scope, did it, Fred? Dr. Fyfe," his voice changed, "you weren't thinking of trying anything, were you? If so, I wouldn't advise it, really I wouldn't. You see, we're on a time schedule. If we don't make our destination the time I told them, I've left instructions—what's to happen to Miss Hinde, I mean."

You might have guessed—they thought of everything. The car stopped as the lights turned red, but Richard made no move. Then they flashed amber, then green; the big car ran onward. They were travelling north, past Hampstead, Highgate—now they'd turned into quite a countrified road, considering you weren't so very far from Piccadilly Circus, that is. The car stopped in front of a fair-sized house with big double gates, Fred got down to open them and they moved up the drive.

Then Fred had opened the door of the car and Charley (if that was his name) told Richard to get out. The door of the house was opened by a nice-looking woman, not unlike Ma Lloyd really, except that she was a lot better dressed and spoke rather differently. Freshly-waved hair, well-kept hands, manner almost cosy.

"We're waiting for you," she said, reminding Richard of the way nurses on a private case sometimes greet a doctor. "We're getting quite impatient."

A man standing at the head of the staircase called, "Got the Doctor there. Bring him up."

Richard stood defiantly, looking around him. Someone—it was Charley—jabbed him in the back, with something hard and small and round. The sense of nightmare was intensified, and for a moment he was back in a dark house, looking at something that resembled an old sack lying at the foot of a stone staircase.

"Get moving," said Charley, all the smoothness gone from his voice. He went up, Pug going ahead. They passed a number of closed doors; there wasn't a sound to be heard from behind any of them. At the top the attic floor, Pug flung open what looked like a cupboard; anyway, it was quite dark inside.

"In here," he said.

"Where's Gillian?" Richard demanded.

"You'll find out. Go on, get in."

He knew then what he was going to find. "You'd like to see Miss Hinde, wouldn't you?" they'd jeered. And, like a fool, it hadn't occurred to him there was no promise he was going to see her alive. He swung round in a wild rage and struck out at the man behind him. Pug plunged forward and caught his arms.

"That'll do. You've given us enough trouble as it is."

He felt a foot in the small of his back and staggered forward, crashing into the dark. Behind him someone laughed.

"Give him a box of matches," said Pug. "They may come in useful. Sorry there's no light," he added. "But you know what these old-fashioned houses are."

Then the door slammed, he heard a key turn in the lock, and a mutter of voices, and again someone laughed. This time it was the woman.

The only difference Sunday made to Crook was that, instead of working in Bloomsbury, he worked in Earls Court. He was hard at it when Mrs. Lloyd got through on the telephone.

"Crook here. Who's speaking? Who? Dr. Fyfe? An inquest? Didn't say whose, I suppose? Well, well, there's one born every minute as they say."

Something that had been perplexing Mrs. Lloyd fell into place. Helping about an inquest, Richard had said, and at the time she'd thought it queer. Now she knew why. Coroners don't hold inquests on Sundays.

"It was a police car," she exclaimed, defensively.

"That's what you think. Chap didn't happen to say what station he'd come from? No, I didn't suppose he had. Lucky for the Doctor, it you ask me, if the inquest doesn't turn out to be his own. Now, now, this is no time for waterworks. Be at home if I drop around? O.K."

He depressed the bar of the telephone and dialled a number. Whatever some of his legal colleagues might think of his methods, he had the supreme virtue, from a client's point of view, of having a friend at every court, even the police court. And so it didn't take him long to learn that no police car had been sent out that afternoon to fetch Richard Fyfe in.

"Don't know what they teach 'em at these posh schools," grumbled Crook ringing up Bill Parsons to let him know how the land lay. "If they wanted him down at the station they wouldn't send a car, not unless he's lost the use of his legs and then it 'ud be an ambulance. Amateurs!"

He made a snorting sound and rushed down the stairs to where the "Superb" was parked round a corner. Mrs. Lloyd had a second shock when she saw him. She cherished the quaint idea that there's something—well—refined—about the legal profession. Anyway, lawyers shouldn't go round looking like bookies' touts. She began to babble something.

"Keep it for your memoirs," urged Crook, pushing past her. "Now, then, happen to notice what this chap looked like?"

"Just like anyone else," she said, feebly, "Oh, dear! It's a pity Dr. Fyfe didn't draw a picture of him instead of the car."

"What's that?" Crook's big brown eyes bulged out of their sockets. "Drew a car?"

"You know how people do, when they're thinking or waiting for someone to come to the 'phone. It was a cat to start with."

"The car?" asked Crook politely, reflecting that where patience was concerned he could beat Job on his own ground.

"Ever so good it was. I mean, you could see at once it was a cat."

"Could you see the other was a car?"

"Oh, yes. Man at the wheel and all."

He coaxed her up the stairs to Richard's room and stood staring at the cat and the dicky-bird and something that, he allowed, might be a dog and something else that quite clearly was a car.

He turned to Mrs. Lloyd as he took the receiver from its rest.

"It could be I got the labels mixed," he told her. "Maybe the dumbcluck this time isn't Dr. Richard Fyfe but a guy called Arthur Crook. Anyway, here's hoping."

Then he got his connection and started talking as rapidly as the waters come down at Lodore. Mrs. Lloyd stood listening and not understanding a word, except that the man she'd taken for a bookie was laying down the law—and how! as Crook himself would have said. When at last he hung up he turned with a smile as endearing as a baby alligator's.

"O.K. by you if I hang around for a while?" he asked. "I'm expecting a car, and this time it'll be the real McCoy."

As Richard pulled himself painfully to his feet a voice he'd never expected to hear again whispered out of the dark. "Richard! Darling, why did you come? I warned you—I warned you—"

"Gillie!" His heart almost stopped beating with excitement. "Where are you? Wait a minute—I've got a torch somewhere."

He pressed the button and a ribbon of light played over the walls of their mutual prison, the prison destined to be their tomb.

"I'm all right. It's just—I can't move."

He saw why, saw the cords round ankles and wrists and plunged forward.

"What have they done to you? My God, I'll have them all strung up for this!"

This was so like the impetuous Richard she loved that she even contrived a laugh. Even death didn't seem so bad with Richard beside her, and she was pretty sure death was their invisible playmate here. Now he was on his knees beside her, tearing at the knots; but it was only when he remembered the penknife in his pocket that he was able to set her free. Funny, he thought, they should have left the knife. It must mean that they were very sure…

"What's that?" he asked, throwing up his head.

Feet were moving across the little landing, going quietly down the stairs.

"Enjoy yourselves, turtle doves!" called a mocking voice. "Make the most of your time together. It won't be long now."

Richard played the beam over the enclosing walls. It was clear that this place had been designed for a box room, a luggage-dump; the walls sloped sharply to meet the floor not twelve feet away; there was no window, no skylight. You couldn't even get much impetus to smash down the door, since there was so little space in which a tall man could stand upright. Still, he thudded and crashed, and the voice, sounding a little farther off now, warned him, "Waste of energy, I assure you. Even if you broke the lock you'll never get past the bolts. Take my tip—take it easy. Remember, the sooner it's over, the sooner to sleep, and you've a nice long sleep ahead."

"What do you suppose they mean to do?" whispered Gillian. "Leave us here—to starve?"

"They won't need to do that. There can't be much air here at the best of times, and now they've blocked the door—I dare say they've put a rug over the crack—yes, I thought as much. We shall be suffocated if we don't get out before long."

"How long?"

"Hard to say. Of course, they may have some other idea in mind."

And, of course, they had.

It was Richard who first noticed the change in the atmosphere; he lifted his head, he sniffed, then he said gently, "Here we go. Gas—seeping in from somewhere."

He flashed his torch again round the walls; but there was no bracket here, no fireplace…

"It's all gas on this floor," explained Gillian. "Mrs. Harton told me."

"Easy as kiss your hand. Make a little hole in the wall, attach a bit of rubber tubing to the nearest gas-jet, turn on the tap—that's what that chap was doing in the room next door—and you can't lose. Or can you? Gillie, we're not going to die here like a couple of rats or rabbits! First thing, let's find out where it's coming from."

A faint hiss guided them to the leak, which was high up in the wall.

"They think of everything, don't they?" said Richard. "There's a bit of piping there—look. Wonder how firm it is."

"You mean, try and knock it out? But that wouldn't help."

"I was wondering if it was firm enough to hold on to. Gillie, *repeat*, we're not going to wait here and be gassed like rats in a hole."

"That's why they gave us the matches!" exclaimed Gillian. "They hoped we should strike one…"

"And blow the place sky-high? You can't say they aren't triers. Gillie, how are you feeling? Do you think if I made a back, you could climb up and stand on my shoulders? You might be able to get a grip on that pipe—thank goodness it's near the corner, so you can get some support from the walls—if we can plug it—a handkerchief would do the trick. And you could wedge it with my propelling pencil. We've got to stop that gas somehow. It's our only chance. Gillie, are you game? Darling!"

He felt it was a shocking thing to ask of her, with her bruised ankles and wrists, and he was preparing arguments and endearments to persuade her, when she surprised him by saying, "Yes, Richard if you say so."

"Darling, what a wife you're going to be. Look, make up your mind, this isn't the end. I believe in miracles…"

Ah, but his miracle's name was Crook, and how could he be sure that Mrs. Lloyd had got in touch? At the time he'd wanted to warn her this wasn't the sort of occasion he'd meant, until he saw the chap's ring, that is. Oh, yes, he'd known he was walking into a trap before ever he left the house, but he'd do the same again, even if he knew this prison was the end of it. There'd been no other way of finding Gillian…

He stooped and made a back, and she climbed up. It was going to be tricky, of course. If she lost her balance in the dark it might be the end for them both. Slowly he straightened up.

"Put your feet in my hands. It's all right, you don't weigh more than a good-sized cat. Now, one foot on my shoulder—lean against the wall…"

It didn't seem possible that she could do it, but she did. Swaying, sick, half-checked by the gas and the darkness and the bad air, she nevertheless reached down for the handkerchief he passed to her—a second clean one was tied round her mouth—and now he released one hand—the other held her firmly round the ankle—and the beam of the torch swung, wavered and lighted on the treacherous bit of pipe.

"Put your head down, darling. That's it. Stuff the handkerchief as far up the pipe as you can."

She wondered dizzily—what will happen? Won't the pipe explode? But Richard was there, and everything must be all right now.

Suddenly she felt herself begin to crumble. "Richard, hold me—I—"

"O.K., sweetheart. I've got you." The torch went back in his pocket; now he had her by both ankles. "Stoop—give me your hands…"

She was coughing helplessly when at last he got her down and held her close in his arms.

"It wasn't any use," she whispered. "And gas would have been quicker."

"Come and lie down by the door. A little air may seep under the rug. They won't think we could plug that pipe."

She lay in his arms, shivering as if she'd never stop, while he comforted her. He didn't say much; they needed all the air there was. But—"I believe in miracles," he repeated.

Only—the miracle would have to come pretty soon if it was to save them.

Charley was making a nice job of re-spraying the *Panther* a tasteful claret-colour, while Fred removed the number-plates—when Mrs. Harton, sitting in the bow-window of the dining-room, saw the first of the police cars come hurrying up the drive.

"Philip!" She turned her head and Pug Mayhew came in. When he saw the car, he said, "Stall 'em, Lena," and tore out to the garage.

"How's she coming? Get away from here. It's the rozzers."

Charley didn't believe him at first. "You're kidding."

"Look out of the window and see if I'm kidding. Lock the door and…" He didn't stop to finish; he'd be wanted in the house.

Lena hadn't turned a hair; she was the toughest of them all.

"Philip," she said, "the police are asking about a Dr. Fyfe. I've told them he doesn't live here…"

"Come to the wrong address," grinned Pug.

"And a Miss—what was the name?—Hinde?"

"Try the Gables down the Avenue. I believe I have heard the name…"

"I believe you have a *Panther*, number ABV 190," the policeman continued, turning to Lena.

"I'm afraid she's up for repairs at the moment."

There was a commotion in the drive and an apparition whirled in who might have been a clown on his day off.

"Such as re-painting?" said Mr. Crook, his hat over one eye and a startled and utterly bewildered Mrs. Lloyd held by one hand. He came forward. "What's that on your coat? Red paint? Careless, very. Come on, sugar. You and me ain't nationalised yet. Leave the red tape to the Civil Service."

He thrust past Mayhew, who made a sharp move to stop him. Crook stuck out a foot as hard as the Rock of Gibraltar and Pug came down with a crash. Crook went storming up the stairs, and Mrs. Lloyd scuttled after him.

"They're here somewhere," said Crook. "Upstairs or downstairs or—no, sugar, they won't be in any room with the door open. Ah, what did I tell you?"

Panting like a grampus he had reached the foot of the last flight of stairs. "See that rug shoved against a door. That's our bit of trouble." He shoved his big, red head over the bannisters: "What the blazes do you chaps think you are? The Big Four? Send some of your thugs up to smash a door. Better bring a hatchet—Black Beauty'll tell you where it is, and if he don't remember, just drop a weight on his feet till he does. That always fetches 'em. And mind," he added, "if you lose either of these I'll charge the lot of you with manslaughter and see the jury brings in a true bill at that."

"It was quite a party," admitted Crook a while later. He was talking to the newly-rescued pair who, while not looking their best, certainly weren't candidates for the mortuary as Pug Mayhew had intended. "Once I saw the Doctor had had the wit to put the number of the car on that sketch he made—right under Smart Charley's nose—the wheels went round faster than the 'Old Superb,' and that's saying something. The police put out a general call for a black *Panther*, number XXX 1278, and they checked the registration. It appears that should have been the number of a *Mortimer* 8 belonging to a fellow called Smith, but Smith's car, which was in his garage, had got a new number—ABV 190. It's an old gag, of course, swapping number-plates, and they must have thought it pretty safe. Who ever notices the number of a police car? You'd tumbled to him by then, I take it?" he added to Richard.

Richard nodded. "The ring gave him away. It's the little things…"

"O.K., buddy. Let's skip the lecture. Well, ABV 190 was the registration number of a black *Panther* belonging to a Mrs. Harton, address as you'd expect. Mrs. Lloyd recognised Charley when they pulled him out of the garage and the police found his finger-prints in your room. It never pays to under-rate the other side," wound up Crook, blissfully arrogant. "'Twasn't as though you hadn't told them I was in on this. Still, we're all good citizens and like to give the police a hand when we can, don't we?"

He got up and held out a huge hand to Gillian. "Still a bit peaky," he suggested. "Know what I'd suggest—speaking as a layman, of course? A bit of medical attention. And the Doctor here," he gave Richard a nudge that nearly broke a rib, "is just the chap to give it you."

And humming gaily, "She's the girl for me," he came rushing down and was reunited to the "Old Superb."

FATHER CHRISTMAS COMES TO ORBINS

Julian Symons

Julian Symons (1912–1994) began his literary career in the 1930s as a left-wing poet and editor of a magazine of twentieth-century verse, and ended it as a doyen of detective fiction. He wrote biographies and books about history as well as a great deal of literary criticism, often (but not exclusively) in the field of crime writing. His study of the genre's history, *Bloody Murder* aka *Mortal Consequences* appeared in three editions over the course of twenty years and proved highly influential. As a crime writer, he won "best novel of the year" awards in both the UK and the US—for different books. *The Colour of Murder*, *The Belting Inheritance*, and *The Progress of a Crime* have all been republished as British Library Crime Classics and illustrate his range as a novelist.

Symons' short fiction falls into two distinct categories. As a critic, he is often regarded as a scourge of traditional detection and as a powerful advocate for the post-war story of psychological suspense, and most of his later short stories are examples of suspense fiction. It tends to be overlooked that he also wrote a considerable number of detective stories in the classic vein, many of them featuring the private investigator Francis Quarles. These stories, written as commercial exercises, often boast neat and entertaining twists. "Father Christmas Comes to Orbins" first appeared in the 1963 "Christmas Number" of the *Illustrated London News*.

"A BEAUTIFUL MORNING, MISS OLIPHANT. I SHALL TAKE A short constitutional."

"Very well, Mr. Payne."

Mr. Rossiter Payne put on his good thick Melton overcoat, took his bowler hat off its peg, brushed it carefully, put it on. He looked at himself in a small glass and nodded approvingly at what he saw. He was a man in his early fifties, but he might have passed for ten years less, so square were his shoulders, so ruler-straight his back. Two fine wings of grey hair showed under the hat. He looked like a retired Guards officer, although he had in fact no closer relationship with the Army than an uncle who had been cashiered.

At the door he paused, eyes twinkling. "Don't let anybody steal the stock while I'm out, Miss Oliphant."

Miss Oliphant, a thin spinster of indeterminate middle age, blushed. She adored Mr. Payne.

He had removed his hat to speak to her. Now he clapped it on his head again, cast an appreciative look at the bow window of his shop, which showed several sets of standard authors with the discreet legend above: *Rossiter Payne, Bookseller. Specialist in First Editions*, and made his way up New Bond Street towards Oxford Street.

At the top of New Bond Street he stopped, as he did five days a week, at the stall on the corner. The old woman put the carnation into his buttonhole.

"Fourteen shopping days to Christmas now, Mrs. Shankly. We've all got to think about it, haven't we?"

A ten-shilling note changed hands instead of the usual half-crown. He left her blessing him confusedly.

This was perfect December weather, crisply cold, the sun shining. Oxford Street was wearing its decorations, enormous gold and silver coins from which depended various precious stones, ropes of pearls, diamonds, rubies, emeralds. When lighted up in the afternoon they looked pretty, although for Mr. Payne's refined taste a little garish. But still, they had a certain symbolic feeling about them, and he smiled at them. Nothing, indeed, could disturb his good temper this morning, not the jostling crowds on the pavements nor the customary traffic jams which seemed, indeed, to please him. He walked along until he came to a large store that said above it, in enormous letters, ORBINS. These letters were picked out in coloured lights, and the lights themselves were festooned with Christmas trees and crackers, and figures of the Seven Dwarfs, all of which lighted up.

Orbins' block went right round the corner into the comparatively quiet Jessiter Street. Now again Mr. Payne went through a customary ceremony. He crossed the road and went down several steps into an establishment unique of its kind, Danny's Shoe Parlour. Here, sitting upon a kind of throne in this semi-basement, one saw through a small window the lower halves of passers-by. Here Danny, with two assistants almost as old as himself, had been shining shoes for almost thirty years. Leather-faced, immensely lined but still remarkably sharp-eyed, he knelt down now in front of Mr. Payne, turned up the cuffs of his trousers, and began to put an altogether superior shine on already well-polished shoes.

"Lovely morning, Mr. Payne."

"You can't see much of it from there."

"More than you think. You see the pavements, they're not spotted; all right, you know it isn't raining. Then there's something in the

way people walk, you know what I mean, it's Christmas in the air."
Mr. Payne laughed indulgently. Now Danny was mildly reproach-
ful. "You still haven't brought me in that pair of black shoes, sir."

Mr. Payne frowned slightly. A week ago he had been almost
knocked down by a bicyclist, and the mudguard of the bicycle had
scraped badly one of the shoes he was wearing, cutting the leather
at one point. Danny was confident that he could repair the cut so
that it wouldn't show. Mr. Payne was not so sure.

"I'll bring them along," he said vaguely.

"Sooner the better, Mr. Payne, sooner the better."

Mr. Payne did not like being reminded of the bicycle incident.
He gave Danny half-a-crown instead of the ten shillings he had
intended, crossed the road again, and walked into the side entrance
of Orbins, which called itself unequivocally, "London's Greatest
Department Store."

This end of the store was quiet. He walked up the stairs, past
grocery on the ground floor and wine and cigars on the first, to jewellery on the second. There were rarely many people in this department, but today a small crowd had gathered around a man who
was making a speech. A placard at the department entrance said:
"The Russian Royal Family Jewels. On display for two weeks in the
Jewellery Department by kind permission of the Grand-Duke and
Grand-Duchess of Moldo-Lithuania." These were not the Russian
Crown Jewels; seized by the Bolsheviks during the Revolution, but
an inferior collection brought out of Russia by the Grand-Duke and
Grand-Duchess, who had long since become plain Mr. and Mrs.
Skandorski, lived in New Jersey, and were on a visit to England.

Mr. Payne was not interested in Mr. and Mrs. Skandorski, nor
in Sir Henry Orbin who was stumbling through a short speech,
but in the jewels. When the speech was over he mingled with the

crowd round the showcase that stood almost in the middle of the room. They lay on beds of velvet, a tiara that looked too heavy to be worn, diamond necklaces and bracelets, a cluster of diamonds and emeralds, a dozen other pieces, each with an elegant calligraphic description of its origin and history. Mr. Payne did not see the jewels as a romantic relic of the past, nor did he permit himself to think of them as things of beauty. He saw them as his Christmas present.

He walked out of the department, looking neither to left nor right, and certainly paying no attention to the spotty young assistant who rushed forward to open the door for him. He walked back to his shop, sniffing that sharp December air, made a little joke to Miss Oliphant, and told her she could go out to lunch. In her lunch hour he sold an American a set of a Victorian magazine called *The Jewel Box*. It seemed a good augury.

In the past ten years Mr. Payne had carried through successfully—with the help of other inferior intellects—six jewel robberies. He had remained undetected, he believed, partly because of his skill in planning, partly because he ran a perfectly legitimate book business, and broke the law only when he needed money. He had little interest in women and his habits were generally ascetic, but he had one vice. He had developed a system at roulette, an improvement on the almost infallible Frank-Konig system, and every year he went to Monte Carlo and played this system. Almost every year it failed—or rather, it revealed certain imperfections which he tried to eradicate. It was to support the system that Mr. Payne had turned from bookselling to crime. He believed himself to be, in a quiet way, a master mind in the criminal world.

Those associated with him were far from that, as he would immediately have acknowledged. He met them two evenings after he had looked at the jewels, in his pleasant little flat above the shop, which could be approached from a side entrance opening into an alley. There was Stacey, who looked what he was, a thick-nosed thug, there was a thin young man in a tight suit whose name was Jack Line, and who was always called Straight Line, and there was Lester Jones, the spotty assistant in the Jewellery Department.

Stacey and Straight Line sat drinking whisky, Mr. Payne sipped some excellent sherry, and Lester drank nothing at all, while Mr. Payne in his pedantic, almost schoolmasterly manner, told them how the job was to be done.

"You all know what the job is, but let me tell you how much it is worth. In its present form the collection is worth whatever sum you like to mention, a quarter of a million pounds perhaps. There is no real market value. But alas, it will have to be cut up. My friend thinks the value will be in the region of fifty thousand pounds. Not less, and not much more."

"Your friend?" the shop assistant said timidly.

"The fence. Lambie, isn't it?" It was Stacey who spoke. Mr. Payne nodded. "How do we split?"

"I will come to that later. Now, here are the difficulties. First of all, there are two store detectives on each floor. We must see to it that those on the second floor are not in the Jewellery Department. Next, there is a man named Davidson, an American, whose job it is to keep an eye on the jewels. He has been brought over here by a protection agency, and it is likely that he will carry a gun. Third, the jewels are in a showcase, and any attempt to open this showcase other than with the proper key will set off an alarm. The key is kept in the manager's office, inside the department."

Stacey got up, shambled over to the whisky decanter, poured himself another drink. "Where do you get all this from?"

Mr. Payne permitted himself a small smile. "Lester works in the department. Lester is a friend of mine."

Stacey looked at Lester with contempt. He did not like amateurs.

"Let me continue, and tell you how the obstacles can be overcome. First, the store detectives. Supposing that a small fire bomb were planted in the Fur Department, at the other end of the second floor from Jewellery, that would certainly occupy one detective for a few minutes. Supposing that in the department that deals with ladies' hats and coats, which is next to Furs, a woman shopper complained that she had been robbed, this would involve the other store detective. Could you arrange this, Stace? These—assistants, shall I call them?—would be paid a straight fee. They would have to carry out these diversions at a precise time, which I have fixed as ten-thirty in the morning."

"Okay," said Stacey. Straight Line moved a toothpick around in his mouth, looking bored.

"Next, Davidson. He is an American, as I said, and Lester tells me that a happy event is expected at any time in his family. He has left Mrs. Davidson behind in America, of course. Now, supposing that a call came through from the hospital for Mr. Davidson. Supposing that the telephone in the Jewellery Department was out of order because the flex had been cut. Davidson would be called out of the department for the few minutes, no more, that we should need."

"Who cuts the flex?" Stacey asked.

"That will be part of Lester's job."

"And who makes the 'phone call?"

"Again, Stace, I hoped that you might be able to provide—"

"I can do that." Stacey drained his whisky. "What do you do?"

Mr. Payne's lips, never full, were compressed to a disapproving line. He answered the implied criticism only by inviting them to look at two plans, one of the layout of the second floor, the other of the Jewellery Department. Stacey and Straight were impressed, as the uneducated always are, by such evidence of planning.

"The Jewellery Department is at one end of the second floor. It has only one exit, into the Carpet Department. There is a service lift, which comes straight up into the Jewellery Department. You and I, Stace, will be in that. We shall have stopped it between floors with the emergency stop button. At exactly ten-thirty-two we shall go up to the second floor. Lester will give us a sign. If everything has gone well, we continue. If not, we call the job off. Now, what I propose…"

He told them, they listened and found it good. Even the ignorant, Mr. Payne was glad to see, could recognise genius. He told Straight his role.

"We must have a car, Straight, and a driver. What he has to do is simple, but he must stay cool. So I thought of you." Straight grinned, took out the toothpick.

"In Jessiter Street, just outside the side entrance to Orbins, there is a parking space reserved for Orbins' customers. It is hardly ever full. But if it is full you can double park there for five minutes—cars often do that. I take it you can—acquire a car, shall I say?—for the purpose. You will face away from Oxford Street, and you will have no more than a few minutes' driving to Lambie's house in Greenly Street. You will drop Stace and I, drive on a mile or two, and leave the car. We shall give the stuff to Lambie. He will pay on the nail. Then we split."

From that point they went on to argue about the split. The argument was warm, but not really heated. They settled that Stacey would get twenty-five per cent. of the total, Straight and Lester twelve-and-a-half per cent. each, and that half would go to the master mind.

Mr. Payne agreed to provide out of his share the hundred and fifty pounds that Stacey said would cover the several diversions. The job was fixed six days ahead, for Tuesday of the following week.

Stacey had two faults which had prevented him from rising high in his profession. One was that he drank too much, the other that he was stupid. He made an effort to keep his drinking under control, knowing that when he drank he talked. He did not even tell his wife about the job, although she was safe enough. But he could not resist cheating about the money, which Payne had unwisely given to him in full.

The fire bomb was easy. Stacey got hold of a little man named Shrimp Bateson, and fixed it with him. There was no obvious risk, and Shrimp thought himself well paid with twenty-five quid. The bomb itself cost a fiver, from a friend who dealt in hardware. It was guaranteed to cause just a little fire, nothing too serious.

For the telephone call Stacey used a Canadian who was grubbing a living at a striptease club. It didn't seem to either of them that the job was worth more than a tenner, but the Canadian asked for twenty and got fifteen.

The woman was a different matter, for she had to be a bit of an actress, and she might be in for trouble, since she actually had to cause a disturbance herself. Stacey hired an eighteen-stone Irish woman named Lucy O'Malley, who had once been a female wrestler, and had very little in the way of a record, nothing more than a couple of drunk and disorderlies. She refused to take anything less than fifty pounds, realising, as the others hadn't, that Stacey must have something big on.

The whole lot came to less than a hundred pounds, so that there was cash to spare. Stacey paid them all half their money in advance, put the rest of the hundred pounds aside, and went on a roaring drunk for a couple of days, during which he managed to keep his mouth buttoned and his nose clean. When he reported on Monday night to Mr. Payne he seemed to have everything fixed, including himself.

Straight Line was a reliable character, a young man who kept himself to himself. He pinched the car on Monday afternoon, took it along to the semi-legitimate garage run by his father, and put new number plates on it. There was no time for a respray job, but he roughed the car up a little so that the owner would be unlikely to recognise it if by some unlucky chance he should be passing outside Orbins on Tuesday morning. During this whole operation Straight, of course, wore gloves. He also reported to Mr. Payne on Monday night.

Lester's name was not really Lester but Leonard. His mother and his friends in Balham, where he had been born and brought up, called him Lenny. He detested this, as he detested his surname and the pimples that, in spite of his assiduous efforts with ointment, appeared in groups on his face every couple of months. There was nothing he could do about the name of Jones, because it was on his National Insurance card, but Lester for Leonard was a gesture towards emancipation.

Another gesture was made when he left home and mother for a one-room flat in Notting Hill Gate. A third gesture, and the most important one, was his friendship with Lucille, whom he had met in a jazz club called the Whizz Fizz. Lucille called herself an actress, but the only evidence of it was that she occasionally sang in the club. Her voice was tuneless but loud. After she sang, Lester always bought her a drink. The drink was always whisky.

"So what's new?" she said. "Lester boy, what's new?"

"I sold a diamond necklace today. Two hundred and fifty pounds. Mr. Marston was very pleased." Mr. Marston was the manager of the Jewellery Department.

"So Mr. Marston was pleased. Big deal." Lucille looked round restlessly, tapped her foot.

"He might give me more money."

"Another ten bob a week and a pension for your fallen arches."

"Lucille, won't you—"

"No." The peak of emancipation for Lester, a dream beyond which his thoughts really could not reach, was that one day Lucille would come to live with him. Far from that, she had not even slept with him yet. "Look, Lester boy, I know what I want, and let's face it, you haven't got it."

He was incautious enough to ask: "What?"

"Money, moolah, the green stuff. Without it you're nothing, with it they can't hurt you."

Lester was drinking whisky too, although he didn't really like it. Perhaps, but for the whisky, he would never have said, "Supposing I had money?"

"What money? Where would you get it, draw it out of the Savings Bank?"

"A lot of money."

"Lester boy, I don't think in penny numbers. I'm talking about real money."

The room was thick with smoke, the Fizz Kids were playing. Lester leaned back and said deliberately: "Next week I'll have money. Thousands of pounds."

Lucille was about to laugh. Then she said: "It's my turn to buy a drink, I'm feeling generous. Hey, Joe. Two more of the same."

Later that night they lay on the bed in his one-room flat. She had let him make love to her. He had told her everything.

"So the stuff's going to a man called Lambie in Greenly Street?"

Lester had never before drunk so much in an evening. Was it six whiskies or seven? He felt ill, and alarmed. "Lucille, you won't say anything? I mean, I wasn't supposed to tell—"

"Relax. What do you take me for?" She touched his cheek with red-tipped nails. "Besides, we shouldn't have secrets, should we?"

He watched her as she got off the bed, began to dress. "Won't you stay? I mean, it would be all right with the landlady."

"No can do, Lester boy. See you at the club, though. Tomorrow night. Promise."

"Promise." When she had gone he turned over on to his side and groaned. He feared that he was going to be sick, and he was. Afterwards he felt better.

Lucille went home to the flat in Earl's Court which she shared with a tearaway named Joe Baxter. He had been sent to Borstal for a robbery from a confectioner's which had involved considerable violence. Since then he had done one short stretch. He listened to what she had to say, then asked: "What's this Lester like?"

"A creep."

"Has he got the nous to kid you, or do you think it's straight up? What he's told you?"

"He wouldn't kid me. He wants me to live with him when he's got the money. I said I might."

Joe showed her what he thought of that idea. Then he said, "Tuesday morning, eh? Until then, you play along with this creep. Any change in plans I want to know it. You can do it, can't you, baby?"

She looked up at him. He had a scar on the left side of his face which she thought made him look immensely attractive. "I can do it. And Joe?"

"Yes?"

"What about afterwards?"

"Afterwards, baby? Well, for spending money there's no place like London. Unless it's Paris."

Lester Jones also reported on Monday night. Lucille was being very kind to him. He no longer felt uneasy. Mr. Payne gave them all a final briefing and stressed that timing, in this as in every similar affair, was the vital element.

Mr. Rossiter Payne rose on Tuesday morning at his usual time, just after eight o'clock. He bathed and shaved with care and precision, and ate his usual breakfast of one soft-boiled egg, two pieces of toast and one cup of unsugared coffee. When Miss Oliphant arrived he was already in the shop.

"My dear Miss Oliphant. Are you, as they say, ready to cope this morning?"

"Of course, Mr. Payne. Do you have to go out?"

"I do. Something quite unexpected. An American collector named—but I mustn't tell his name even to you, he doesn't want it known—is in London, and he has asked me to see him. He wants to try to buy the manuscripts of—but there again I'm sworn to secrecy, although if I weren't I should surprise you. I am calling on him, so I shall leave things in your care until—" Mr. Payne looked at his expensive watch, "not later than mid-day. I shall certainly be back by then. In the meantime, Miss Oliphant, I entrust my wares to you."

She giggled. "I won't let anyone steal the stock, Mr. Payne."

Mr. Payne went upstairs again to his flat where, laid out upon the bed, was a very different set of clothes from that which he normally wore. He emerged later from the little side entrance looking quite unlike the dapper retired Guards officer known to Miss Oliphant. His clothes were of the shabby nondescript ready-to-wear kind that might be worn by a City clerk very much down on his luck, the sleeve and trouser cuffs distinctly frayed, the tie a piece of rather dirty string. Curling strands of rather disgustingly gingery hair strayed from beneath his stained grey trilby hat and his face was grey too, grey and much lined, the face of a man of sixty who has been defeated by life. Mr. Payne had bright blue eyes, but the man who came out of the side entrance had, thanks to contact lenses, brown ones. This man shuffled off down the alley with shoulders bent, carrying a rather dingy suitcase. He was quite unrecognisable as the upright Rossiter Payne. Indeed, if there was a criticism to be made of him, it was that he looked almost too much the "little man." Long, long ago, Mr. Payne had been an actor, and although his dramatic abilities were extremely limited, he had always loved and been extremely good at dressing up. He took with him a realistic-looking gun that in fact fired nothing more lethal than caps. He was a man who disliked violence, and thought it unnecessary.

After he left Mr. Payne on Monday night, Stacey had been unable to resist having a few drinks. The alarm clock wakened him to a smell of frizzling bacon. His wife sensed that he had a job on, and she came into the bedroom as he was taking the Smith and Wesson out of the cupboard.

"Bill." He turned round. "Do you need that?"

"What do you think?"

"Don't take it."

"Ah, don't be stupid."

"Bill, please. I get frightened."

Stacey put it into his hip pocket. "Shan't use it. Just makes me feel more comfortable, see."

He ate his breakfast with a good appetite and then telephoned Shrimp Bateson, Lucy O'Malley and the Canadian, to make sure they were all on. They were. His wife watched him fearfully. Then he came to say goodbye.

"Bill, look after yourself."

"Always do." Then he was gone.

Lucille had spent Monday night with Lester. This was much against her wish, but Joe had insisted on it, saying that he must know of any last-minute change.

Lester had no appetite at all. She watched with barely-concealed contempt as he drank no more than half a cup of coffee, and pushed aside his toast. When he got dressed his fingers were trembling so that he could hardly do up his shirt buttons.

"Today's the day, then."

"Yes. I wish it was over."

"Don't worry."

He said eagerly, "I'll see you in the club tonight."

"Yes."

"I shall have the money then, we could go away together. Oh no, of course, I've got to stay in the job."

"That's right," she said, humouring him. As soon as he had gone she rang Joe, to say that there were no changes.

Straight Line lived with his family. They knew he had a job on, but nobody talked about it. Only his mother stopped him at the door and said, "Good luck, son," and his father said, "Keep your nose clean." He went to the garage and got out the Jag.

*

Ten-thirty. Shrimp Bateson walked into the Fur Department with a brown paper package under his arm. He strolled about pretending to look at furs, while trying to find a place to put down the little parcel. There were several shoppers and he went unnoticed, but it was not easy to find a place. He stopped at the point where Furs led to the stairs, moved into a window embrasure, took the little metal cylinder out of its brown paper, pressed the switch which started the mechanism, and walked rapidly away.

He had almost reached the door when he was tapped on the shoulder. He turned. An assistant was standing with the brown paper in his hand.

"Excuse me, sir, I think you've dropped something. I found this paper—"

"No, no," Shrimp said. "It's not mine."

"Oh, but really, sir—"

There was no time to waste in arguing. Shrimp turned and half-walked, half-ran, through the doors and to the staircase. The assistant moved slowly after him. People were coming up the stairs and Shrimp, in a desperate attempt to avoid them, slipped and fell, bruising his shoulder. The assistant was standing hesitantly at the top of the stairs when he heard the whoosh of sound and, turning, saw flame. He ran down the stairs then, took Shrimp firmly by the arm and said, "I think you'd better come back with me, sir."

The fire bomb had gone off on schedule, setting light to the curtains and to part of a store counter. One or two women were screaming, assistants were busy saving the furs. Flack, one of the store detectives, was on the spot quickly, and organised the fire extinguishers. They got the fire in hand in five minutes.

The assistant, full of zeal, brought Shrimp along to Flack. "Here's the man who did it."

Flack looked at him. "Firebug, eh?"

"Let me go. I had nothing to do with it."

"Let's talk to the manager, shall we?" Flack said, and hauled Shrimp away. The time was ten-thirty-nine.

Lucy O'Malley looked at herself in the glass, and at the skimpy hat perched on her enormous head. Her near-crocodile handbag, of a size to match her person, had been put down on a chair nearby.

"What do you feel, madam?" the assistant asked, ready to take her cue from the customer's reaction.

"Terrible."

"Perhaps it isn't really you."

"It looks bloody awful," Lucy said. She enjoyed swearing, and saw no reason why she should restrain herself.

The assistant perfunctorily and dutifully laughed, and moved over again towards the hats. She indicated a black hat with a wide brim. "Perhaps something more like this?"

Lucy looked at her watch. Ten-thirty-one. It was time. She went across to her handbag, opened it, exclaimed.

"Is something the matter, madam?"

"I've been robbed."

"Oh really, I don't think that can have happened."

Lucy had a sergeant-major's voice, and now she used it. "Don't tell me what can and can't have happened, young woman. My money was in here, and now it's gone. Somebody's taken it."

The assistant, who was young and easily intimidated, blushed. The department supervisor, elegant, eagle-nosed, blue-rinsed, moved across like an arrow and asked politely if she could help.

"My money's been stolen," Lucy shouted. "I put my bag down for a minute, twenty pounds in it, and now it's gone. That's the class of people they get in Orbins." She addressed this last sentence to another shopper, who moved away hurriedly.

"Let's look, shall we, just to make sure." Blue Rinse took hold of the handbag; Lucy took hold of it too, somehow the bag's contents spilled on to the carpet.

"You stupid bitch," Lucy roared.

"I'm sorry, madam," Blue Rinse said icily. She picked up handkerchief, lipstick, powder compact, tissues. Certainly there was no money in the bag. "You are sure the money was in the bag?"

"Of course I'm sure. It was in my purse. I had it five minutes ago. Someone here has stolen it."

"Not so loud, please, madam."

"I shall speak as loudly as I like. Where's your detective, or haven't you got one?"

Sidley, the other store detective for the second floor, was pushing through the little crowd that had collected. "What seems to be the matter?"

"This lady says twenty pounds has been stolen from her handbag." Blue Rinse just refrained from emphasising the word "lady."

"I'm very sorry. Shall we talk about it in the office."

"I don't move until I get my money back." Lucy was carrying an umbrella, and she waved it threateningly. However, she allowed herself to be led along to the office. There the handbag was examined again and the assistant, now tearful, was interrogated. There also Lucy, having surreptitiously looked again at the time, put a hand into the capacious pocket of her coat, and discovered the purse. There was twenty pounds in it, just as she had said. She apologised, although the apology went much against the grain for her, declined the suggestion that she should return to the hat counter, and left the store with the consciousness of a job well done.

"Well," Sidley said. "I shouldn't like to tangle with her on a dark night."

The time was ten-forty.

The clock in the Jewellery Department said just after ten-thirty when a girl came running down, out of breath, and spoke to the manager. "Oh, Mr. Marston, there's a telephone call for Mr. Davidson. It's from America."

Marston was large, and inclined to be pompous. "Put it through here, then."

"I can't. There's something wrong with the line in this department, it seems to be dead."

Davidson had heard his name mentioned, and came over to them. He was a crew-cut American, tough and lean. "It'll be to do with my wife, she's expecting a baby. Where's the call?"

"We've got it in administration, one floor up."

"Come on, then." Davidson moved off at what was almost a run, and the girl trotted with him. Marston looked after them disapprovingly. He became aware that one of his assistants, Jones, was looking rather odd.

"Is anything the matter, Jones? Do you feel unwell?"

Lester said that he was all right. The act of cutting the telephone flex had filled him with terror, but with the departure of Davidson he really did feel better. He thought of the money, and of Lucille.

Lucille was just saying goodbye to Joe Baxter and his friend Eddy Grain. They were equipped with an arsenal of weapons, including flick knives, chains and knuckledusters. They did not, however, carry revolvers.

"You'll be careful," she said to Joe.

"Don't worry. This is going to be like taking chocolates from a baby, isn't it, Eddy?"

"S'right," Eddy said. He had a limited vocabulary, and an almost perpetual smile. He was a terror with a knife.

The Canadian made the call from the striptease club. He had a girl with him. He had told her that it would be a big giggle. When he heard Davidson's voice—the time was just after ten-thirty-three—he said, "Is that Mr. Davidson?"

"Yes."

"This is the James Long Foster Hospital in Chicago, Mr. Davidson, Maternity Block."

"Yes."

"Will you speak up, please. I can't hear you very well."

"Have you got some news of my wife?" Davidson said loudly. He was in a small box beside the store switchboard. There was no reply. "Hallo. Are you there?"

The Canadian put one hand over the receiver, and ran the other up the girl's bare thigh. "Let him stew a little." She laughed. They could hear Davidson asking if they were still on the line. The Canadian spoke again.

"Hallo, hallo, Mr. Davidson. We seem to have got a bad line."

"I can hear you clearly. What news is there?"

"No need to worry, Mr. Davidson. Your wife is fine."

"Has she had the baby?"

The Canadian chuckled. "Now, don't be impatient. That's not the kind of job you can hurry."

"What have you got to tell me then? What are you ringing for?"

The Canadian put his hand over the receiver again, said to the girl, "You say something."

"What shall I say?"

"Doesn't matter. We've got the wires crossed or something. Tell him you're the Admin Block."

The girl leaned over, picked up the telephone. "This is the Admin Block. Who are you calling?"

In the box sweat was running off Davidson. He hammered with his fist on the wall of the cabinet. "Damn you, get off the line. Put me back to the Maternity Block."

"This is the Admin Block. Who do you want?"

Davidson checked suddenly. The girl had a Cockney voice. "Who are you? What are you playing at?"

The girl handed the telephone back to the Canadian, looking frightened. "He's on to me."

"Hell." The Canadian picked up the receiver again, but it had been left uncovered, and Davidson had heard these words, too. He dropped the telephone, pushed open the door of the box, raced for the stairs. As he ran he loosened the revolver in his hip pocket. The time was coming up to ten-thirty-eight.

Straight Line brought the Jaguar smoothly to a stop in the space reserved for Orbins' customers, and looked at his watch. The time was ten-thirty-one. Nobody questioned him, nobody so much as gave him a glance. Beautiful, he thought, a nice smooth job, really couldn't be simpler. Then his hands tightened on the steering wheel. He saw in the driving mirror, just a few yards behind him, a policeman standing. Three men in long robes were evidently asking him for directions, and he was consulting a London place map. Well, Straight thought, he can't see anything of me except my back, and in a couple of minutes he'll be gone. There was plenty of time. Payne and Stacey weren't due out of the building until ten-thirty-nine or ten-forty. Plenty of time. But there was a hollow feeling in Straight's stomach as he watched the policeman in his mirror.

Several minutes earlier, at ten-twenty, Mr. Payne and Stacey had met near the service lift beside the Grocery Department on the ground floor. They had met thus early because of the possibility that the lift might be in use when they needed it, although from Lester's observation it was used mostly in the early morning and late afternoon. They did not need to use the lift until ten-thirty, and they would be very unlucky if it was permanently in use until that time. If they were so unlucky—well then, Mr. Payne had said with the pseudo-philosophy of the born gambler, they would have to call the job off. But even as he said this he knew that it was not true, and that having gone so far he would not turn back.

The two men did not speak to each other, but moved steadily towards the lift by way of inspecting chow mein, hymettus honey and real turtle soup. The Grocery Department was full of shoppers, and they were quite unnoticed. Mr. Payne reached the lift first, pressed the button. The doors opened. They were in luck. Within seconds they were both inside. Neither man spoke. Mr. Payne pressed the button which said "Two" and then, when they had passed the first floor, the one that said "Emergency Stop." Jarringly the lift came to a stop. It was now immobilised, so far as a call from outside was concerned. It would be moved only by calling in engineers who would free the emergency stop mechanism—or, of course, by operation from within.

Stacey shivered a little. The lift was designed for goods, and was roomy enough to take twenty passengers, but he had a slight tendency to claustrophobia which was increased by the thought that they were poised between floors. He said, "I suppose that bloody thing will work when you press the button."

"Don't worry, my friend. Have faith in me." Mr. Payne opened the dingy suitcase, revealing as he did so that he was wearing rubber gloves. Inside the suitcase there were two long red cloaks, two fuzzy white wigs and thick white beards, two pairs of outsize horn-rimmed spectacles, two red noses, two hats with large tassels. "This may not be a perfect fit for you, but I don't think you can deny that it's a perfect disguise."

They put on the clothes, Mr. Payne with the pleasure he always felt in dressing up, Stacey with a certain reluctance. The idea was clever, all right, he had to admit that, but he hated the thought of making himself look a Charlie. When he looked in the lift's small mirror at himself as Father Christmas, however, he was pleased to find that he was totally unrecognisable. Deliberately he took the Smith and Wesson out of his jacket, and put it into the pocket of the red cloak.

"You understand, Stacey, there is no question of using that weapon."

"Unless I have to."

"There is no question," Mr. Payne repeated firmly. "Violence is never necessary. It is a confession that one lacks intelligence."

"We got to point it at them, haven't we? Show we mean business."

Mr. Payne acknowledged that painful necessity by a downward twitch of his mouth, indiscernible beneath the beard.

"Isn't it time, yet?"

Mr. Payne looked at his watch. "It is now ten-twenty-nine. We go—over the top, you might call it—at ten-thirty-two. Compose yourself to wait, Stacey."

Stacey grunted. He could not help admiring his companion, who stood peering into the small glass adjusting his beard and moustache, and settling his cloak more comfortably. When at last Mr. Payne nodded, said, "Here we go," and pressed the button that said "Two," resentment was added to admiration. He's all right now, but wait till we get to the action, Stacey thought. His gloved hand on the Smith and Wesson reassured him of strength, potency, efficiency.

The lift shuddered, moved upwards, stopped. The doors opened. Mr. Payne placed his suitcase between the lift doors so that they would stay open and keep the lift on the second floor. They stepped out.

To Lester the time that passed after Davidson's departure upstairs and before the lift doors opened was complete and absolute torture. The whole thing had seemed so simple as Mr. Payne outlined it to them. "It is a matter of timing," he had said, "Timing pure and simple. If everybody plays his part properly, Stace and I will be back in the lift within five minutes. Planning is the essence of this, as of every scientific operation. Nobody will be hurt, and nobody will suffer financially except—" and here he had looked at Lester with a twinkle of his frosty eyes, "—except the insurance company. And I don't think the most tender-hearted of us will worry too much about the insurance company."

That was all very well, and Lester had done what he was supposed to do, but he hadn't really been able to believe that the rest of it would happen. He had been terrified, but with the terror was mixed a sense of unreality. He still couldn't believe, even when Davidson went away to the telephone upstairs, that the plan would go through. He was showing some costume jewellery to a thin old woman who kept roping necklaces around her scrawny neck, and while he did so he kept looking at the lift, above which was the department clock. The hands moved slowly, after Davidson left, from ten-thirty-one to ten-thirty-two. They're not coming, Lester thought. It's all off. A flood of relief, touched with regret but with relief predominating, went through him. Then the lift doors opened, and the two Father Christmases stepped out. Lester started convulsively.

"Young man," the thin woman said severely, "it doesn't seem to me that I have your undivided attention. Haven't you anything in blue and amber?"

It had been arranged that Lester would nod or shake his head to signify that Davidson had left the department, or that things had gone astray. He nodded his head now as though he had St. Vitus's Dance. The thin woman looked at him, astonished. "Young man, is anything the matter?"

"Blue and amber," Lester said wildly. "Blue and amber." He pulled out a box from under the counter and began to look through it. His hands were shaking.

Mr. Payne had been right in his assumption that no surprise would be occasioned by the appearance of two Father Christmases in any department at this time of year. This, he liked to think, was his characteristic touch, the touch of—not to be unduly modest about it—genius. There were a dozen people in the Jewellery Department, half of them looking at the Russian Royal Family jewels, which had proved less of an attraction than Sir Henry Orbin had hoped. Three of the others were wandering about in the idle way of people who are not really intending to buy anything, and the other three were at the counters, where they were being attended to by Lester, a girl assistant whose name was Miss Glenny, and by Marston himself.

The appearance of the Father Christmases aroused only the feeling of pleasure experienced by most people at the sight of these slightly artificial figures of jollity. Even Marston barely glanced at them. There were half a dozen Father Christmases in the store during the weeks before Christmas, and he assumed that these two were on their way to the Toy Department, which was also on the second floor, or to Robin Hood in Sherwood Forest, which was this year's display for children.

The Father Christmases walked across the floor together as though they were in fact going into Carpets and thence along to the Toy Department, but after passing Lester they diverged. Mr. Payne went to the archway that led from Jewellery to Carpets, and Stacey abruptly turned behind Lester towards the manager's office. Marston, who was trying to sell an emerald brooch to an American who wasn't sure whether his wife would like it, looked up in surprise. He had a natural reluctance to make a fuss, and also to leave his customer, but when he saw Stacey with a hand actually upon the door of his own small but sacred office he said to the American: "Excuse me a moment, sir," said to Miss Glenny "Look after this gentleman, please" (by which he meant that the American should not be allowed to walk out with the emerald brooch), and called out—although not so loudly that the call could be thought of as anything so vulgar as a shout—"Just a moment, please. What are you doing there? What do you want?"

Stacey ignored him. In doing so he was carrying out Mr. Payne's instructions. At some point it was inevitable that the people in the department should realise that a theft was being carried out, but the longer they could be left without realising it, Mr. Payne had said, the better. Stacey's own inclination would have been to pull out his revolver at once and terrorise anybody likely to make trouble, but he did as he was told.

The manager's office was not much more than a cubby hole, with papers neatly arranged on a desk, and behind the desk half a dozen keys hanging up. The showcase key, Lester had said, was the second from the left, but for the sake of appearances he took all the keys. He had just turned to go when Marston opened the door, and saw the keys in Stacey's hand. The manager was not lacking in courage. He understood what was happening at once and, without speaking, tried to grapple with the intruder. Stacey drew the Smith and Wesson from his pocket and struck Marston with it hard upon the forehead. The manager dropped to the ground. A trickle of blood came from his head.

The office door was open, and there was no point in making further attempt at concealment. Stacey pointed the revolver and spoke. "Just keep quiet, and nobody else will get hurt."

Mr. Payne produced his cap pistol and said, in a voice as unlike his usual cultured tones as possible, "Stay where you are. Don't move. We shall be gone in five minutes."

Somebody said, "Well, I'm damned," but nobody moved. Marston lay on the floor, groaning. Stacey went to the showcase, pretended to fumble with another key, then inserted the right one. The case opened at once. The jewels lay naked and unprotected. He dropped the other keys on to the floor, stretched in his gloved hands, picked up the jewels, and put them into his pocket.

It's going to work, Lester thought unbelievingly, it's going to work. He watched, fascinated, as the cascade of shining stuff vanished into Stacey's pocket. Then he became aware that the thin woman was pressing something into his hand. Looking down, he saw with horror that it was a large, brand-new clasp knife, with the dangerous-looking blade open.

"Bought it for my nephew," the thin woman whispered. "As he passes you, go for him."

It had been arranged that if Lester's behaviour should arouse the least suspicion he should make a pretended attack on Stacey, who would give him a punch just severe enough to knock him down. Everything had gone so well, however, that this was not necessary, but now it seemed to Lester that he had no choice. As the two Father Christmases backed across the room towards the service lift, covering the people at the counters with their revolvers, one real and the other a toy, Lester launched himself feebly at Stacey, with the clasp knife demonstratively raised. At the same time Marston, on the other side of Stacey and a little behind him, rose to his feet and staggered in the direction of the lift.

Stacey's contempt for Lester was increased by the sight of the knife, which he regarded as an unnecessary bit of bravado. With his left fist he punched Lester hard in the stomach. The blow doubled Lester up. He dropped the knife and collapsed to the floor, writhing in quite genuine pain.

The delivery of the blow delayed Stacey, so that Marston was almost on him. Mr. Payne, retreating rapidly to the lift, shouted a warning, but the manager was on to Stacey, clawing at his robes. He did not succeed in pulling off the red robe, but his other hand came away with the wig, revealing Stacey's own cropped brown hair. Stacey snatched back the wig, broke away, and fired the revolver.

Perhaps he could hardly have said himself whether he intended to hit Marston, or simply to stop him. The bullet missed the manager and hit Lester, who was rising on one knee. Lester dropped again. Miss Glenny screamed, a man cried out. Marston halted.

Mr. Payne and Stacey were almost at the lift when Davidson came charging in through the Carpet Department entrance. He drew the revolver from his pocket and shot, all in one movement. Stacey fired back wildly. Then the two Father Christmases were in the service lift, and the door closed on them.

Davidson took one look at the empty showcase, and shouted to Marston: "Is there an emergency alarm that rings downstairs?"

The manager shook his head. "And my telephone's not working."

"They've cut the line." Davidson raced back through the Carpet Department to the passenger lifts.

Marston went over to where Lester was lying, with half a dozen people round him, including the thin woman. "We must get a doctor."

The American he had been serving said "I am a doctor." He was bending over Lester, whose eyes were open.

"How is he?"

The American lowered his voice. "He got it in the stomach."

Lester seemed to be trying to raise himself up. The thin woman helped him. He sat up, looked at them, said "Lucille." Then blood suddenly rushed out of his mouth. He sank back.

The doctor bent over again, looked up. "I'm very sorry. He's dead."

The thin woman gave Lester a more generous obituary than he deserved. "He wasn't a very good assistant, but he was a brave young man."

Straight Line, outside in the Jag, waited for the copper to move. But not a bit of it. The robed men were pointing to some particular spot on the map, the copper was laughing, they were having some sort of stupid joke together. What the hell, Straight thought, hasn't the bleeder got any work to do, doesn't he know he's not supposed to hang about? He looked at his watch. Ten-thirty-four, coming up to ten-thirty-five—and now, as the robed men moved away, what should happen but that a young teenage girl came up, and the copper was bending over towards her with a look of idiotic goodwill. It's no good, Straight thought, I shall land them right in his lap if I stay here. He pulled away from the parking space, looked again at his watch. He was obsessed by the need to get out of the policeman's sight. Once round the block, he thought, just once round can't take more than a minute, and I've got more than two minutes to spare. Then if he's still here I'll stay a few yards away from him with my engine running. He moved away down Jessiter Street towards the square at the bottom. A moment after Straight had gone, the policeman, who had never even glanced at him, moved too.

By Mr. Payne's plan they should have taken off their Father Christmas gear in the service lift and walked out at the bottom as the same respectable, anonymous citizens who had gone in, but as soon as they were inside Stacey said: "He hit me." A stain showed against the scarlet right arm of his robe.

Mr. Payne pressed the button to take them down. He was proud that, in this emergency, his thoughts moved with clarity and logic. He spoke them aloud.

"No time to take these off. Anyway, they're a good disguise in the street. Straight will be waiting. We step out and into the car, take them off there. Davidson shouldn't have been back in that department for another two minutes."

"I gotta see a doctor."

"We'll get to Lambie first. He'll fix it." The lift whirred downwards. Almost timidly, Mr. Payne broached the subject that worried him most. "What happened to Lester?"

"He stopped one." Stacey was pale.

The lift stopped. Mr. Payne adjusted the wig on Stacey's head. "They can't possibly be waiting for us, there isn't time. We just walk out. Not too fast, remember."

The lift doors opened, they walked the fifty feet to the Jessiter Street exit. They were delayed only by a small boy who rushed to Mr. Payne, clung round his legs and shouted that he wanted a present. Mr. Payne gently disengaged him, whispered to his mother, "Our tea break. Back later," and moved on.

Now they were outside in the street. There was no sign of Straight or the Jaguar.

Stacey began to curse. They crossed the road from Orbin's, stood outside Danny's Shoe Parlour for a period that seemed to both of them endless, but was in fact thirty seconds. People looked at them curiously, two Father Christmases wearing false noses, but they did not arouse great attention. They were oddities, yes, but oddities who were after all in keeping with the time of year and the Oxford Street decorations.

"We've got to get away," Stacey said. "We're sitting ducks."

"Don't be a fool. We wouldn't get a hundred yards."

"Planning," Stacey said bitterly. "Fine bloody planning. If you ask me—"

"Here he is."

The Jag drew up beside them, and in a moment they were in and down Jessiter Street, away from Orbins. Davidson was on the spot less than a minute later, but by the time he had found passers-by who had seen the Father Christmases get into the car, they were half a mile away.

Straight began to explain what had happened, Stacey swore at him, Mr. Payne cut them both short.

"No time for that. Get these clothes off, talk later."

"You got the rocks?"

"Yes, but Stace has been hit. By the guard. I don't think it's much."

"Whatsisname, Lester, he okay?"

"There was a fight. Stace caught him with a bullet."

Straight said nothing more. He was not one to complain about something that couldn't be helped. His feelings showed only in the controlled savagery with which he now drove the Jag.

While he drove Mr. Payne was taking off his own Christmas outfit and helping Stacey off with his. He stuffed them, with the wigs and noses, back into the suitcase. Stacey winced as the robe came over his right arm, and Mr. Payne gave him a handkerchief to hold over it. At the same time he suggested that Stacey should hand over the jewels, since Mr. Payne would be doing the negotiating with the fence. It was a mark of the trust that both men still reposed in Mr. Payne that Stacey handed them over without a word, and that Straight did not comment.

They turned into the quiet Georgian terrace where Lambie lived. "Number 15, right hand side," Mr. Payne said.

Joe Baxter and Eddy Grain had been hanging about in the street for several minutes. Lucille had learned from Lester what car Straight was driving. They recognised the Jag immediately, and strolled towards it. They were just up with the car when it came to a stop beside Lambie's house. Stacey and Mr. Payne got out.

Joe and Eddy were not, after all, very experienced. They made an elementary mistake in not waiting until Straight had driven away. Joe had his flick knife out and was pointing it at Mr. Payne's stomach.

"Come on now, Dad, give us the stuff and you won't get hurt," he said.

On the other side of the car Eddy Grain, less subtle, swung at Stacey with a shortened length of bicycle chain. Stacey, hit round the head, went down, and Eddy was on top of him, kicking, punching, searching.

Mr. Payne hated violence, but he was capable of defending himself. He moved aside, kicked upwards and knocked the knife flying from Joe's hand. Then he rang the doorbell of Lambie's house. At the same time Straight got out of the car and felled Eddy Grain with an effective rabbit punch.

During the next minutes several things happened. At the end of the road a police whistle was blown, loudly and insistently, by an old lady who had seen what was going on. Lambie, who also saw what was going on and wanted no part of it, told his manservant on no account to answer the doorbell or open the door. Stacey, kicked and beaten by Eddy Grain, drew his revolver and fired four shots. One of them struck Eddy in the chest, and another hit Joe Baxter in the leg. Eddy ran away down the street holding his chest, turned the corner, and ran slap into the arms of two policemen hurrying to the scene. Straight, who did not care for shooting, got back into the Jag and drove away. He dropped the Jag as soon as he could, and went home.

When the police arrived, with a bleating Eddy in tow, they found Stacey and Joe Baxter on the ground, and several neighbours only too ready to tell confusing stories about the great gang fight that had taken place. They interrogated Lambie, of course, but he had not seen nor heard anything at all.

And Mr. Payne? With a general *mêlée* taking place, and Lambie clearly not intending to answer his doorbell, he had walked away down the road. When he turned the corner he found a cab, which he took to within a couple of hundred yards of his shop. Then, an anonymous man carrying a shabby suitcase, he went in through the little side entrance.

Things had gone badly, he reflected as he became again Mr. Rossiter Payne the antiquarian bookseller, mistakes had been made. But happily they were not his mistakes. The jewels would be hot, no doubt, they would have to be kept for a while, but all was not lost. Stace and Straight were professionals, they would never grass. And although Mr. Payne did not, of course, know that Lester was dead, he realised that the young man would be able to pose as a wounded hero and was not likely to be subjected to severe questioning. Mr. Payne was whistling "There's a Silver Lining" as he went down to greet Miss Oliphant.

"Oh, Mr. Payne," she trilled. "You're back before you said. It's not half-past-eleven."

Could that be true? Yes, it was.

"Did the American collector—I mean, will you be able to sell him the manuscripts?"

"I hope so. Negotiations are proceeding, Miss Oliphant. They may take some time, but I hope they will reach a successful conclusion."

The time passed uneventfully until two-thirty, when Miss Oliphant came into his little private office. "Mr. Payne, there are two gentlemen to see you. They won't say what it's about, but they look, well, rather funny."

As soon as Mr. Payne saw them, before they produced their warrant cards, he knew that there was nothing funny about them. He took them up to the flat, he tried to talk his way out of it, but he knew it was no use. They hadn't yet got search warrants, the Inspector said, but they would be taking Mr. Payne along anyway. It would save them some trouble if he would care to show them...

Mr. Payne showed them, gave them the jewels and the disguises. Then he sighed at the weakness of subordinates. "Somebody—grassed, I suppose."

"Oh, no. I'm afraid the truth is you were a bit careless."

"*I* was careless." Mr. Payne was scandalised.

"Yes. You were recognised."

"Impossible."

"Not at all. When you got out into the street, afterwards, there was a bit of a mix-up so that you had to wait, isn't that right?"

"Certainly, but I was disguised."

"Danny the shoe cleaner knows you by name, doesn't he?"

"Yes, but he didn't even see me."

"He didn't need to. Danny can't see any faces from his basement, you know that, but he did see something, and he came to tell us about it. He saw two pairs of legs, wearing some sort of red robes. And he saw the shoes. He recognised one pair of shoes, Mr. Payne. Not those you're wearing now, but that pair on the floor over there."

Mr. Payne looked across the room at the black shoes, shoes so perfectly appropriate to the role of the shabby little clerk that he had been playing, and at the decisive, fatally recognisable sharp cut made by the bicycle mudguard in the black leather.

THE TURN-AGAIN BELL

Barry Perowne

Barry Perowne was the pen-name of Philip Atkey (1908–85). Born in Wiltshire, he went to school in Oxford, and in 1932 he married his cousin Marjorie. Marjorie's father, Philip's uncle, was Bertram Atkey, a crime writer whose literary career seems to have exerted some influence on his nephew. Bertram's series characters included Smiler Bunn, variously described as a "society swindler" and "gentleman-adventurer", and Prosper Fair (a "vagabond sleuth" who happened to be the Duke of Devizes in disguise). In the early 1960s, Perowne wrote a number of "continuation" stories featuring Prosper Fair.

Perowne shared his uncle's interest in writing about well-born rogues, and in 1933 he published his first book featuring A. J. Raffles, the famous "amateur cracksman" originally created by E. W. Hornung. He'd been approached by Montague Haydon, editor of *Thriller* magazine, to write a new set of Raffles stories, rather along the lines of the thrillers by Leslie Charteris about Simon Templar, "the Saint". *Thriller* closed after war broke out, but Perowne returned to Raffles after the war. This time he worked more in the vein of Hornung's original short stories, and his pastiches achieved considerable popularity. He also wrote stand-alone crime stories, and the films *Blind Spot* and *Walk a Crooked Path* were based on his work. "The Turn-Again Bell" first appeared in *The Sphere*, 12 November 1959.

T HE SMALL, FLINT-BUILT, ELEVENTH-CENTURY CHURCH, WITH its square Norman tower, stood isolated on a knoll overlooking a wide common. It was the day before Christmas Eve and the early darkness was closing in. On the mounds and stones of the churchyard the snow lay deep. The yew trees stood black and white in the freezing stillness.

In the cellar under the church, the furnace glowed snugly red and threw the Rector's shadow slanting across the wall. The furnace was old and cranky and, now that he had managed to get it working properly for once, the Rector was reluctant to leave its warmth.

He stood leaning on the flue-rake and gazed down with faded blue, thoughtful eyes at the burning coke. A tall, white-haired man, his leathery face and gaunt build were the legacy of many years spent tramping the lanes, fields and bridlepaths, in fair weather and foul, of his straggling, sparsely-populated parish.

He was a widower and he was thinking about his three sons. He was seeing them, pictured there in the red depths of the furnace, as small boys addicted to wigwams, catapults, and tadpoles in jars of duckweedy water. There was a girl in the picture, a grey-eyed, russet-pigtailed small girl with scratched knees, a hanger-on of the three boys, an adhesive nuisance who trailed them round wherever they went.

He smiled slightly to himself as the small, blue flames danced over the crackling coke.

He saw his sons grown lankier, graduated to guns and fishing-rods and, resigned to the presence of that inevitable girl, extending to her the priceless boon of their masculine tolerance.

A burning cinder fell from the furnace and the Rector pushed it under the grating with his flue-rake.

In the fire, he saw his sons more or less grown up, no longer just tolerating that girl, who had grown into a very pretty girl indeed, but arguing fiercely among themselves, even fighting ferociously, for the privilege of taking her on some expedition or other in a dangerous, noisy racing car which they had jointly constructed.

"All those rows about Iris," muttered the Rector. "Scandalous!"

To complicate matters, the girl's father, Stephen Colvey, had been divorced from his first wife. He had lived, in those days, in a different part of the country. When he had sought to marry again, the vicar there, a man of strong views about divorce, had declined to officiate at the ceremony. Colvey, also a man of strong views, had sworn never to set foot inside a church again in any circumstances. He had married the girl, who had become Iris's mother, in a registrar's office, and he loathed and abominated clergymen.

In consequence, when he had moved into the Rector's parish, he had done his utmost, first to keep his only daughter away from the Rectory boys, then to keep the Rectory boys away from his only daughter. But he was a busy man, a company director, away from home a good deal, and Iris's mother was unprejudiced and good-humoured; and school holidays were long and kids were kids. So Colvey never had had a hope, really, and the Rector often had wondered how it would all come out in the end.

He had the answer, now.

THE TURN-AGAIN BELL   305

They all had gone their ways, those young people—Iris to a job in London, Donald into the Navy, Douglas to farm in Canada, Derwent to pump Persian oil. But Iris now was home to spend Christmas with her parents, and Donald would be arriving shortly, on leave. And the Rector was to marry Iris and Donald, in the church here, on Boxing Day. And that was the answer.

The Rector was very well pleased with it—delighted, in fact. He took out his watch, peered at it in the furnace-glow. He was wearing a clerical collar, an old cardigan, pepper-and-salt tweed trousers tucked into rubber boots. Iris, with that taste early instilled in her by his vigorous sons, had a racy little car of her own now. She had gone in it to meet Don's train, at the town ten miles away.

"Surely you're coming with me?" she had asked the Rector.

"No, my dear, I've a lot of things to do," he had told her. "I'll expect you both at the rectory about teatime."

He had felt that they would like to have their meeting to themselves. But he saw that it was pretty well teatime now and, hanging up the flue-rake, he put on his jacket, wound his voluminous scarf round his neck. He shovelled some more coke into the furnace. He wanted the church reasonably warm over Christmas, if possible. How they had got on in the eleventh century, he couldn't imagine. Hardier congregations, perhaps.

He adjusted the damper and hoped that the fire would keep in all night, but there was no telling. Like everything else, from the cellar here to the belfry, the furnace was in urgent need of repair. He went up the cellar steps into the vestry. In the pitch darkness, he felt for his coat and cap, put on the coat, took his flashlamp from the pocket.

He went into the dark church, where the whiteness of the snow, drifted deep on the sills outside, gave to the tall, stained-glass windows a faint, ghostly radiance. A few of his diminutive congregation, including Iris, had dressed a Crib, and he shone his light on to it for a moment, thinking what a great pity it was that Stephen Colvey refused to walk up the aisle with his only daughter and give her away. It wasn't a chance he was likely to have again; to a man with an only daughter, it happened once in a lifetime. Colvey's rejection of it, his infliction of a new hurt because of an old one, was a pity. Father and daughter loved each other, the Rector knew that, and Colvey's deliberate absence could make a difference between them. And once it had happened, it couldn't be repaired; it could remain as a secret regret in both of them as the years went by.

The Rector shook his head as he went into the porch. He opened a low, arched, heavy, iron-studded door to the left. The ray of his flashlamp shone on the tufted ends, the sallies, of four ropes hanging motionless above flagstones worn by the feet of centuries of bell-ringers.

Inevitably, about a church as old and out-of-the-way as this, many legends clustered. There was one about a Christmas bell and the Rectors of this parish. It was said that, once in the incumbency of each Rector, there came a time when, over Christmas, he would hear one of the church bells sound a single stroke, loud and clear, for no known reason. He would feel impelled to turn from whatever he was doing and go to the church to see who had rung the bell. There would be nobody there, the four ropes would be hanging motionless, and nobody else would have heard the bell ring. Nobody but the Rector. When it happened, he'd know that it was the last Christmas he would see and there would be a new Rector within a twelve-month.

The circle of torchlight shone through the arched doorway on to the four ropes hanging motionless, their shadows printed on the wall of flints.

He had been more than thirty years in the parish, but he never had been able to discover the origin of that legend. There was one documented instance, however, of an attempt to take advantage of the legend. A man with a hatred for the Rector of the time had rung one of the bells loud and clear in the night, at Christmas, intending to lie in wait, with a flintlock pistol loaded and primed, for the Rector to answer the summons. But the man must have been holding the pistol in his hand as he pulled on the bell-rope, for the Rector found, on reaching the church, that there had been an accident and his enemy lay on the flagstones under the bell-ropes with half his head blown off.

The circle of light from the flashlamp shone on the worn flagstones.

From remembering the legend, as he always did at Christmas, the Rector thought again of his sons. As boys, they had learned to be good bell-ringers. When they were all three at home, the bells were rung as they should be. Don, even by himself, could chime three, one with each hand, a third with his foot through a loop of the rope. But chiming was an art; the Rector himself never had got the knack of it and, as he had no bell-ringers now, all that the village had heard of the bells for a long time was when, for services, he clocked the one that had a cord attached to its clapper.

He shut the belfry door, then the outer door of the church. As he put on his cap, he looked out over the common, wide and white under a glimmer of starlight. Here and there shone the dot of a lighted window, but there was no one about. His walk home took him, as it always did, about five minutes from the church to the crossroads, where he turned left, then three minutes more to the Rectory gate.

*

Crunching up the snow-crisp drive, he knew that Iris and Don hadn't arrived yet, for the front windows of the rambling old house were in darkness, except for the jumping of firelight behind the curtains. There was a light in the potting-shed, off to the side of the garden. The Rector went over to the shed and found his gardener-handyman, Jim Collins, in there, plucking a brace of pheasants by the light of a stable-lamp.

"How are they, Jim?" the Rector asked.

"Hung just right, sir," Collins grinned. "They don't get pheasants in the Navy."

"No, Don'll enjoy those," said the Rector. "I'll take the rest of the game round the parish in the morning."

He always got his hands on as much game as he could; there were old people in the parish who were glad of a bit of game, especially at Christmas.

He let himself into the house by the side door. The bootjack was kept just inside, in the lamplit passage. The dining-room, on the left, was in darkness, but the serving-hatch between the passage and the kitchen, on the right, was open, and he heard Amy Collins, his housekeeper, talking to someone in there. Amy was Jim Collins's wife; the two of them made up the Rectory staff.

"Getting older, of course," the Rector heard Amy saying, as he took off his boots, "but still walks twenty miles or more round the parish most days. Made of whipcord, he is, I know that, but what with his boys all away now, and him getting older—well, all I'm saying is, I'm just a bit gladder, each year, once Christmas is safely over. I can't help it. I feel we're round the corner then, Ella, and safe for another twelve-month."

It was her sister Ella that Amy had in there with her, the Rector realised; Ella must have dropped in for a cup of tea. They were talking about that old legend of the bell.

Ella laughed. "You mean to say you actually *worry*, come Christmas, about that old wives' tale, Amy?"

"I always remember what our own aunt told us," Amy said. "She worked for the previous Rector. I always remember her telling how she went to bed late one Christmas Eve and, what with cooking and baking and everything, she was overstrung and couldn't sleep, and she heard the Rector's bedroom door open—long after midnight, it was—and she heard him go downstairs and go out by the side door."

The Rector straightened up, frowning, one slipper on, one in his hand. This was something about the legend of the old bell that he never had heard before. He couldn't help listening.

"Aunt thought he might have gone to visit someone sick," Amy said. "She come down to the kitchen here and made herself a cup of cocoa. She was sitting at this table here, drinking her cocoa, when she heard the Rector come in. He hadn't been gone long. She went to the hall, and he was taking his coat off, and she asked if he'd like a cup of cocoa. I always remember aunt telling it—the queer way he looked at her and said, as though he was hoping against hope, 'Did the bell wake you?'"

"Ah, now, Amy," Ella said, her tone uneasy.

"He'd been over to the church," Amy said—because he'd heard the bell. But aunt hadn't slept a wink and she knew very well that no bell had rung—at least, not for any human being to hear, except the Rector. But she said, yes, it was the bell that woke her. He went on looking at her in that queer way, and he said, 'I'm afraid you're not telling me the truth.' He knew what it meant, of course. They both did. I remember aunt saying she never had known him so quiet and kind and gentle as he was the next few months. But it was his last Christmas, you can't deny it, Ella. We had a new Rector—our present Rector—within a twelve-month."

"I'll tell you what it is, Amy," Ella said. "With his boys all away, and the Rector alone, you and Jim sit here in the kitchen of this old house, night after night, and just listen to the clock tick. You ought to get a television to bring a bit of life into the place. If you had a television, you'd see the scientific side of things and not be so superstitious."

"That," said Amy, "is one thing I'm not. All I'm saying is, with the Rector not getting any younger, I don't like Christmas and I'm glad to get round the corner on the safe side of it, that's all I'm saying."

That Amy, and perhaps Jim, too, actually worried about him at Christmas, because of that old legend of the bell was news to the Rector. It disturbed him. He put on his other slipper and, walking along the passage, stooped to look through the serving-hatch.

"Good evening, Mrs. Wilby," he said to Ella. "Amy, I think we might light all the lamps now. The car'll be here any minute."

Thinking about what he had heard, he went to his study, lighted his pipe thoughtfully, then from his rolltop desk took his bank passbook and his statements from the Ecclesiastical Commissioners. He was doing some close figuring over these when he heard that speedy red car of Iris's coming up the drive. He rose and, with a broad smile, went to greet his eldest son and his daughter-in-law-to-be. His Christmas had begun.

Over tea by the fire, he heard Don's news of Gibraltar, the Cameroons, Simonstown, Mombasa and the Red Sea ports. All the wide world outside this parish. Amy kept coming in with fresh relays of hot water and buttered toast. She was plump, rosy, white-haired, and looked the soul of common sense. It was hard to believe that she actually was troubled, uneasy, about a legendary bell. But the Rector had heard what he had heard.

When she had cleared away the tea things, he filled his pipe and glanced at Iris and Don. They were leaning back contentedly on his old leather couch, and they were looking at each other, with the firelight on their faces, and their fingers lightly linked. The Rector twisted a spill for his pipe.

"Are you two doing anything special tomorrow?" he asked. "Or d'you think you could drive over to the town and do something for me?"

"We'd love to, Uncle John," Iris said. She had called him that, despite her father's anger, ever since she was a small girl. "What d'you want us to do?"

The Rector lighted his spill at the fire. He thought of the four bell-ropes hanging motionless above the flagstones in the dark, cold belfry.

He said, "I want you to buy a television set. You know more about these things than I do. It's for Amy and Jim—a Christmas present."

He puffed his pipe alight. He wasn't at all sure that television didn't tend to keep people comfortably at home, instead of coming to church. Still, perhaps Ella Wilby was right, and modern science could help lay an old, grim superstition.

Iris and Don went off in the red car on their errand next morning, and the Rector went off on his—on foot. He looked pretty much of an old poacher, trudging gauntly over the white landscape of Christmas Eve with a big, bulging game-bag over his shoulder, but the game wasn't poached. It was wangled out of people who had been shooting in the neighbourhood. Some of them were out today. He heard an occasional gun report as he went from one cottage to another where old couples lived; and he admired the Christmas trees in their windows, praised their paper-chains, and agreed sincerely with them, over a glass of whatever was going, that the world was changing fast, no denying it.

His game-bag considerably lighter, he was heading along a foot-path towards an outlying cottage when four men with guns came out of the spinney alongside the path. Three of them greeted him cordially and insisted on replenishing his game-bag with a hare and four pigeons. But the other man stood apart.

"Good morning, Mr. Colvey," the Rector said.

Stephen Colvey nodded, his handsome face cold, his eyes hard. And the Rector went on his way, pondering. He knew that when Don had gone to see Colvey about marrying his daughter, Colvey had said only, "Iris is twenty-four. I have no say in the matter." There had been no relenting in Colvey's face this morning. He'd rather estrange himself completely from Iris than set foot inside a church. The Rector saw that there was no hope at all of Colvey being present to give his daughter away—to a clergy-man's son.

The Rector and Don rang the bells that night—not the clocking of a single bell, but a real, long Christmas ring that carried far out over the common and the straggling parish. The Rector tried not to think of the bitterness with which Colvey would listen to the bells—if he listened at all.

Afterwards, when he was left alone in the church—Don was taking Iris home—the Rector went down into the cellar to make up the furnace. He found that it had gone out. He had to rake it out com-pletely and relight it, working by the ray of his flashlamp balanced on the coke-pile. At last, the coke in the furnace began to crackle, a red glow spread through it, the small blue flames danced over it. He watched it for a while, leaning on the shovel, thinking of Colvey and the wedding, and of what Amy and Jim would say when they saw their television set in the morning.

He looked at his watch in the furnace-glow. It was very late. Soon, in houses all over the parish, kids—very light sleepers on this particular night, as he knew from experience—would be waking up to speculate in piercing whispers on the peculiar angles and bulges of pendant stockings fingered in the dark.

The Rector left the church and headed for home. There had been a new, light fall of snow, under which the criss-crossing tyre-ruts were frozen hard. The night was clear and cold, the stars were bright. Trudging along, hands deep in his coat pockets, his shadow slanting on the snow, he was about halfway to the crossroads, when he heard a bell in the church tower clang once, loud and clear.

The Rector stood quite still, listening. About him was the white glimmer of snow and starlight. All was silent. He felt the measured, slow thumping of his heart, and his mouth was dry. He turned slowly and looked back at the church on the knoll. The tower was a square, black block against the stars.

He continued to look up at the tower as he walked back to the church. He went up the slope of the path, where the snow was shovelled back in banks to either side. He paused for a moment outside the west porch, under the tower, then he opened the door, stepped inside, stood listening in the darkness. All was still.

He took his flashlamp from his pocket, opened the heavy, creaking door to the right, shone the ray of the flashlamp on to the four bell-ropes. The sallies hung motionless above the worn flagstones.

He went in and, shining the flashlamp upward ahead of him, climbed the ladder up into the belfry. He shone the torch round over the bells with their headstocks, stays, grooved wheels that took the ropes. The bells swung in ancient iron-and-timber frames, and one of these had partially collapsed. The bell hung askew, with its clapper against the rim.

The Rector nodded to himself. From the cellar to the belfry, he thought, there were things that needed urgent attention. The bells hadn't been rung for a long time as they had been rung tonight. This was the result.

He climbed down the ladder. As he closed the porch door behind him, and started home again, he thought ruefully of the power of legend. He had known very well, from the sound the bell had made, just what had happened. Yet he had felt that dryness of the mouth, that thump of his heart, that start of sweat in his palms—

He turned to the left, at the crossroads, and he felt exactly those things again. A sports car, glimmering red against the snow, was tilted in the ditch, one wing and headlight smashed, the headlight glaring into the hedge.

He felt a clutch of fear. "Iris?" he said. He ran forward, clumsily, slipping in his heavy rubber boots on the ruts frozen in the snow. "Iris?"

But it was a man in the car. The top was up, and he was a shadow sitting behind the wheel. "It's all right," he said. "It's not Iris. It's Colvey. This door's jammed and the other one's wedged against the hedge. Nothing like a real good skid to make your knees and spine feel like wet string. I've been sitting here, all snug, till I felt like making the effort to force this damned door open. If you'll just give a good yank from outside and I give a shove from inside—"

They got the door open and Colvey ducked out. He swayed. The Rector caught him by the arm. "Are you all right?"

"Perfectly," Colvey said. "I'm not hurt. And I'm not drunk. Not now, anyway. Though I've been having a drink with a few friends. My own car's in the doubtful hands of George Hann, at the garage, so Iris said to use hers, she was going out but would just as soon walk. Very handsome gesture by a daughter. And now I've turned the apple of her eye—or *one* of the apples of her eye—into another job for George Hann. Not a very handsome gesture by a father, I fear."

He was not entirely sober, in spite of what he said. He probably had spent the evening trying to drown the thought of the wedding from which he had shut himself out.

He looked along the road. "My God!" he said. "Look at those skidmarks in the snow—two or three hundred yards of 'em, all over the road. It's damned lucky you weren't walking along here to your Rectory gate ten minutes earlier. You'd have been hit for six. You'd have had it, Rector."

The Rector felt that dryness in his throat. "And you'd have killed a man while you were drunk in charge of a car," he said. "I wonder how you'd have felt about it—through the years? I wonder how Iris would have felt about it?"

Colvey turned on him with sudden violence. "You parsons!" he said. "What's this—a sermon? It didn't happen, and a miss is as good as a mile. Leave it at that."

"Gladly," the Rector said. He looked at the long, raking skidmarks in the snow, at the tilted, red car with its single headlight glaring into the hedge. He said slowly, "But I think you should know, Colvey, why it didn't happen—*why* I wasn't walking along this stretch of the road to my gate at precisely the time your car hurtled along here, skidding from side to side, completely out of control. You see, I was halfway to the corner there when I heard something that made me turn and go back to the church."

"You heard something?" Colvey said.

"I heard a bell ring," said the Rector, and there was a wonder in him—"of its own accord."

They stood there on the road, looking at each other, with the whiteness of the snow all about them, and the world asleep.

"There's some old legend," Colvey said, "about a bell that—"

"I climbed up and looked at the bells," said the Rector. "They were rung tonight as they've not been rung for a long time. The result was a partial collapse of one of the iron-and-timber frames—and the bell rang."

They looked at each other in silence.

"D'you think anybody else heard that bell ring?" Colvey said, after a moment.

"I think it most unlikely," the Rector said. "I think only I—the Rector—heard the bell that rang, at Christmas, of its own accord. According to the legend, of course, that makes this my last Christmas. I was saved for my last Christmas. And, of course, it may well be my last Christmas. Yours, too. And anybody else's. Regardless of legends. We don't know—any of us. But at least it's in our power not to make ourselves and others—people we love—needlessly unhappy. You know what I'm talking about, Colvey."

"Yes," Colvey said. He turned, looked at the car, and shrugged, almost jauntily. "Well, seeing what I've done to her car, I suppose the least I can do is—" He stopped. "No," he said, in a different tone. "No, I'll walk up the aisle with Iris's hand on my arm—but not because of the car."

The Rector nodded. "I know." He felt as though a weight had been lifted from him. "The only thing is—I'm afraid we shan't be able to manage a full wedding peal, in the circumstances."

Colvey looked at him with a sudden smile. "I'll make allowances," he said—"in the circumstances." He reached into the car, switched off the headlight. "The car's well clear of the road. I'll leave it where it is and get along home now. I'll telephone George Hann in the morning. Good night, Rector."

"Good night," the Rector said. "Happy Christmas, Colvey."

"Same to you, Rector."

The Rector stood peering after Stephen Colvey until he was gone, then walked back slowly to the church. In the darkness there, with the drifted snow outside making the stained-glass windows glimmer faintly, he knelt for some time in one of the pews.

Then, as he was there, he went halfway down the cellar steps. He felt warmth from the cellar, saw that it was lighted with a dim, red glow.

So finally, at peace with himself, this one of the many Rectors the parish had known walked on home, and the small, flint-built, eleventh-century church, on the knoll overlooking the common, was left alone in the wide, white silence under the stars.

MORE CHRISTMAS
SHORT STORIES

A Christmas party is punctuated by a gunshot under a policeman's watchful eye. A jewel heist is planned amidst the glitz and glamour of Oxford Street's Christmas shopping. Lost in a snowstorm, a man finds a motive for murder.

This collection of mysteries explores the darker side of the festive season from unexplained disturbances in the fresh snow, to the darkness that lurks beneath the sparkling decorations.

With neglected stories by John Bude and E.C.R. Lorac, as well as tales by little-known writers of crime fiction, Martin Edwards blends the cosy atmosphere of the fireside story with a chill to match the temperature outside. This is a gripping seasonal collection sure to delight mystery fans.